GYPSIES

ROBERT

CHARLES

WILSON

BANTAM BOOKS

NEW YORK · TORONTO · LONDON · SYDNEY · AUCKLAND

All of the characters in this book are fictitious, and any resemblance to actual persons, living or dead, is purely coincidental.

This edition contains the complete text
of the original hardcover edition.
NOT ONE WORD HAS BEEN OMITTED.

GYPSIES

A Bantam Spectra Book/published by arrangement with
Doubleday

PRINTING HISTORY
Doubleday edition published January 1989
Bantam edition/November 1989

ISBN 0-553-28304-9

Published simultaneously in the United States and Canada

Bantam Books are published by Bantam Books, a division of
Bantam Doubleday Dell Publishing Group, Inc. Its trade-
mark, consisting of the words "Bantam Books" and the por-
trayal of a rooster, is Registered in U.S. Patent and Trademark
Office and in other countries. Marca Registrada. Bantam
Books, 666 Fifth Avenue, New York, New York 10103.

PRINTED IN THE UNITED STATES OF AMERICA

O   0 9 8 7 6 5 4 3 2 1

One turns in all directions and sees nothing. Yet one senses that there is a source for this deep restlessness; and the path that leads there is not a path to a strange place, but a path home.

—Peter Matthiessen,
The Snow Leopard

Part One

LAND'S END

Chapter One

·······················

Alone in her bed, Karen White dreamed a familiar dream.

There are dreams that are like capsules of life, that sum up a thing and define it. Karen's dream was one of those. A bucket from the dark well of her past, it came up brimming.

In the happier part of her life the dream had recurred very occasionally; now—with all the trouble —it came more often.

The dream never changed. She might have invented all or none of it. It recalled a time in her life in which illusion and reality were more fluid, when certainties were few—a frightening time.

After midnight now—Gavin gone for good and

3

Michael still not home—she dreamed the dream again.

In the dream she is a child, coming awake before dawn in her bedroom in the old house on Constantinople Street.

The room is dark. A summer night. The window is open and a welcome breeze rivers through the flyspecked screen. On an impulse, or drawn by some sound, she rises, pads barefoot across the floor, and pulls the gently hissing curtains back.

The air feels good. She yawns and blinks, then gapes in startlement: Laura and Timmy are out on the lawn.

They are her younger brother and sister. Karen herself is nine—two years older than Laura and four years older than Tim. She imagines she is mature: how childish they seem, tiptoeing through the high dandelion-specked grass by moonlight. But it's late. Past midnight, not yet dawn. What are they doing out at this terrible hour?

As she watches, they see her at the window.

Laura, the impetuous one, points, and Karen feels suddenly spotlit.

Tim, who turned five last December, waves her away. *Go on*, he seems to be saying with his hands. *You don't understand. Go back to sleep.* She reads disgust in his small round face and is tempted just to give in . . . whatever they're doing, does she really want a part of it?

But Laura is signaling, too; Laura is smiling. "Hey," she calls out hoarsely, a kind of whisper: it drifts up through the open window. "Hey, Karen! Karen, *come on!*"

Frightened, but feeling a tickle of curiosity, Karen tiptoes down the dark stairs. Mama and Daddy are asleep. Heavy presences in the deeper darkness of their bedroom, the door ajar: she feels as much as sees them. Daddy is snoring; she sees the outline of his shoulders, his eyeglasses abandoned on the night-stand. His snores are labored and masculine.

He'll be so mad, Karen thinks, if he catches us. She resolves to scold her brother and sister. Tim especially: he's the troublemaker. A bad streak in him, Daddy says. At five, he already reads ferociously. Devours comic books off the rack, because Daddy won't let him buy them or bring them home. The man at the drug-store always yells when he catches Tim reading that way. Tim, predictably, doesn't care.

Tim is behind all this, Karen thinks.

The house on Constantinople possesses a postage-stamp backyard which abuts a gully. It's an old Pitts-burgh row house on a hilly street. Some light filters through from the front. Beyond the back fence, with its rusty iron scrollwork, fireflies dance at the beckon-ing verge of the ravine. It's dark, it should be scary—it *is* scary—but Tim and Laura are already prizing open the twisted coat hanger which latches shut the old wire-mesh fence.

They have been told not to go into the gully.

Breathless and feeling fragile in her nightclothes, Karen comes abreast of the younger children. She wants to demand an explanation, shepherd them back to their beds. *You're the oldest,* Daddy has told her, *you bear the responsibility. You have to look out for them.* But Laura holds her finger to her lip, smiles a furtive smile as Tim jimmies the gate.

One by one they file across the lane and down a moist path into the dark of the woods. They navigate by moonlight and intuition. Karen guesses at the path and watches Laura's pale shape in front of her. Walk-ing, she realizes she is shoeless. The damp pressed earth shocks her feet; trees drape clammy leaves against her cheeks. The house retreats with all its warm reassurances until it is invisible behind them.

"Here," Tim says finally, his high-pitched voice strangely authoritative. There is a clearing in the wood, a weedy gap between two stands of elm. They stop and wait.

The waiting does not seem strange. There is an electricity in the air, a humming in the earth. Karen can see stars now, obscured by a haze of city light but shining, rippling. There are night motions in the underbrush. Raccoons, she tells herself. A sow bug crawls over her foot.

"Do it now," Laura whispers. "Now, Tim."

Tim cocks his head at her—so adult-seeming in this light that he resembles a wizened old man—and nods.

He raises his hand.

Karen thinks for a moment he is playing band conductor: it's that kind of gesture, dramatic and a little bit childish. She shakes her head and peers closer.

But he is not conducting. She should have known. His hand radiates light.

Solemnly, he draws a big upside-down letter U in the air. An arch, each leg grounded in the dewy soil, as tall at its apex as a five-year-old can reach. His hand moves slowly and his face is screwed into a fierce knot of concentration. It would be comical, except that a miracle is taking place. As he finishes the arc the air enclosed within it seems to ripple.

Tim steps back now, mopping his forehead.

The cold light fades. But the U shape remains: a wedge of darker darkness.

"I told you," Tim says, addressing Laura, sparing not even a glance for Karen. His child's voice is merciless: *"Apologize."*

"Sorry," Laura says. But she's not contrite. Her voice betrays her fascination. "Can we go through? Really?"

"No!" Karen says suddenly. Her voice is loud in the darkness. She knows what this is; she knows what Daddy would say. Bad bad bad. "Nobody go near it!"

She hears the sound of her own panic.

Tim regards her contemptuously. "You shouldn't even be here."

It makes her angry. "Go back to bed!"

She is nine. He is five. He ignores her. "You go back to bed," he says.

The coldness in his voice shocks her.

Laura looks between them. Laura is the younger sister and—Karen has acknowledged it—the prettier. Laura has big eyes and a child's full lips.

Karen, at nine, is a little bit pinched, somewhat narrow of face. Mother says it's a worrier's face.

My little worrywart, she says.

"We'll all go," Laura says decisively. "Just a little way." Her small hand closes on Karen's arm. "Not far."

And before Karen can stop it—before she can think about it—they step through the arch.

It's hard for her to understand. A moment before they were deep in the wooded ravine; now they're in some dark, hard place. There are cobbles underfoot and the sound of her breathing echoes back from narrow walls. An alley. She blinks, aghast. There is garbage collected in steel barrels. A rat—clearly a rat and not a raccoon—noses through the litter. Streetlights at the mouth of the alley cast long unpleasant shadows.

"The ocean," Laura says to Tim. "You said we could see the ocean."

"This way," her brother says.

Karen's heart pulses against her ribs. That's crazy, she thinks, *what* ocean, there's no ocean, we live in

Pittsburgh. In *Pennsylvania.* She retains a vivid memory of her school geography. The only bodies of water around Pittsburgh are the Allegheny and Monongahela rivers, mingling to create the mighty Ohio. She has taken a boat ride; she remembers the old steel-girder bridges and the awe they inspired in her. There is no ocean here.

But they turn a corner and follow this cobbled street, which she does not recognize, and she smells a salt tang in the air, something bitter, ozone, and there are faint cries which might be nesting gulls.

The street itself is so strange she feels she *must* remember it. The buildings are odd, three- and four-story structures with the crosshatched look of the fairy-tale houses in her Golden Books, their brick chimneys gap-toothed against the cloudy sky. (But hadn't there been stars?) The wind is cool, worse than cool, *cold,* and she's dressed only in her nightie. Her bare heel skids against a residue of fish scale down among the dark cobbles and she clutches Laura's arm.

They ascend a hill.

The city is spread out suddenly before them.

Karen's confusion becomes total: this is *not* Pittsburgh.

Not Pittsburgh, but a very large city nevertheless. Much of it is this same kind of gingerbread architecture, winding narrow roads punctuated by factories and mills that are the only illuminated buildings, their high wired windows spilling red and yellow furnace light. Farther off, where the land rises, the city seems more modern; she can see tall buildings like the buildings downtown—in Pittsburgh—but these are cheerless black obsidian slabs or squat, chalky structures. Atop one of them, a dirigible is moored.

But more marvelous than this is the sea.

From where they stand the road runs down to the

docks. There are rows and rows of wooden warehouses. Inside their cavernous frames Karen sees people moving. It's reassuring, in a way, seeing people here. It suggests some sort of normalcy. If she cried out for help, someone might hear. Beyond the warehouses, a long lighted pier runs out across the oily water. A few ships are docked; some have high wooden masts, some do not. One is immense, as big as an oil tanker.

The strangeness of the scene begins to affect her. She has the feeling of having come, somehow, very far from home. She's lost—they're all lost. She thinks of the arch Timmy drew in the dark air of the ravine, their only door . . . can they find it again? Or has it vanished?

"All right," she says. "We've seen it. There it is. Now we have to go home."

"She's afraid," Timmy says to Laura. "I told you."

But Laura looks at her sympathetically. "No . . . Karen's right. We should get back." She shivers. "It's *cold.*"

"It's always cold here."

Karen doesn't stop to wonder what he means. "Let's go," she says.

Timmy sighs elaborately but cooperates, outvoted. They turn back. The narrow street, from this direction, seems completely new. Inside Karen the spring of panic has coiled tighter . . . what if they *are* lost?

But no, she thinks, that's the alley there. She pulls Laura tighter so as not to lose her. She grabs for Timmy's hand. He resists a moment, then relents.

Daddy's faith was not misplaced. She *can* protect them.

But as they approach the mouth of the alley, a man steps out from the shadows.

He is looking directly at them. He is tall and dressed in a gray suit and hat. He looks ordinary, like the men she has seen riding the trolleys to work. But there is something in the intensity of his gaze, in the way he smiles, that amplifies her fear. A gust of wind plucks at his overcoat; a few flakes of snow swirl past.

"Hi," he says. "Hello there."

They stand still, transfixed. The man's voice echoes down the empty street.

Still smiling, he takes a few sauntering steps closer. It occurs to Karen that there is something familiar about his face, the lines of it, the wide eyes . . . something she cannot place.

"We have to go back," Timmy says—for the first time, a note of uncertainty in his voice.

The man nods agreeably. "I know. Everybody has to go home sometime, right? But look! I have presents for you."

He reaches into his overcoat. Timmy waits, studious but unafraid. Karen thinks, *He knows this man. He's been here before.*

The man produces from the depths of his coat a glass paperweight—the kind you shake and it snows inside. He hands this to Tim.

Tim stares, transfixed.

"The kingdoms of the Earth," the man says.

Tim takes the gift, holds it solemnly.

The overcoat is magic, fathomless. The grinning man reaches in once more and produces—"Presto!" he says—a small pink plastic hand mirror, the cheap kind you can buy at the five-and-dime. He extends the mirror to Laura.

"Go on," he says gently. "A getting-to-know-you present."

A part of Karen wants to shout *no*. But Laura, frowning, takes the gift and regards it.

"Fairest in the land," the man says, smiling.

And Karen cowers, knowing she is next.

The man looks directly at her. He is like the men on TV shows, like Eliot Ness in "The Untouchables": ruggedly handsome. The smile is very convincing. But his mild gray eyes are as cold as the snow and as empty as the street.

He reaches into his coat again.

This time: a baby doll.

A naked plastic baby doll about the size of her thumb. It's not much. But, curiously, she's drawn to it. The expression on its crudely formed face attracts her. It seems to be asking for help.

Overcome, she snatches the doll and pockets it.

"Your firstborn child," the man says softly.

The words set off silent alarms inside her. It's like waking up from a dream. "Come *on,*" she says, taking charge at last. She tightens her grip on Timmy and Laura, their small, fleshy arms. "Now," she cries. "Run! Come on!"

They duck around the gray man into the alley.

The darkness obscures the doorway. She hunts it out with some sixth sense. Beyond it, she can smell the wet night warmth of the ravine.

She steps through, pushing Tim and Laura ahead of her. The sky on this side is beginning to show dawn. "We have to hurry," she says. "Up the hill! GO!"

There is no longer any question of disobeying. Daylight priorities have begun to assert themselves. The two smaller children scurry ahead.

Karen pauses a second to look back.

The door—Tim's door—has begun to disappear. It fades; the borders become indistinct. But for a lingering moment she can see through to the other side, to that cold fish-smelling wharf city, the alley mouth, the gray man gazing at her. He makes no move to follow. He smiles blandly.

The image shivers.

He raises his hand and waves.

The doorway bursts like a bubble, and Karen flees toward the house.

The dream ended there. She woke from it shivering and reached for the bedside clock.

12:45, the bright digital readout announced.

Third night in a row now. The dream had never come so often or so intensely. That must mean something, she thought; but what?

No. Dreams don't mean anything.

She scooted over to Gavin's side of the bed, her arm extended toward him. But the bed, of course, was empty.

It had been empty for almost a month now.

She felt stupid and ashamed of herself, ashamed of the transient wish her body had betrayed. It was a rough time, she thought, yeah, but things were holding together, this was no time to freak out. Silently, she recited the litany she had invented for herself:

It's only a dream.

Dreams don't mean anything.

And even if it isn't a dream, it happened a long time ago.

Quarter to one and Michael still wasn't home. She would have heard him at the door; she always did. Well, but it was Friday night . . . she hadn't given him a specific curfew. In the past it hadn't been necessary. Mike was just fifteen, had few friends, had only recently showed any real interest in girls. The blossoming-out was good and Karen had encouraged it—it was a distraction from the divorce. But she wondered now whether it might not be too *much* distraction.

"Worrywart," she said out loud.

She sat up and wrapped a housecoat around herself.

Sleep was out of the question anyway, at least till Mike was home. She groped her feet into her slippers and shuffled across the bare bedroom floor. Gavin had insisted on exposed wooden floors. Gavin was all sleek austerity and polished pine. Karen thought she might have preferred broadloom. There was something comforting about broadloom. She liked it on her feet. It softened the hard corners of things—it was warm.

In the new place, Karen told herself firmly, we will have broadloom. Wall to goddamn wall.

The move was inevitable. She had household money from Gavin, but it barely covered her expenses. No matter how the divorce was settled, she and Michael would need a new place. She had already begun a haphazard program of packing: the bedroom was full of Mayflower boxes. She hated their shapes, the cumbersome bulk of them along the wall, the nagging reminder that her life could so quickly and utterly come apart.

Downstairs, she warmed up milk and made herself a cup of cocoa. She poured a little more milk in the pan and then set it off the burner—maybe Michael would want a cup.

She switched on one floor lamp and the TV set in the austere pine living room.

Not much on TV at this hour. David Letterman browbeating some guest, a crop of old movies. She stretched out on the sofa with the remote control and punched up the news network.

A bus had been firebombed in the Middle East, the civil service strike was in its second week, a hurricane was threatening the Gulf coast—business, in other words, as usual. She switched off the sound but left the set on for its flicker, the comforting illusion of a second presence in the room. She checked the clock on the face of the VCR.

1:05.

She tightened the belt on her housecoat and took her journal and pen from the end table. Since Gavin moved out she had been keeping the journal, a sort of diary and notebook: it gave her somebody to talk to, even if it was only herself.

The dream again, she wrote.

She pressed the nibbled end of the Bic against her teeth and frowned.

Meaningless, she wrote. *Or so I want to believe. But it comes back so often.*

Trying to think what was really happening those days. The old house on Constantinople. It would have been 1959, 1960 maybe. No real memories (unless the dream is a memory). But I do remember the house. The bedroom I shared with Laura, Timmy's room, Mother and Daddy's room with the big wooden bureau and Grandma Fauve's afghan carpet. The stairs, the mantel clock, the big RCA Victor TV set.

She hesitated, then wrote:

The doll.

Memory, she wondered, or flotsam from the dream?

"Baby," she whispered to herself. The doll was named Baby.

Remember Daddy looking at Baby. "Where'd you get this, Karen?"

His big eyes, and the stubble on his cheek.

"From a man," I said.

"What man? Where?"

I could never lie to him. I told him about Timmy, the ravine, the door, the dark city.

He was angrier than I've ever seen him. I waited
for him to hit me. But he stormed off to Timmy's room
instead.

Timmy screamed . . .

She remembered huddling in her bed clutching
Baby against herself. Daddy had beaten Tim with a
belt and Tim had screamed. But the memory was in-
complete, diaphanous; the harder she fished for it, the
slippier it became. Well, damn, she thought.

Pretty soon after that they had moved out of Constantinople Street. From Constantinople they had
moved to—she thought about it—the apartment in
the West End. Right. Then a year in Duquesne, and a
dozen places after that.

"We're like gypsies," her mother told her one
time. "Never in one place for long."

Karen set aside the journal, more depressed than
ever.

1:15, the clock said.

At 1:23 she heard the key in the front door. She
picked up her cup, wanting to look casual; the cocoa
was stone cold.

The door closed. Michael stepped in from the
foyer.

Karen said, not angrily, "You're late."

"I know." He shrugged out of his worn leather
jacket, hung it on a peg. His dark hair was disarrayed
and there were rings under his eyes. "I'm sorry, Mom.
I didn't know you'd be up."

"I was just restless. You want some hot chocolate?"

"I should hit the sack."

"One cup," Karen said, wondering at the desperation in her own voice: am I that starved for company?
"Helps you sleep."

Her son smiled wearily. "Okay. Sure."

They sat in the kitchen, uneasy in the tall-backed

vinylette chairs. A wall of sliding doors looked out over the dark backyard. Karen felt the shades of her dream moving like a separate creature inside her. She got up, pulled the drapes, sat back down with her hands clamped around the cup. Her fingers were cold.

Michael had his feet up on the opposite chair. He was good-looking, Karen thought, in a fragile way. His dark hair made his skin look pale; he was thin, young-looking for his age. The paraphernalia of teenage toughness—jacket, tight Hanes T-shirt, faded jeans— wore uneasily on him.

She cleared her throat. "You saw a movie?"

He nodded.

"With Amy?"

"Right. Dan and Val drove us downtown."

"Good movie?"

"I guess it was all right. Car-chase flick. You know." He forced a smile. "Boom. Crash."

"Doesn't sound too great." She ventured her best guess: "Having problems with Amy?"

"Amy's okay."

"You seem down, is all."

"Not because of Amy."

"What, then?"

He looked at her across the table—his serious look. "You want to know?"

"If you want to tell me."

He sat back in the chair with his hands in his pockets. "I saw that guy again."

The words fell like stones in the still air of the kitchen. The refrigerator hummed into silence. Outside, there was a shrill of crickets.

September now. Autumn closing in.

"We were driving home," Mike said tonelessly. "We turned onto Spadina. He was there. Standing in front of a Chinese restaurant. The place was closed. It was dark. He was just standing there. Like he was waiting, you know? And he saw me. Four people in the car, but it was me he was looking at." He pushed the cocoa away, put his hands flat on the table. "He *waved*."

Karen didn't want to ask, but the question had its own momentum: "Who? Who waved?"

Michael peered into the darkness. "You know, Mom."

The Gray Man.

Chapter Two

....

1

Michael skipped breakfast next morning.

"Straight to school," Karen said. "And straight home. All right? I don't want to be worrying about you."

"Straight home," Michael said—offhandedly, but with a seriousness under that, maybe even a little fear.

But that was good, wasn't it? It would make him cautious.

She stood at the window with the curtain tucked back and watched her son walk down this empty suburban street until he was lost from sight, down beyond the intersection of Forsythe and Webster, where the McBrides' big maple tree was shedding its leaves.

The mailman dropped a letter through the slot in the door: the letter was from Laura.

Karen carried it downtown, beside her on the front seat of her little Honda Civic, to the restaurant where she had agreed to meet Gavin. When he was late—predictably late—she took the letter out of her purse and turned it over in her hands a couple of times. The envelope was of some thick, clothy paper, like vellum; the return address was a P.O. box in Santa Monica, California.

California. She liked the look of the word. It radiated warmth, security, sunshine. Here in this Toronto restaurant everybody was dressed in fall grays and fall browns, fashionable downtown people scattered among these mirrors and tiles like leaves. Cold air prickled on her arms whenever the door swept open.

She opened the envelope slowly, with a halting motion that was eager and reluctant at once.

Dear Karen, the letter began.

Open loops and dark fountain-pen ink. The words as she read them took on Laura's throaty contralto.

I got your note and have been mulling it over. Since you ask—and I know it's none of my business—here are some thoughts.

First off, I am sincerely sorry about you & Gavin. Is it any consolation to say I think you are 100 percent correct on this? (Even if the divorce isn't—as you say—your own idea.) We gypsies aren't cut out for middle-class life.

I know the whole thing must come as a blow. And of course there's Michael. Fifteen years old—dear God, is that possible? I really would like to meet my only nephew. Is he as cute as his pictures? (Don't tell him I said that.) But I take it for granted. A heartbreaker. Is he adjusting?

I'm convinced that we ought to be more than Christmas-card relatives. It would be nice to see both of you again.

Yes, big sister. These are hints.

Karen, listen: they play old songs on the radio and I think of you. "Cast Your Fate to the Wind." Remember? It's better advice than you think.

I'm serious. Auntie Laura could use your company.

I can put you up for a week, a month, whatever. On short notice or immediately.

If you can't say yes, say maybe. Ask and I'll send directions, but RSVP.

It was signed in Laura's unmistakable, overflowing script. Karen smiled in spite of her misgivings, reading it.

P.S., it said, under the bottom fold of the paper. *The age of miracles is not over.*

Her smile faded.

She looked up and saw Gavin standing across the table. He gazed at her loftily and said, "You look like shit."

She sighed. It was the kind of opener he seemed to prefer these days. "Well," she said, "you don't. You look impeccable." It was true.

Gavin was nervous about clothes. He studied the fashion columns in *Esquire* as solemnly as a general planning a military campaign. He was tall, with a build he had developed at the racquetball club across the street from his office; he smelled of Brut and antiperspirant. "Seriously," he said, pulling up his chair, peering at her. "Are you sleeping okay? You look tired."

"Well, I am . . . hell, yes, I *am* tired."

"I didn't mean anything by it."

"No," she said. "I know." It was just his way of talking. *Truce,* she thought desperately. What was important now was that Michael was in danger. "We're here to talk."

To talk. But it sounded ominous, so they ordered lunch instead. It was a restaurant Gavin knew, close to his office. He was in his element here. He ordered a seafood salad and a light beer. Karen ordered cottage cheese and fruit. Gavin talked a little about his work; Karen told him how Michael was doing in school. They were talking, she thought, and that was a beginning, but they were not *talking*—she didn't mention the Gray Man.

There had been a time when talking to Gavin was easy. They had met at Penn State, where Karen was a year behind him in a B.A. course. Gavin was dissatisfied—not randomly rebellious in the way that was fashionable then, but looking for a way to inject meaning into his life. He was a Canadian, and he had resolved to go back home and study law. Law, he said, was a point of entry into people's lives. It was where you could apply leverage, make a difference, change things for the better. We all want to change the world, Karen thought, recalling the Beatles tune, lately a TV ad for Nike shoes. Maybe Nike was one of Gavin's clients.

The divorce was still pending. They were, in Gavin's preferred language, "separated." "Separated" meant he had left her last May to live with his girlfriend in her lakefront apartment. It had come as a shock: the separation, the girlfriend, both. Gavin cheated as impeccably as he dressed; Karen had never suspected. He just told her about it over breakfast one morning. *It's not working between us. I know that, you know that.* Very cool. *I'm moving out. . . . Yes, I have somewhere to go. . . . Yes, there is a woman.*

She hated it. All of it. She hated the fact of his infidelity and she hated this feeling that her role had been defined for her: the jealous wife. Well, she told herself, to hell with that. I can be as cool as he can.

So she had gone along blithely: no yelling, no major scenes. Now she wondered if that was not simply another kind of surrender. Gavin, a lawyer, understood life as gameplaying, rough sport played in earnest, and what he had achieved with Karen was a kind of checkmate. Because she concealed her feelings he wasn't forced to deal with them.

She had been bluffed and outmaneuvered.

No more. Too much at stake now for fuzzy thinking. She had made a list before she left the house: *Questions to ask.* Gavin was pressing to begin the legal proceedings, and she knew she shouldn't agree to anything before seeing her own lawyer—as soon as she found one—but she wanted to raise the question of the house.

She wanted to move. She *needed* to move. Not only did the house contain what had become sour memories, but there was the problem of the Gray Man. She was vulnerable and alone in the big suburban house; she felt encircled there, besieged. For Michael's sake, it was vital that they leave . . . and she wondered if they should not move out of the city entirely. The problem was that she had no independent income. Last week she'd gone to see an employment counselor and when he asked for a résumé Karen was forced to admit she hadn't worked outside the home for as long as her son had lived. Her prospects, the man informed her, were limited.

And now the household money was low and she didn't want to ask Gavin, again, for cash. Come the divorce, she guessed he would be paying support. But that was in the future.

So she had worked out a plan. They would sell the house. With her share of the income Karen could relocate and take a vocational course, programming or something. And the support payments, when they finally began, would keep her and Michael fed.

It had seemed like a good plan when she worked it out at home; now, here in the restaurant, she was less certain. Gavin embarked on some story about the firm, office politics, it was endless; the waiter stole away with her half-eaten cottage cheese and replaced it with coffee and she realized, panicking, that lunch was almost over, time had run out, her courage had failed. "The house," she said abruptly.

Gavin sipped his coffee, rested a knuckle thoughtfully against his chin. "What about it?"

She stammered out her plan. He listened, frowning. She didn't like the frown. It was his patient look, his *concerned* look, the look she imagined him exercising on his clients. She thought of it as his *yes, but* expression: Yes, but it will cost more than you think. Yes, but we'll have to go to court.

"It's a good idea," he said when she finished. "But not practical."

He sounded so sure of himself. The finality of it was crushing. She mumbled something about common property, the divorce laws—it wasn't *his* house, not entirely—

"Nor yours." He drained his cup. "I explained this years ago, Karen. The house is a tax write-off for my mother. She bought it out of Dad's estate. In the eyes of the law, we're tenants. The house doesn't belong to either of us."

She had some vague memory of this. "You said that was a technicality."

"Nevertheless."

She sat upright, shocked at her own disappointment, the depth of the frustration welling up in her. "Don't tell me it's impossible. We could work something out." But this was too much like pleading. "Gavin—I made *plans*—"

"It's not up to me." He added, "It's the way things are. But you always had trouble with that, right? Dealing with reality—it was never your long suit."

Her coffee cup twisted in her hand. The coffee spilled out; the cup crashed against the saucer. She pushed herself away from the sodden table.

"For Christ's sake," Gavin said tightly.

He had always hated scenes.

She drove away dazed.

Home, she felt feverish. She poured herself a drink and sat down with her notebook. Her mind felt busy but blank, a motor revving in a motionless car. She turned to a clean page and wrote:

Dear Laura,

It was like automatic writing, unwilled, a conspiracy between pen and fingers. She surprised herself by continuing:

Invitation accepted. Michael & I arriving by the time you get this. We'll be staying at that hotel in Santa Monica, you remember the one, same as last time. Or I'll leave a message at the desk if there's no room. Look for us there.

Love—

And signed it. And put it in an envelope, and addressed the envelope, and marked it SPECIAL DELIVERY and loaded it with stamps.

She would mail it later. Or maybe not. Well, she thought, *probably* not. It was a dumb idea, an impetuous idea; she was only disappointed because of Gavin.

She crumpled the envelope. Then, "Well, damn," she said, and unfolded it and put it in her purse.

Outside, the light was failing.

She looked at her watch.

It was after six o'clock. Michael was late.

2

Michael left school at a quarter after four and began the walk home alone.

He had evaded Dan and Valerie on his way to the lockers. He didn't want company, he didn't want a ride. It suited his mood to be alone.

He wondered, not for the first time, whether solitude might not be his natural condition.

It was only September, but autumn was setting in in a serious way. He lived six long suburban blocks from the school and the shortest route home took him down two winding residential streets and across a power company right-of-way, past high-tension towers that sang in a demented high-pitched buzz whenever the weather turned cold. He walked that way now, no buzzing today but only a silence, the sound of his feet in the brown summer grass.

He liked this place, the isolation of it, the trees and wild meadows and high steel towers. On the left, there were box homes under construction, beams like naked ribs; on the right, an old stand of wild maples. Down the middle ran this meadow, gently rolling pastureland gone to seed at the foot of the power-line gantries. Walking here, he felt suspended between worlds: school and home, tract and countryside.

Real and unreal.

He pushed his hands down into his jacket pockets

and rested a minute against a length of Frost fence. Off among the trees, a cicada began to hum. The wind, already an autumn wind, tousled his hair.

He felt sad for no reason he could understand.

The sadness was connected with his mother and connected with the divorce—a word Michael had only just permitted into his vocabulary. No doubt, it was connected somehow also with the Gray Man.

The worst thing, he thought, was that there was nobody to talk to about it. Especially not at home, especially not these days. You just couldn't say certain things. Everything was fine, until somebody said the wrong word—literally, a word, like "divorce"—and then there would be a chilly silence and you understood that this terrible thing, this obscenity, must never be mentioned again. He couldn't say "divorce" to his mother: it was taboo, an unword.

On TV, he thought, it would be easy. She would ask him how he was feeling, he would admit something—guilt, pain, it wouldn't matter, *something*—maybe cry a little—there would be that release. Roll credits. Out here, however, here in the real world, it wasn't practical.

And it wasn't just the divorce. Michael didn't have much trouble with the idea of divorce; half his friends had divorced parents. Much more problematic was the notion of his father living with someone else, a woman, a stranger—trading his family for that. It was hard to imagine his father's life meandering on like a river, with Michael and his mother becoming something abandoned in the course, an elbow lake or an overgrown island. Michael wasn't angry—at least not yet—but he was bewildered. He didn't know how to react.

Hate him for leaving?

It didn't seem possible.

Hate his mother for driving him away?

But that was not an allowable thought.

Maybe it didn't matter. Maybe he wasn't affected by it. That was possible. He had, God knows, other problems.

But he recalled the moment last week when he had crept into his mother's bedroom, opened the top drawer of her desk, and copied out the telephone number she had written on the last page of her address book . . . the number of Michael's father's new home, the lakeside apartment Michael had never seen.

Strange thing to do, for someone who wasn't affected.

But "divorce" wasn't the only unmentionable word around Michael's house. Deeper and more disturbing was this business of the Gray Man.

Michael thought of him as the Gray Man. He had come up with the description when he was six, back when the Gray Man started to appear in his dreams. Gray because of the slate-gray clothes he always wore; gray, too, because a kind of grayness seemed to radiate from him, like an aura, a gray aura. Even his skin was chalky and pale. Michael understood very soon that talking about these dreams disturbed his mother, that any other nightmare might elicit a hug or permission to sleep with the light on, but that the Gray Man would only invoke these frightened looks and frightened denials. No, there's no such thing. And stop asking me.

But it was a lie.

He *did* exist. Out here in the world, out in the real world, a real Gray Man.

Michael had seen him for the first time when he was ten years old. They were driving cross-country

and they had stopped at a gas station along the highway somewhere out in Alberta. A hot day, car windows down, nothing but blank space and blue horizon
and this shanty filling station, some old guy pumping
gas, and in the shade of the plankboard souvenir store,
obscure amidst all this clutter and dust: the Gray Man.
The Gray Man peered out from under a gray slouch
hat with a fixed, attentive look Michael remembered,
too vividly, from his dreams.

Terrified, Michael looked to his mother, but his
mother had seen the Gray Man at the same time and
she was terrified, too. He could tell by the way she was
breathing, tight little gulps of air. Dad was paying the
pump jockey, attention focused on his credit card as it
ratcheted through the stamper in the old man's hand,
worlds away. Michael opened his mouth to speak but
his mother laid a warning hand on his arm. Like a
message: *Your father won't understand.* And it was
true. He knew it without thinking about it. This was
something he shared with his mother, and only with
his mother. This fear. This mystery.

The Gray Man didn't move. He just watched. His
face was calm. His eyes radiated a profound and scary
patience. He watched as Michael's father started the
car, watched as they accelerated down the highway.
I'll wait, the eyes promised. *I'll be back.* And Michael
returned the stare, kneeling on the rear seat, until the
Gray Man and the gas station both had vanished in the
sun haze.

The horizon made him feel safe again. The Gray
Man lost in an ocean of space: it was like waking up.

He knew better than to ask about it. What both-
ered him most was seeing his mother so scared. Her
fear persisted all that day; she was not reassured by
distance. And so he was carefully silent. He didn't
want to make things worse. "You're awfully quiet to-

day, kiddo," his father said. "Sure you're feeling all right?"

"Yes."

No.

He was confused. How *did* he feel?

Frightened, obviously.

But there was something else: he recalled it all these years later, here in the power company meadow. He felt it again.

Curiosity? But that was too mild a word. More like—

"Fascination."

The word hovered in the cool September air like some dark bird.

Startled, Michael turned.

Briefly, the world seemed to go in and out of focus.

He thought, *I should have been safe here.* This was home turf, his own territory. It was certainly not a place for the Gray Man, who was a lurker, an alley person, a shadow person. But here was the Gray Man only yards away, slouch hat pulled down against the sunlight, the same man Michael had seen at the gas station in Alberta five years ago, not appreciably older but maybe—it was a sour joke—maybe a little grayer.

Michael took a shocked step backward and felt the fence press into his spine.

The Gray Man spoke. "You don't have to be afraid." His voice was rough, old, but deep and calming. He smiled, and the smile made his angular face seem less scary. His eyes, small in their battlements of brow and cheekbone, remained fixed. A thin line of scar tissue ran from brow to ear and up into the shadow of the hat. "I only want to talk."

Michael suppressed an urge to run. With animals,

they said, you should never show your fear. Did the same rule apply to nightmares?

"Going home?" the Gray Man asked. "Home to your mother?"

Michael hesitated.

"Your mother," the Gray Man said, "doesn't talk much, does she?"

Michael reached out and wrapped his fingers in the links of the fence, steadying himself. He felt weak, bewildered. His legs felt tremulous and distant.

The Gray Man stood beside him. The Gray Man was tall and calm. The Gray Man put a hand on his shoulder.

"Walk with me," the Gray Man said.

Michael's attention was tied up now in the Gray Man's voice, the sweep and cadence of it; he wasn't conscious of the route they were following, the places they passed. By the time he thought to look around they had left the power company meadow far behind.

"You feel different," the Gray Man said. "You're not like other people." His hand on Michael's shoulder was firm, fatherly.

The words brought back a flicker of fear. "Because of you," Michael said accusingly. "You—"

"Not because of me. But we can start there. What is it you call me?"

"The Gray Man." It was silly. It was a childish thing to say out loud in the cool September air. But the Gray Man's laugh was indulgent, amused.

"I have a name. Well, I have lots of names. Sometimes—" His voice lowered a notch. "Sometimes I'm called Walker."

"Walker," Michael repeated.

"Walker. Tracker. Finder. Keeper."

Like a song, Michael thought absently.

"What matters is that I know things about you. The things your mother won't talk about."

Michael asked in spite of himself, "What things?"

"Oh, all kinds of things. How lonely you feel. How *different* you feel. How you wake up sometimes . . . you wake up sometimes in the night, and you've been dreaming, and you're afraid because it would be so easy to wake up *inside* a dream. As if dreams were real, a place you could go, maybe a place you visited once."

And Michael nodded, strangely unsurprised that the Gray Man knew this about him. It was as if he had passed beyond fear and surprise into an altogether stranger realm. Sleepwalk territory, Michael thought.

They walked past darkened houses and brittle, silent trees. There was no wind. He didn't recognize the neighborhood; he wondered fleetingly how far they had come. Nowhere near home, anyway. There was no neighborhood like this near home.

"We don't go to the obvious places," the Gray Man said, and Michael felt included in that *we:* a brotherhood, a special few. "We don't walk where other people walk. You know that already. Deep inside yourself . . . you know that."

He had never spoken about it. Seldom even thought about it.

But yes, it was true.

"You could walk out of the world if you wanted to." The Gray Man stopped and bent at the waist and looked into Michael's eyes. "The world has angles other people don't see. Corners and doors and directions. You could step sideways and never be seen again. Like this."

And the Gray Man moved in a direction Michael could only just perceive. Not away, exactly, but somehow . . . *beyond*.

And Michael took a tentative step after.

"This," the Gray Man said, smiling now. "This. *This.*"

A step and another step.

Michael felt an electricity flowing in him, a tingling sense of power. He was dizzy with it. Angles, he thought. Angles and corners and doors. A door in the air.

He could see the place the Gray Man was standing now, a cobbled hilly street, a horizon of hard blue sky and old industrial smokestacks, a faint smell of fish and salt in the air. He could not hear the Gray Man's voice but saw him beckoning, a subtle but unmistakable motion of his pale hand. This way. This way. Only a step, Michael thought. This quiet miracle. It was only a step away . . .

"Michael!"

The sound came from far away. But his attention wavered.

"Michael!"

Closer now. Reluctantly, with a sense of opportunities lost, faltering, he turned away from the Gray Man, the cobbled street, the cold blue sky.

The sky he faced now was dark. A few stars blinked above the blue nimbus in the west. He *did* recognize this neighborhood: old houses and a slatboard grocery store on the corner, a mile or more from home and school.

His mother's Civic was at the curb. The door opened and she was framed in it, breathless and frightened, beckoning him in. It was like the gesture the Gray Man had made. He wondered how much she had seen.

But he turned back to look for the Gray Man and the Gray Man was gone . . . no blue sky, no cobbled street, only a tattered hedge, this cracked slab of side-walk.

Strange, he thought. Strange. He was so close.

His mother tugged him into the car. She was trembling but not angry. Shaking his head, still dazed, he buckled the shoulder strap around himself in an automatic motion as she gunned the car away from the curb.

"We're leaving," she said between her teeth. "We're leaving *tonight.*"

"Leaving?"

"We're going to California."

3

Karen stopped at the house long enough to pack a couple of cases, drove north to the airport, and left the car in the garage. God knows when she'd be back to claim it. But, technically, the little Civic belonged to Gavin, anyway. Let him worry about it.

She managed to buy two one-way tickets on a red-eye flight to Los Angeles, departing a couple of hours before dawn. They waited the night out in the gate lounge, Michael stretched out over a bench. He looked dazed and sleepy against the comfortless vinyl. Karen hugged herself, watching him. The air conditioning was relentless.

After midnight she remembered the letter in her purse, the one she had written to Laura. She stood up, laid out her coat over her sleeping son, and went to the rest room in the lounge. Her face in the mirror was haggard and thin, cheekbones projecting under pale skin. It was the face of some stranger, some fugitive.

She dictated her letter over the phone to a telex

agency. The telegram might make it across the continent before they did.

She had to wake Michael when it was time to board the plane. His eyes were heavy; he leaned instinctively against her. Long time since he had done that.

She did not want to think of how far she had driven to find him, or of how lost he had looked, standing on that broken sidewalk with one foot out of the world—or of the shadow she had seen beyond him, tall and patiently smiling.

4

Michael slept through the long plane trip.

He woke once a little after dawn. His mother was asleep; most of the plane was asleep. A sleepy-looking stewardess moved up the aisle, smiled absently at him, moved on. The drone of the aircraft filled his head.

He looked down through the window and saw the desert. He guessed it was the desert. It was swept with morning light, stark with shadows, a complex undulating wilderness. It was pathless, strange and empty, another world. Canyons and arroyos; arid Triassic seabed. Full of hidden angles, Michael thought, curious corners.

You could walk out of the world if you wanted to.

And it was true.

Angles, Michael thought. Angles and corners and doors.

Chapter Three

....

1

Later, when Karen explained why she had come, her sister Laura said, "I can take you to a place. A safe place. It's where I live."

And Karen turned to face the window of the hotel room. A crescent of beach, tousled palm trees, the murmur of the traffic. "You mean," she said, "not *here*."

"Not here. No. But not far away."

Coming into California was like walking into a memory.

She had spent a week here in 1969. It was a bad time; she had argued with her sister; they had not parted amicably. Times change, Karen reminded herself. But the streets had not, the hotel in Santa Monica had not, not in any significant way. Michael sat dazed beside her in a miasma of vinyl and stale cigar smoke as the cab barreled down these broad, gray freeways from the airport. Involuntarily, she recalled odd bits of knowledge she had picked up over the course of a lifelong magazine addiction. Fact: palm trees are not native to Southern California. Fact: without irrigation, these endless stucco housing tracts would be as dry as the city of Beirut. But most of all she was struck by the quality of the sunlight, its angularity, a kind of light you never saw back East. It was not a brighter light but whiter, opalescent; it made hard shadows that faded, in the distance, to a wash of gray.

And of course the ocean. She remembered the ocean, the reach of it, how it filled the horizon. She stepped out of the taxi into this strange sunlight and marveled a moment at the distance she had come.

They were alone in the hotel for a few days. Michael didn't talk much. He seemed to understand why they had come, the urgency of the trip, and Karen figured he was disoriented by it: certainly she was. He asked one morning why Aunt Laura hadn't met them and Karen explained about the post office box—"She won't have picked up her mail yet." And so they waited in the room, ordered their meals from room service, left a message at the desk when, one afternoon, they went out to walk along the beach. Karen guessed she had become very Canadian in the years she had spent in Toronto, because the people she saw along the littered beach seemed very strange to her. A man wearing roller skates and a striped tank top bowled her off the sidewalk and, as she sat bewildered in the sand, looked over his shoulder and said something abusive. The words, thank goodness, did not register.

I'm a stranger here, she thought. I don't belong here. No future in this place.

She was grateful Michael hadn't seen. He was at a stall buying hot dogs. They ate silently, staring out at the ocean. Michael had always been quiet, Karen thought, but this new silence was disturbing. He seemed to be bracing himself for the next inevitable disaster. She sympathized with this intuition that their troubles might not have ended: it was her intuition, too.

And then they walked back to the hotel, and found Laura was waiting in the lobby.

Karen saw her first. She had that privilege, for a moment, of seeing without being seen. She found herself wanting to prolong it, to avoid announcing herself. Looking at her sister Karen felt a strange sensation of double vision, of time turning back on itself.

Laura was older, of course. But the two decades since 1969 had been kind to her. She was lightly tanned, very California, her hair cut boyishly short. Her figure was good. She was wearing a white sundress, a gaudy headband tied at the back, and cheerful bracelets at her wrists. As she turned, the bracelets chimed.

Their eyes met, and Karen thought for a fleeting moment: *I could have been like that*. She looks like me, Karen thought, but airier, lighter. Karen had always thought of herself as solid, earthbound; her sister looked as delicate as the wind.

She wondered, Is this *envy?* Am I *jealous?*

"Aunt Laura," Michael said, seeing the recognition that leaped like a spark between the women.

Laura came across the tiled lobby with a mad grin and hugged them both.

They had lunch in the hotel coffee shop. Laura devoured a massive salad. "It's the smog," she said. "I'm not used to it. It does weird things to my appetite."

Michael looked at her oddly. "I thought you lived here."

Laura exchanged glances with Karen.

"Not *here,*" Laura said. "Not exactly."

Karen left Michael in the hotel room to pack—and to catch the end of a Dodgers game on TV—while she and Laura took a brief stroll down the boulevard.

"I don't know," she said. Everything seemed strange and sudden now, the appearance of her sister, these old connections and older barriers. She felt a kind of panic, the urge to back off a step, to reconsider. "I'm grateful for the invitation. And it's what we came here for. Of course. To see you . . . to visit. But I'm concerned about Michael."

Laura said, "He doesn't know?"

Karen thought, We always did this, didn't we? Talked in these ellipses. We do it still. "There was never any need for him to know."

They found a bench overlooking the tarry beach. Offshore, against the white glare of the horizon, a tanker moved toward port.

"I'm not like you," Karen said. "I'm even less like Tim. I never wanted it—to be able to do what we do. I didn't ask for it and I didn't ever want it."

"None of us asked for it. What are you saying, that Michael doesn't know *anything?*"

"Why? Why force it on him? If he can live without knowing, why make him conscious of it?"

"Because it's in him," Laura said calmly. "It's part of him. You *must* feel it."

Maybe she could. Maybe she had felt it from the first, since his birth, before his birth: that he was different in the way she was different, that the frightening ability to walk between worlds was there in him—enclosed, like the bud of a flower, but real and potent.

But it was not something she wanted to consider. She said, "I worked hard, you know, to give him a normal life. Maybe you don't know what that means. I guess it never mattered to you. But a *normal life* . . . it was the best thing I could give him. Do you understand that? I don't want to throw it away."

Laura put her hand on Karen's arm. The gesture was calming, and it seemed for a moment as if she and not Karen were the older sister. "Don't blame yourself. He forced the issue. Not Michael but—what do you call him? The Gray Man."

The memory was like a weight.

"Stay with me," Laura said. "At least a while. It's been too long since we saw each other. And I want to get to know my nephew. And I want you both to be safe."

"Is it really very far?"

"We can drive there."

"What's it like?"

"Like here. Very much like here. But nicer."

"All right," Karen said sadly. "Yes."

2

They checked out and loaded up the luggage in Aunt Laura's car—a car Michael could not identify, probably foreign. It was small and boxy and the name

Durant was written on the gas cap. The trunk swallowed all their luggage effortlessly.

They were on the road an hour before the change began.

It was a long drive. They followed the San Diego Freeway south past slummy instant suburbs and forests of desiccated palm trees, past oil wastelands and cracked concrete underpasses scrawled with Hispanic graffiti. Laura didn't talk much, seemed to be concentrating on the driving. It was coming on for dusk, rush-hour traffic, blinders pulled down to keep out the setting sun. Michael felt the tension rising in the enclosed space of the car.

He understood that something important was happening. They were going to Aunt Laura's place to visit, to stay a while, that had been established . . . but more than that. His mother's anxiety was obvious. She sat beside Aunt Laura with her spine rigid and her head held almost primly forward. And he could see the concentration gathering in Laura herself, a tensing of muscles.

They left the freeway on an off ramp and turned west toward the ocean, through a range of scrubby brown hills. There was more housing going up along these dry ravines. Billboards for Model Homes. Who would live here? Michael wondered. Why? What was there to draw all these people?

And then they came within sight of the ocean, a gray flatness, shabby roadside stalls and businesses, salt air and the rancid smell of diesel oil.

The change began as the sun was setting.

Michael thought at first it was a trick of the light. The sunset seemed to suffuse the car through the windows on the right. It was momentarily blinding, the way a lance of sun off hot, still water is blinding. But not only that. He felt a surge of something *inside him,* a disorientation, as if he had been blindfolded and spun a dozen times around. For a fraction of a second Michael thought he was falling, that the car was plummeting through empty space. He blinked twice and held his breath. Then the tires bit pavement again, the suspension bottomed and then steadied. The brightness faded.

But the memory lingered. This was a *familiar* feeling. When had he felt it before? Just a little while ago, he thought . . . in Toronto. With the Gray Man.

Like this, Michael thought: a stepping outside and beyond, through the secret doors of the world; and he looked outside with sudden startlement: *Where are we now?*

But the world—this road—looked the same. Or nearly the same. It might be imagination, but it seemed as if some of the shabbiness had gone. The storefronts were a little cleaner, a little brighter. The air (he was almost certain) felt fresher, the sunset brighter but less gaudy.

He caught Laura's eye in the rearview mirror.

She looked at him and nodded solemnly, as if to say, *Yes, I did that. Yes, it's real.*

He cleared his throat and said, "Where are we going?"

"My place," Laura said calmly. "I told you." A sign announced the distance in miles to a town called Turquoise Beach. "That's it . . . that's where I live."

3

Karen had never been good at dealing with the unexpected. She was cautious, therefore, in evaluating this place Laura had brought her to. Turquoise Beach.

A name not on any map she had ever seen, though she supposed you could go to a gas station—here—and buy a map that would have Turquoise Beach marked on it. And other strange places.

They arrived after dark, but the town, what she could see of it, was an innocuous old seaside town, Victorian buildings and newer stucco storefronts. There was something quaintly bohemian about the beaded curtains fronting doorways and the stained glass shining from upper-story apartments. They drove down a crowded beachfront main street, cafés and patio restaurants open to the warm night. A tiny storefront window proclaimed ALL KIND OF SHELLS. The one next door offered ANTIQUES, HURRICANE LAMPS, DRIFT GLASS—SALE! And the people on the street were almost as quaint. They were dressed in what Karen thought of as gypsy fashion: faded Levi's, quilted shirts in bright colors. There was a woman with feathers braided into her long dark hair.

Beyond this hub was a network of shadowed streets and quiet houses, a similar mix of Victorian brickwork and airy wood-frame buildings. Laura, humming to herself, turned west toward the ocean and parked at last in a patch of gravel adjoining a three-story slatwood house. "We're the top two floors," she said, climbing out.

Karen stood in the coolish night air feeling suddenly alone in this new world, reminding herself that it really *was* that, a new world. Did Gavin exist in this place? If she phoned their old number in Toronto, would he answer?

Did Canada exist, or had the borders been redrawn?

Strange. It made her shiver. She listened to the faint rushing of waves against the shore, prosaic and real. And the stars, she thought: the stars were still the same.

Laura came abreast of her holding two suitcases. Karen said quickly, "Here, let me have one." But a bearded man bustled out of the front door of the house and took the case out of her hand. "You must be Karen," he said.

Laura said, "This is Emmett. Emmett lives downstairs. Emmett is *helpful.*" Emmett smiled somewhat shyly.

He's courting her, Karen thought. But wasn't someone always? Laura had always attracted men. Laura had a knack with men.

Whereas Karen had married the first man who showed any interest in her . . . who had left her to live with his girlfriend by the lake. "Hello, Emmett," she said.

Michael came around the car with his own suitcase weighing him down. Emmett wisely didn't offer to take it; instead he said, "Let me show you the stairs. Mike—right?"

Michael followed him into the house.

"He's nice," Karen said.

"So? You approve?"

"My first impression is good."

Laura smiled. "Emmett and I are pretty much loners. But we've been circling a little bit. There are—" She made a seesaw gesture with her hand. "Possibilities."

Karen said hopefully, "You have coffee?"

"Costa Rican. Fresh-ground."

"I want a *big* cup of coffee. And a shower." And a bed, she thought privately. Something soft. With clean sheets.

"Can do. *Told* you it was nice here."

And Karen understood that they had begun to be sisters again. After all these years. In this strange place.

4

They sat around Aunt Laura's old kitchen table for an hour before bed, the two women talking about nothing in particular, sipping coffee from porcelain mugs. Michael watched with a growing impatience. He felt excluded: not from the conversation so much as from what was left unsaid. Between them, he thought, they *know*. They *understand*.

When he couldn't take it anymore, he stood up. It had been a long day and his head was buzzing. But he felt the urge to say something, to make them acknowledge the thing that had happened. This was taboo: but the world was different now; he felt the words come welling up.

"You ought to explain," he said. And into the sudden silence: "I mean, I'm not blind. I don't know where we are, but I know you can't get here from the hotel. Not down the regular roads." Roads, he thought, angles, doorways. "I felt it," he said. "You should explain."

His mother looked away, folded her hands in her lap, regarded her folded hands wordlessly. Michael felt a sudden remorse. But his Aunt Laura wasn't angry or surprised. She looked at him steadily from her place by the window.

"Soon," she said quietly. "I promise. All right?"

The gratitude he felt took him by surprise: it was that intense. "All right," he said.

Because, the thing was, she meant it. He could tell.

"But bed now," Laura said. "I think that's a good idea for all of us. Can you find your room?"

Upstairs and to the right.

Tired as he was, Michael lay awake for a time in his new bed in the dark, listening to the night sounds of his aunt's house and the quiet pulsing of the surf. The house was quiet. For a long time, there were no voices from the kitchen.

Chapter Four

. . . .

1

A stranger to this world, Karen decided her wisest
course would be to understand the immediate neighborhood.

She found an old Texaco road map in one of Laura's cluttered kitchen drawers. On the map, the town
of Turquoise Beach was a black dot nestled in a curve
of coastline between Pueblo de Los Angeles and San
Diego. Pueblo de Los Angeles sounded strange, but
everything else—she was not very familiar with California—seemed roughly in its place. Across the border
from San Diego was a Mexican city called Ciudad Za-

ragoza. Was that right? San Francisco was familiar and reassuring, but what about the large towns marked Alvarado, Sutter, Porziuncola? She couldn't find Hollywood: should it have been on the map? Still . . . the familiar outweighed the strange.

I'll get used to it, she thought. In time, I'll know where I am. As a gesture toward the future, Karen taught herself the layout of her sister's apartment. Two bedrooms up and a futon in the spare room downstairs, a large central living room with polished wooden floors and broad windows overlooking the sea. Paperback books on homemade shelves and gauzy curtains that moved in a daily breeze from the west. On the living room wall Laura had hung a poster print of the Edward Hopper painting of a lonely Pittsburgh diner.

The beach was undemanding, so Karen followed it north for a mile or so one morning. Beaches were not susceptible to change. Rock and water and sand would not surprise her. The littoral was a complex terrain of black stone and tide pools, which discouraged casual sunning but was good for beachcombing. Karen felt an instinctive liking for the people she saw that overcast day, picking their way along the waterline with somber expressions and knitted sweaters. From a promontory overgrown with sea grass she was able to sit and look back at the town, its quiet grid of roads, to identify Laura's tall house among all the others. *Home,* she thought tentatively. But the word was only hypothetical. She tasted it with her tongue and wondered whether it would ever make sense again.

The wind came in from the sea, and she shivered and began the long walk back.

The next day Laura drove her into town for lunch. Michael said he'd be okay at the house with Emmett. They were tossing an old softball down by the water; Emmett grinned and nodded. Emmett was a musician (Laura said), but trustworthy; yes, he would make sure Michael was fed.

By day, the town of Turquoise Beach seemed even more cheerfully low-rent. Laura explained that it was pretty much a bohemian town. The oldest houses, she said, dated from the twenties. There had been a successful cannery operation in Turquoise Beach from 1923 through the Depression, and the cannery barons had built these brick Victorian-style houses on the hills overlooking the sea. When the cannery closed for good, in the fifties, Turquoise Beach had almost closed with it. But it struggled on as a very marginal resort town, too far from the city to attract much tourist trade, a weathering anachronism, increasingly home to literary hermits and similar eccentrics.

By the mid-sixties it had become a booming seaside bohemia. Aldous Huxley had lived out his last years in a big red-brick house on Cabrillo; the poet Gary Snyder was supposed to have spent some winters here. In the seventies a lot of arts-and-crafts businesses had moved in, and so Turquoise Beach—in its small way—had prospered. Today many of the residents were perfectly straight, middle-class types employed at the new aerospace plant up the highway. But the atmosphere persisted.

Laura parked along the main street, which was called Caracol Street, and Karen followed her sister into a café restaurant with folding chairs and tiny tables that spilled out onto the sidewalk. It was past one and the lunch crowd had faded. Twice, Laura nodded and smiled at people passing in the street. But for the most part they were alone—it was a place where they could talk.

Laura said, "You like it so far?"

Karen wondered what to say. She decided it was not a decision she could make. Not yet. She said, "I want to know more about it."

"The town? The world? What?"

"I guess—the world."

"Tough question. Where to begin?"

"Anywhere," Karen said. "Anything." But what *did* she want to know, really? "Is there a Canada?"

"Yes."

"Is there a Soviet Union?"

"Yes . . . but the borders are a little different."

"Have there been wars?"

"Yes."

"The same wars?"

"Not quite."

"Are there atomic bombs?"

"Very few. Is that the kind of thing you want to know?" Laura put down her napkin and looked thoughtful. "Geopolitics. Well, let's see. The Yalta Conference came out a little differently. The Beirut Accords banned the proliferation of nuclear weapons in 1958, and the ban is enforced, and with a vengeance. Poland is a member of the EEC. Turkey is a Moslem nation, but Iran isn't. Uh—"

Karen shook her head. "It doesn't matter. What you're saying is that it's a more peaceful world?"

"I think that's the most basic thing. Yes, it's more peaceful. And no, I don't know why, exactly. There's no process, nothing obvious that stops wars from happening. They *do* happen. World War II happened . . . although the Holocaust was a much more limited event, and Japan was wise enough to stay out of it entirely. Still, the European war was bloody, Americans died in trenches. All the awfulness, barring Hiroshima. But some peace came out of it. Nobody looking for enemies, nobody wanting enemies. No McCarthy era. America was prosperous and maybe complacent in those years, but not hysterical."

Karen said—it came out sounding more skeptical than she intended—"No more bad guys?"

"Plenty. There's racism, there's religious intolerance, there's conformity. There are famines. But the *scale* of it is different. Just slightly shifted. I would call it a gentler world. No CIA, no military advisers in Third World countries, and the crime rate is pretty low —although everybody complains about it." She smiled. "And the weather is nice."

Karen tried to think of all the things that had frightened her in her daily life. "Pain," she said. "Disease. Death."

"We're not in paradise. But you can get into a hospital without taking out a second mortgage."

"Drugs." The great parental nightmare.

"There are drugs," her sister said. "But I've never heard of a real heroin problem outside the worst urban neighborhoods. Not as much alcoholism either. Not too much demand for cocaine or amphetamines. Life's, you know, a little slower. But you can buy small amounts of marijuana. Legally."

Karen said, "A great place to run away to."

"Hey, if that's what you're doing, it's nothing to be ashamed of. Sometimes you have to run away."

You should know, Karen thought, and was instantly ashamed of herself. She said, "It *is* nice. Well, obviously." Added, "You're happy here?"

Her sister did not immediately answer. Karen understood that she had asked one of the basic questions, one of the dangerous ones. Abruptly Laura became her little sister again, and Karen thought old, unanswerable thoughts: *I should have protected her . . . I should have . . .*

"I'm as happy," Laura said carefully, "as I can

imagine myself being. And I wouldn't go back. Not to stay. This is home now."

Home. That word again.

Karen said, "Then I was wrong . . . all those years ago."

Laura put her hand across the table, bracelets jangling. "That's not what I meant."

But the awareness of that old argument hung in the air between them. Karen turned to face the street, hoping to shake this sudden melancholy, or something worse than melancholy. But the street, Caracol Street in this odd town in this peculiar world, seemed abruptly foreign. A shrill and passing thought: *You shouldn't have come here. It was bad to come here.* Daddy's voice echoing in her head.

She thought of Laura twenty years ago, in the hotel in Santa Monica.

2

It was 1969, a bewildering year. Karen was working on an English degree at Penn State, commuting home odd weekends. Tim was restive in high school; Laura was in her second semester at UC Berkeley and —Karen's mother said—in serious trouble.

Karen had come home for the Easter break. Home that year was the house in Polger Valley, an old steel town in the Mon Valley, its ancient mills revived by the war in Vietnam. Daddy had taken work at the foundry; Karen's mother was working part-time at the hairdresser. Karen had mostly paid her own tuition at Penn, with only a little help from her parents. Laura's college had taken a respectable bite out of the savings, though, and Tim's education remained in doubt—he was bright but refused to take a job. The draft was a threat, but Tim claimed he would find a way to fail the physical, or maybe run off to Canada . . . and maybe he would; but it was Karen's idea that he said these things mostly to make Daddy angry. Then Tim could storm out of the house and commiserate with his long-haired friends. Tim, who wore an American flag stitched upside down to the back of his denim jacket, was a lightning rod for conflict.

Daddy was sulking the weekend Karen came home; Tim was absent. The scenario was familiar.

Her mother took her aside after dinner. Lately, Karen had acquired some perspective toward her parents. They were adults, and she was an adult; she should be able to talk to them in an adult way.

At least that was the theory. In practice it was more difficult. But she tried to be objective.

"We had a letter from Laura," her mother said.

Her voice was restrained. She didn't want Daddy hearing this. Daddy was in the room he called the den, a tiny room off the downstairs hallway, watching TV. Karen and her mother sat in the kitchen. The kitchen, Karen thought, was the most reassuring room in the house, and therefore the best room for bad news. Karen focused this moment in her mind: dishes stacked on the drainboard, her mother in a flower-print housedress, the envelope clutched in one hand. "Laura's not in Berkeley anymore."

Karen blinked. Not in Berkeley? "Well, where is she? Is she coming home?"

Mama shook her head and handed Karen the letter.

The letter was very brief. It explained that Laura had dropped her courses and moved in with some friends, that "you might not be hearing from me too often," that "I want to find a place for myself in my own way." The return address on the envelope was in Los Angeles.

Her mother said, "I haven't mentioned this to Daddy. You know how he is."

He would be angry, Karen thought. Her new objectivity allowed her to understand that Daddy was often angry with his children. She had not yet fathomed the reason why.

Her mother did something astonishing then. She reached into the pocket of her housedress and took out two one-hundred-dollar bills and pushed them across the kitchen table toward Karen.

Karen looked at the money, bewildered.

"Take it," Mama said. "Household money. It doesn't matter. Take it and go out there. Find her and try to talk some sense into her."

I have finals, Karen thought. I have to study. I can't take the time.

But she could not bring herself to say any of this.

Instead, faintly awed, she took the money and folded it into the pocket of her Levi's. It made an uneasy presence there.

Her mother said, "You always were the sensible one."

She booked tickets and a hotel room through a travel agent. The process was frightening—she had never traveled so far in her life. "Is this a vacation?" the travel agent asked. "I don't know," Karen said. "I guess so."

She rented a car at the Los Angeles airport, mapped out a route to the hotel and followed it scrupulously, showered, and then drove to the address Laura had written on the envelope.

She was dismayed when she saw the house. It was a single-story box at the foot of a canyon road. The blank walls had been painted canary yellow; the paint was peeling. A motorcycle was parked in front.

She knocked on the frame of the screen door. There was a pause, then the door wheezed open. The man inside was tall and very thin. He was wearing a sweatshirt and tight, threadbare jeans. He had a beard.

"Hey," he said. He seemed confused. "You look like Laura."

"I'm her sister." Karen's eyes began to adjust to the dimness. The room was a mess. An open mattress, a water pipe, bundles of clothes . . . "Can I talk to her?"

"Laura? Laura's not here. Hasn't been here for a couple of days." Blankly: "You want to come in?"

Karen shook her head. She took a notebook and a pen from her purse and scribbled the address of the hotel. "Will you give this to her?"

The man shrugged. "If she shows up." He hesitated. "It's Karen, right?"

Karen paused on her way down the concrete steps. "You know me?"

"She talked about you."

And so there was nothing to do but wait. The waiting made her feel guilty, passive. She ought to be doing something. But what? Hire a detective? It was ludicrous. And she couldn't afford it. She waited by the phone and tried to bury herself in the texts she'd brought with her. Faulkner and Sir Walter Scott. The books blended in her mind, a weird double exposure, all these strange families haunted by the past. When the phone finally did ring—a day before her return ticket came due—she jumped as if she'd been slapped.

She yanked up the receiver and said, "Laura?"

"It's no good you coming here, you know." Small,

distant voice. "I mean, I appreciate it. But it's pointless."

She gripped the phone with all her strength. "I want to see you."

"I appreciate that. I don't know if it's possible."

"Today," Karen said. "I'm leaving in the morning."

There was a long silence then, the ticking and whispering of the Bell exchanges.

"All right," Laura sighed. "You're at some hotel?" She repeated the address.

"I'll be over later."

Click and hum.

Karen was faintly shocked when she saw her sister, though obviously she should have been expecting this: Laura looked like a hippie.

"Hippie" was a word Karen had heard mostly from the TV news. Scruffy people in protest parades. Drug abusers. At Penn State she had kept herself aloof from that kind of thing. She had a circle of friends, mostly women from her English courses, mostly conservative. She had seen joints circulating at sorority parties, passed from hand to hand like votive candles, but that was as radical as it got. They were all against the war, all politically progressive, never too much involved. They took a secret pride in their levelheadedness.

Like me, Karen thought. She was the sensible one. She had sensible friends.

Laura wore ancient denims and a T-shirt that had been dyed a blinding variety of colors. Her hair was braided and she had painted what looked like the signs of the zodiac on her fingernails. Karen felt strangely outmaneuvered by this, this visible declaration of eccentricity. She might be able to talk her sister out of a

bad idea, a stupid plan: but a wardrobe was too concrete. That's why they dress this way, she thought, to
bother ordinary people.

Laura came into the room and sagged limply into
a chair. "My guess," she said, "is that you're here because Mama sent you. Right? 'Go find Laura, talk some
sense into her.' " Laura mimicked the broad Mon Valley cadences of her mother's speech.

Karen felt stung. "Mama gave me the money,
yes."

"So you think she's right? I'm crazy?"

"You don't have to be defensive about it. I don't
know—*are* you crazy?"

"Yes. It's a common condition."

"You want to be talked out of it?"

"No. Very much no."

"You look tired," Karen said.

"I am. I've been making arrangements." Added,
more guardedly, "Did you read the letter? I'm going
away."

"Going where?"

"You'd probably prefer I didn't say."

Karen thought this was probably true.

"You look pretty wild," she said desperately.

"I guess I do." Laura peered at Karen then, and
Karen saw something suddenly gentler in her sister's
face. "I'm sorry about all this mysterioso stuff. Do you
want me to explain? If you came for an explanation—"

An explanation would be better than nothing.
"But let's walk," Karen said. "I'm sick of this room."

They took Cokes out along the beach.

"I came out to Berkeley," Laura said, "mostly because of all the stuff I'd been hearing about California.
Sounds stupid, right? Well, it was. Stupid and naïve.
But it was important to me . . . the idea that somewhere in the world there were people who used the

word 'freak' and didn't mean something cruel by it. It was always Tim who talked about us that way. Remember? 'We're freaks,' he would say. 'We ought to get used to that.'"

Karen said, "Tim always had a cruel streak. He had no cause to say that. Anyway, that was a long time ago."

"It was when we were in high school. And the thing is, he was right."

Karen turned toward the ocean. "You don't believe that."

"I do believe it. And *you* believe it." She touched Karen's arm. "I'm sorry. I know how you hate this. But we have to talk about it. We've spent too long not talking about it. We're freaks and we've been freaks since we were born. That's why Daddy hates us so much. That's why he beat us whenever he caught us doing what we can do."

Karen's consternation was immense. She tried to summon the objectivity she had cultivated at school. In her psych. course, all this would have seemed very simple. But words like "Daddy" and "freak" lay in uneasy proximity and she dared not inspect them too closely. "Those old dreams," she stammered, "those old games—"

"They weren't dreams. They aren't games." Laura sighed, hesitated, seemed to consider how to proceed. Began again patiently: "When you're told long enough, and hard enough, and early enough, that something is bad, and unmentionable, and dirty, then you believe it. You can't help but believe. *I* believed it. But I was lucky enough to get beyond all that."

(Karen thought, But you never *did* believe it. You were like Tim. Rebellion was always easy for you.)

Laura said, "At Berkeley, everybody was doing acid—"

"LSD?" Karen was horrified.

"Don't believe what you read in the papers. I mean, it doesn't live up to Leary's rap either. But it taught me a few things. I was able to stand outside myself, really look at myself for the first time." She became fervent. "The sense of *possibilities*—I think that's what we're really all about, you and me and Tim. We can see what other people can't."

"Possibilities," Karen said dully: but this was all way beyond her control . . .

"Worlds," Laura said. "Isn't that what everybody's looking for? A better world? You know, I used to go down to the Haight with some friends. And there was this same feeling—a better world *is* possible. You know what the Haight is now? A ghetto full of teenage crank addicts. That whole thing is dying. Dead. Everybody's gone off—to the desert, to Sonoma, to Oregon. The *vision* is dead. So I came down here with some people who wanted to set up a community, a more creative way of living together—we used those words. You saw the house? A pit. And Jamie's gone back to her parents, and Christine is pregnant, and Donald's in Canada dodging the draft, and Jerry has a very bad needle habit. So the dream dies, right?"

Karen was appalled. Drugs and needles and communes. It sounded squalid.

Laura said, "But it doesn't *have* to die. I have this ability, this freakish ability to walk sideways off the planet. And I am convinced that there *is* a better world out there somewhere. Out in that tangle of could-be's. Not a dream, and not any of those hellish places Tim was always opening up. I mean a *good* place. A place where people care about each other, where stupidity doesn't claw us all down."

Karen folded her hands in her lap. "I think Mama was right. I think you *are* crazy."

"Oh, Karen, come on. If anyone's living in a dreamworld, it's you. You remember that night in the old house on Constantinople? When we went down the ravine, and Timmy opened a door into that old cobble city by the sea? How cold it was, and that man—"

"We made that up," Karen said, more loudly than she had meant to. On the beach, a strolling couple glanced toward her.

She stared at the ground.

"Well, I remember it," Laura said softly. "I remember Timmy getting beat for it. Then me. Then you. You worst of all. Because you're the oldest. Our protector. That's what they wanted you to be. Karen's supposed to know better. Karen—"

"Stop it."

"You just can't admit it, can you?"

"No," Karen snapped.

"No. Because admitting would mean admitting so much else. That the world is stranger than it looks. That Daddy doesn't know best. That when Daddy beats you it doesn't mean he loves you. Maybe the opposite. And maybe that's the worst thing of all."

Karen stood up. There was sand on her dress. She felt prim and ridiculous brushing it off. Her hands trembled.

Laura said, "Going home?"

"Don't make fun of me!"

"No . . . oh, Karen, I'm sorry. But you don't have to go."

"I have exams."

"You don't have to have exams."

"What?"

"Come with me. We could do it together. Cross some borders."

She's serious, Karen thought. My God, she's serious.

She clutched the strap of her purse. "I never wanted a better world. I don't *need* one. Don't you understand that? All I want is to be normal."

And in the morning she flew back to Pennsylvania and did not see her wild sister again for twenty years.

She sat in the café on Caracol Street with this oppressive memory tugging at her. The Laura facing her now across this table was older—not repentant but certainly less wild. "You were right," Karen admitted, "about a lot of things."

"I think each of us believed the other was running away."

"Maybe we were."

"Maybe we still are." Karen frowned. Laura continued, "There are so many questions we never asked. Never let ourselves ask. How come we can do what we do? Are we freaks of nature, genetic misprints? Or something else? And there's Tim. I haven't heard from him since he left home back in '72—have you?"

"No. Nobody in the family has." But this was still perilous talk. "I don't think it matters what we are. The past is the past."

Laura shook her head. "It *does* matter."

She put down a bill and change for lunch; they threaded their way out of the restaurant. The sun was shining down Caracol Street from the west. Laura shaded her eyes and said, "It will matter to Michael."

Chapter Five

....

Emmett was a pretty neat guy, Michael decided.

Emmett played acoustic guitar for a Latino folk band called Rio Negro and also did some solo stuff in the local Turquoise Beach clubs. His apartment, which was the floor downstairs from Aunt Laura, looked like a music shop. He had all kinds of stringed instruments hanging on pegs or just leaning up against the walls. Emmett showed Michael how to tell the difference between a flamenco guitar, a classical guitar, and a steel guitar; showed him a Dobro, an F-style mandolin, an old long-necked Vega banjo—"the Pete Seeger model." Michael wandered through the clutter in dumb amazement. He said, "I took a few lessons a year or so ago . . . I know some chords."

Emmett said, "Yeah? Well, hey, there's an old Gibson over there if you want to try it. Doesn't look like much but it plays okay."

Michael held the guitar reverently.

Garage-sale material, he thought, but the joints were good and the strings felt new. He finger-picked a G, Em, C. His fingers felt clumsy but the chords rang out.

Emmett fetched down his own guitar, a twelve-string Martin. "I have handmade guitars, I have foreign guitars. But I keep coming back to this old Martin. Bitch to tune, but I love the sound it makes." He perched on a window seat with the Venetian blinds and the sea behind him and played complex runs that made Michael feel hopelessly amateur. Emmett smiled through his beard. "You want to play something?"

Michael said he might be able to chord along to some old folkie stuff. *Union Maid* or *Guantanamera* or something on that order. "Chord along, then," Emmett said, and Michael tried gamely to keep up as Emmett launched into *The Bells of Rhymney*. His voice was a rough, strong baritone and Michael was amazed at the sincerity he brought to the old Seeger protest tune. *"Is there no future, cry the brown bells of Merthyr—?"* It made him shiver.

They played through half a dozen songs until Michael's fingers were sore. Emmett grinned massively. "Not bad," he said. He reached into the pocket of his shirt and took out something Michael was able to identify as a joint. He lit it, inhaled, extended his hand.

Michael maintained his cool. "It might be better if you didn't tell my mom."

"About the smoke?"

Michael nodded.

"She disapproves?"

"She would."

Emmett said, "Okay, then . . . our secret."

Michael toked carefully. He had smoked a couple of times in Dan's basement, weekends. He managed not to cough. But the sweet, pungent smoke went through him like a wind. He felt instantly light-headed.

He made a move to hand Emmett back the old Gibson guitar. Emmett said, "Keep it."

Michael goggled.

"It's not an heirloom. Long as you play it, hang on to it. If you get tired of it I'll take it back."

He cradled the guitar in his lap. Afternoon sunshine glinted off the varnish. It was a better guitar than Emmett made it out to be. The pain in his fingers had retreated, so Michael hugged the Gibson against his chest and picked out a few bars of an old Paul McCartney song, *Yesterday*.

Emmett nodded appreciatively. "That's pretty. You make that up?"

"What, you never heard it?"

"Nope. Should I?"

"The Beatles," Michael said. "You know? Lennon and McCartney? *Sergeant Pepper, Abbey Road?*"

"New one on me," Emmett said happily. "These guys play at your school?"

And so Michael was reminded again that he had come a long way in that car trip with Aunt Laura.

It was so easy to forget. It was not as if they were in a foreign country. Everybody spoke English, everybody drove on the right side of the road. But, he thought, it *was* a foreign country. The concept was familiar from the science fiction he'd read: a "parallel world."

Easy to say. Less easy to deal with. He had played ball with Emmett on the beach; he had watched TV;

he had behaved—these last few days—as if everything were normal. He understood that his mother wanted that from him, and for now—at least for a while—he was willing to give it. And it worked, this illusion-making: for hours at a time he really *would* forget what had happened in the car, or before that, back home, with the Gray Man.

But then his mind would circle back and he would recall that he was a stranger here. And the questions would crowd in. Obviously Laura possessed this ability, to step sideways out of the world, and by implication so did his mother, and you could take that a little further: maybe *he* did, too.

So what did that make them? A family of monsters? Wizards? Space aliens?

The weed had dried out his throat; his voice was husky. He said, "Do you think there's anything strange about my mom?"

Emmett seemed nonplussed by the question. "Too soon to tell, sport. What do you think?"

Michael shook his head: it was irrelevant. "How about Laura?"

"I'm fond of her," Emmett said guardedly. "Is that what you want to know?"

"No, no . . . I mean, what would you think if I said she was a witch?"

"I would say you had better reconsider your vocabulary." Added, "Maybe I want my guitar back."

"I don't mean it that way. I mean, like—magic powers and so forth."

"Magic?" Emmett seemed amused. "Your mom was right, kiddo. You should probably avoid this stuff."

So Michael went for a walk up the beach, by himself.

He brought along Emmett's guitar—his guitar

now. He carried the battered Gibson carefully, mindful that the weed had left him a little off balance. He picked his way among the rocks for what seemed like an endless time, but when he looked back the house was still plainly in sight. He perched himself on a flat piece of shale where he could keep an eye on his aunt's place, so he would know when his mom got back—but where he would not necessarily be seen—and played aimless quiet finger chords. The dope was obviously pretty strong. Parallel-world marijuana. He closed his eyes and stretched out across the face of the rock, letting the afternoon sun roll over him.

I am what my mother is. I am what Aunt Laura is.

Inescapable logic. The "what" remained uncertain.

There was a tingling sensation in his extremities; his fingers seemed to tremble. Michael pressed his palms against the hot, sandy surface of the stone. Hot shale and beach tar. *Hanging on,* he thought. *Anchoring myself here.*

All an illusion, of course: the solidness of things, the *realness* of things. What was a world if you could drive a car out of it? And he recognized that this was an old fear, that he used to go to bed with this fear, the fear that he might accidentally dream himself off the planet.

It had never happened. Not by accident. But maybe he could do it on purpose.

It was a possibility he had never dared consider. Considering it now—even in the privacy of his own mind—sent shivers through him. The strange tingling in his hands increased; if it were a sound, he thought, it would be a high-pitched whine.

He whispered, "Do it."

Nobody to hear him but the sea and this cloud-rippled sky.

Emmett's dope had trampled his inhibitions. Roll with it, he thought. Why not? Why not *now*, why not *here?*

"Do it."

He sat up and held his arms out in front of him. He was aware of the sound of the sea washing in against the rocks, a distant gull wheeling and diving. He pressed thumb against thumb, forefinger against forefinger, so that a circle of sea and sky was framed by his hands. Like a private TV screen, he told himself. The tingling revved into a sensation like electricity. Four zillion volts screaming along his spine, now concentrated in this circle of air. It was a heady feeling.

So what's on TV?

He narrowed his eyes.

Imagine a storm there. A vortex, a whirlpool, and the whirlpool is the sum of all things possible, doors and angles opening out from this locus in a hundred thousand directions. Pick one out of the multitude. Feel it. Follow it.

He closed his eyes and opened them.

He looked between his fingers at a green and red world.

It might have been the same seacoast. But in the landscape he could see through the frame of his hands there was no ocean. Green was the green of algae, of decaying sea wrack, and it occupied a long plain fading to the horizon. Red was the red of oxides and dust, the lifeless shore. He shifted his hands toward the place the town would be and saw a crater that was like the Astrodome turned upside down. Figures moved in the charred rubble around it: wheeled figures, derricklike torsos of shining silver. Machines.

The machines were singing to themselves.

Change, Michael thought hastily.

He paged again through the book of possibilities.

A better world this time. A world off the cover of an old *Popular Science:* winged cars, domed buildings, obsidian piers that stabbed across the water. There was a harbor full of boats with blinding white sails. A banner flew from a flagpole yards away, red with black insignia, a leaf and a hammer in silhouette.

Michael was sweating but mesmerized.

Change, he told himself.

An empty shore this time, no boats or people, young seals playing in the tide pools. The seals put their noses up as if they sensed his presence.

Change.

Snow swirling down on dark, spiral structures of riveted iron . . .

Change.

. . . men in furs building a fire . . .

Change.

. . . a sea full of ships as big as cities . . .

Change . . .

He stopped when he was exhausted.

He fell back against the reassuring blankness of the rock.

His head was spinning.

It's all really out there, he thought. All those places and a million others.

And it was not just seeing them. He could have gone there. Walked there across the thinnest of barriers.

He understood that he had a lot to learn. He was shotgunning his attention in a dozen directions, and maybe that wasn't good. Moreover, he couldn't toke up every time he wanted to do this—and he knew that he wanted to do it again. But at least he had proved this to himself: anything they could do, he could do.

He thought, It runs in the family.

No secrets anymore.

He turned back to the house in time to see Aunt Laura's car pull up. His mother climbed out, already scanning for him, anxious as she was so often anxious these days.

But things had changed.

Michael stood up, held Emmett's battered Gibson guitar by the neck, brushed the sand off the seat of his pants, and began the walk back home.

Chapter Six

....

1

Michael kept quiet over dinner that night. His mom was quiet, too, frowning into the broad Oriental bowl Aunt Laura had set out for her. It was Laura who did most of the talking, between chopping ginger or tending the wok.

She talked about her work. Laura was a potter, had a kiln in the big shed out back, did clays and porcelains that fetched big prices in the tourist stores out along the highway. She was thinking about maybe a new floral pattern . . . something simple. Classic. Oh, and the Chinese cabbage was fresh today. (Every-

thing smells so good, Michael's mom said listlessly.)
And wasn't the weather nice? (The weather was nice.)
And so on.

But every once in a while Laura would look at
Michael in a thoughtful way, and he was aware of it
and began to feel self-conscious. He understood that
his aunt's secret talent was strong and obvious, once
you knew what to look for—a kind of glow or aura—
and Michael wondered whether he had acquired the
same look.

But nobody said anything.

He woke up next morning anxious to test himself
again. He sat impatiently through the breakfast ritu-
als, watched a little morning TV, wore out his calluses
on the new guitar. He wanted to get away without
attracting attention. The situation was tight, Laura
and his mother moving around the house in restless
circles; he might have given up, but a couple of hours
before lunch his mom announced she'd do the shopping today, it was only fair, and took off in Aunt Laura's car with a grocery list and a handful of the weird
State Bank bills that passed for cash in Turquoise
Beach. Michael waved at the Durant and then saun-
tered around to the rear of the house, planning to cut
past the pottery studio and along the open beach
again. But when he came around the shed he saw Aunt
Laura standing by the cane fence waiting for him, and
it was too late then to turn back.

He liked Aunt Laura. She was only a couple of
years younger than his mom, but it seemed like more.
She was easy to be around. She was happy most of the
time. It was a contrast. He had begun to understand,
these few days they had spent here, how unhappy his
mom had been since the divorce. Their house in Toronto had been a deep well of silences. How long since
she had really smiled? A long time.

Aunt Laura smiled. She smiled now, standing by the broken-down fence in her Levi's and tank top. She had on a pair of round-lens sunglasses, the kind Michael thought of as Lennon glasses. "Beachcombing?" she said, and the tone of the question was half amused, half serious.

He was embarrassed. "Sort of."

"You know," she said, "we really ought to talk."

"I'd like that," he said. "Sometime. Sure. But—"

"Talk about you, Michael," she said. "About what you can do. About what you were doing out on the beach yesterday."

He could only stare.

She had made an educated guess about her nephew's long walk yesterday, based on hints, the way he looked, some cryptic comments Emmett had passed on. Judging by the expression on his face, she was on the money.

The amazing thing, Laura thought, was that it hadn't happened sooner.

She regarded her nephew as objectively as she could. Reasonable specimen of the genus adolescent male. Gaunt in his blue sweatshirt and faded jeans, cropped hair, Nike runners speckled with dry sand. He was beginning to build up a tan; a mild case of adolescent acne was on the retreat. His eyes were dark and sometimes furtive in a way that reminded her of Karen. Karen had had this same habit of dodging uneasy truths; although in Michael it was less pronounced.

She thought, A family trait.

My nephew, she thought. Karen's child. The only generation we have produced . . . unless Tim has been off siring wizards.

She walked him along the quiet back streets near

home. Turquoise Beach was a town of gardeners, and she liked the tropical greenery spilling out of these trellises and yards: bougainvillea, ground ivy, blooming aloes. Mornings like this, the air was full of wild perfume.

She thought, *It would be very hard to leave this place.*

But they had not reached that cusp quite yet.

She said, "Did your mother ever talk about home? About your grandmother and grandfather, what it was like living there?"

Obviously Michael had not adjusted to the idea of this interview. He shook his head. "Not much." Which means, Laura thought, probably never.

She gathered her thoughts. How to communicate this in a way that would make sense to a fifteen-year-old? Too much old pain here. Hard to make a good story of it. She said, "There were the three of us, your mother and me and Tim. And your grandmother and grandfather. We moved a lot, but Daddy had this little copperplate sign he used to hang up wherever we lived—'The Fauves.' To me it always sounded like some exotic species of animal. And I guess I used to think of us that way sometimes, as a separate species."

Michael's look was wary but understanding.

"Mama and Daddy were what you would call plain people. Mon Valley, Ohio River people. I still hear it in the way Karen talks . . . I hear it in myself sometimes. Daddy worked different places. Mills, mostly, back when the steel industry was good. He was a welder and he could stand in on a lathe. But he drank and got fired a lot. We lived in Duquesne a couple years, then different places around Pittsburgh. The thing about him was, he was hard to be with. He led kind of a sad, sour life. He laid a lot onto us kids." She drew a breath and saw that Michael was still attentive.

"I think it was easiest for me. I was pretty. I was the middle kid. Tim was the boy, so he had to live up to a lot of expectations. And Karen—well, your mother was the oldest, and maybe that was the worst. Everything Tim and I did wrong, she took the rap for it."

Michael ventured, "It must have been hard . . ."

"Being what we are?" But obviously that was what he meant. The crux. Even now, this was hard to talk about: she could never have said these things even to someone like Emmett. "Harder than you know. When we were little we played games. We called it 'making windows' or 'making doors.' We understood, I guess by some kind of instinct, that it was a thing to keep secret. So we did it at night, in the dark, or out in the ravine back of the old house on Constantinople. And sometimes . . . sometimes we got caught."

She had dropped her voice to a whisper. Michael walked on beside, eyes fixed on the laces of his shoes.

"Daddy said it was the worst thing a person could ever do. The worst sin. It was a sin so bad it wasn't even in the Bible, except where it said about suffering a witch to live. It was bad and it would get us in trouble . . . or it would kill us."

"He said that?"

"In so many words. Often. And sometimes with his fists."

Michael returned to his study of the sidewalk.

Laura said, "We all took it to heart, of course. But for me—certainly for Tim—the temptation was still there. It came naturally to us. We were *good* at it. And so we still did it sometimes, opened windows and doors, when we were certain we wouldn't get caught. Did it and then prayed God would forgive us. But Karen took it all very much to heart. All of us believed Daddy, but Karen believed him with this awful, fierce intensity . . . I think it blinded her. I think in a way she still believes him."

They walked along the shaded street to a corner and turned left. They passed a couple more of these tall, old houses, then a blankness of sea grass and rock. The pavement stopped at a black-and-yellow sawhorse with the words CAUTION—ROAD ENDS printed on it. Beyond that was a grassy headland, a fifty-foot drop to the sea. The water down below churned white against the rocks.

Laura sat and hugged her knees. Michael crouched against a rock, gazing off across the water.

She said, "You're not used to thinking about your mother this way."

"I guess not."

"It takes some getting used to."

He seemed very thoughtful. She let the silence stretch out. This was a place she liked to come and she was content here.

Michael picked a blade of grass and shredded it between his fingers. He said, "Is that all there is?"

"How do you mean?"

"I've never heard of anybody else who could do this. Have you? I mean, it's not even like ESP or witchcraft, something you can read about in a library book. So we were all born this way, right? But *why?* Where does it come from?"

She shrugged. "We never found out."

"You mean," he said, "you never asked."

"There was never anyone we *could* ask. Not Mama or Daddy, for sure. They didn't have the talent. You could look at them and *know* they didn't. Their parents? I met Grandma Fauve one time. She lived in an old house in Wheeling with three cats and a Doberman chained to the toolshed. She was normal as any old lady. Too, I think I would have known if Mama or

Daddy came from a home where there were people like us. There's a way of *not* talking about things . . . and neither of them talked like that."

"Then it's a mystery."

"Yes," Laura said. "It's a mystery."

"Do you think we could ever figure it out?"

The question touched a nerve. She arched her back and turned her face to the sea wind. The wind came up these bluffs like a river; every August you could see people out here with kites. But the weather had changed. Too cool for that now.

She turned to her nephew and said, "We may have to."

Before they went home, Laura said, "Show me what you can do."

Michael was reluctant at first. It was something private, something he had only just discovered. But he thought about what she'd told him—it was more than his mother had ever said—and guessed he owed her this.

But maybe he couldn't do it. Maybe he'd lost the knack. Maybe he had to be stoned to be able to do it . . . maybe he was too nervous.

He held his arms out in front of him, joined forefingers and thumb as he had yesterday. Nothing happened. Desperately, Michael searched himself for a trace of the electricity he'd been able to conjure down by the shore. He remembered how it had felt, the way it seemed to come, not *from* him, but *through* him, sourced up through the ground, a strange voltage of granite and limestone and seabed, magma and tectonics. And, remembering, he began to feel it again, faintly at first, a tingling, and then something more intense. He opened the vortex of possibility between his hands, thinking, *Yes.*

He showed her the devastated, oceanless world he had discovered yesterday. He showed her the empty world: today the seals were clustered far up the littoral and a gray rain was falling. And he showed her places he had never seen before, worlds that were nothing like Turquoise Beach: desert worlds, an ocean unbroken by land, a sky of high lavender clouds . . . more. He was dimly aware of her standing just outside the periphery of his vision, peering over his shoulder; her gasps of awe, faintly perceived, made him happy. He thought, *She sees it, too.* It wasn't a hallucination, and he wasn't crazy, and he wasn't alone. Giddy with it now, he flashed through a half dozen changes, until a sense of fatigue—a kind of interior exhaustion—forced him to stop.

Michael sagged against a boulder. His head throbbed. He took a deep, satisfying breath and said, "How's that? Is that okay?"

Laura looked at him as if from a great distance. Her voice was ragged, faint. She said, "It's more than I could ever do . . ."

2

Karen's argument with her sister happened in the evening, but the frustration had been building all that day.

It was their third week in this house. Part of the strain she felt was no doubt simply the stress of living in close quarters with Laura, who was still nearly a stranger to her. Part of it was the adjustment that inevitably followed any wrenching change.

But part of it was more than that. Part of it was a dislocation more profound. This world Laura inhabited was, curiously, almost *too* familiar. Just when Karen began to feel at home, she would stumble over some incongruity that left her head spinning. Yesterday, for instance. She had been lined up at the grocery store when she overheard the checkout girl telling a clerk that John F. Kennedy had died—in retirement, in New England, at the age of seventy-two. A stroke, she said. "Well, I admired that man. Although he *was* a Catholic."

FORMER PRESIDENT JOHN FITZGERALD KENNEDY DEAD, the headlines in the *L.A. Times* said. Funeral services were announced for Sunday. Dignitaries to gather in Washington. President Bartlett expresses grief, and so on and so forth.

All those years ago, Karen thought. Who was I mourning for?

Can a bullet really be undone? By *wishing?*

She was dazed for hours, puzzling over it.

But not just that. There was the atmosphere of Turquoise Beach itself, the easy lifestyle Laura seemed so content with. Karen was less pleased by it. It was aimlessly hedonistic, and she was not sure she wanted Michael exposed to it much longer. He had taken a liking to Emmett, Laura's downstairs boyfriend: Emmett, who played music for a living, and whom Karen had observed down by the beach at night smoking grass.

All this contributed to Karen's stress. But it was Laura who started the argument, when she insisted on talking about Michael.

Michael had gone to bed. Laura was up finishing the dishes. Karen had put on her nightgown and robe but couldn't sleep; so she sat in the kitchen under the cool fluorescence of the ceiling lights, listening to the wet clack and rattle from the sink.

Laura declined her offer to dry and said, "You really ought to talk to him, you know."

"Michael's doing fine," Karen said. "He's adjusted well these last few days."

"I don't think platitudes are too useful right now, do you? You know what I mean."

"The talent," Karen said. "Does it always have to come around to that?"

"This time it does. Haven't you thought about how confusing this all must be for him? Not just Turquoise Beach, but all that mess before you left—the Gray Man. What's he supposed to think about it?"

I would prefer, Karen thought, that he *didn't* think about it. She knew how ridiculous that would sound. But it would be simpler—"It would be simpler," she said, "if we could just lead a normal life here."

"Normal!" Her sister dropped a plastic gravy boat into the drainer. "You hold up that word like it's some kind of holy relic! I mean, I *understand*—but Christ, Karen, I'm not sure 'normal' is something you and I can aim for!"

"For Michael's sake—"

"I'm *talking about* Michael's sake. He's a smart kid, he's curious, and I think he deserves whatever explanation we can give him."

Karen was silent a while. Finally she said, "I was hoping to keep him above all this."

"It's a little past that."

Laura dried her hands and sat at the small butcher-block table.

"Michael is a bright, curious kid. He should be talking to you about all this, not me."

Karen looked up sharply. "He's talked to you?"

"Yes."

"What did you tell him?"

"The truth."

Karen was shocked. "Everything? I mean—back home, Tim and Daddy, all that?"

"All that."

She was mortified. All this had happened behind her back. "He's hardly ready! He's only fifteen!" It was like a conspiracy. "Jesus, Laura, he's my son! I have a right to make some choices!"

"He's your son. And I'm sorry if I interfered. But he's also a very confused young person badly in need of answers. He *should* have come to you . . . but he didn't. He didn't feel like he could."

"So instead he came to you? *Why?*" She felt wounded. "Because you inhabit this hippie utopia here? So what did you tell him? That everything would be okay if we all wore tie-dye and denim a little more often?"

Laura stood up and went back to the sink. She faced the window, which was full of night, and Karen could see her face reflected there, lips pressed tightly together.

Laura said, "This is the best I could do. You understand that? I think . . . whatever this talent we have is, I think it's connected somehow with imagination. The ability to see what isn't there, at least the shape of it, the outline. I wanted to find the best place I could, a place to live, a *sane* place—I wanted to dream it into existence. And this is the best I could do." Her shoulders moved in a shrug. "Maybe I didn't do too well."

"I didn't mean—"

"Maybe Michael could do better. Did you ever consider that?"

She was taken aback. "Michael?"

"It's obvious enough. Look at him sometime. I mean, really look." Laura turned away from the window. Her fingers were tight against the rim of the

counter. "I think he's more talented than any of us
. . . more talented even than Tim."

But it was not something Karen wanted to think
about.

Bad enough that Michael had to know about all
this. Bad enough that she had brought him here; bad
enough that Laura had dragged him into all that old
family misery. Bad but, okay, maybe understandable.
He *was* a part of it, and maybe she should have talked
to him.

But she had not wanted to admit to herself that
Michael himself might have the talent.

Had not allowed herself to admit it. It was the
Great Unthinkable. The last time she had considered
the idea—the memory came rushing back—was when
she was pregnant. Michael had not been Michael then,
had only been this presence inside her, an awkward
weight, a coiling of life against her belly. Lying in bed
at night, feeling him kick, she had allowed the
thought: *What if he is like me?* She guessed it was like
having one of those genetic diseases, that disease
Woody Guthrie had. It had corrupted her life and
might corrupt her child's.

Could she bear that?

She had pressed herself against Gavin, who was
sleeping soundly, until his warmth suffused her body.
She resolved then, drifting toward a troubled sleep,
that she would not even consider the possibility. Their
child would be normal. She would make him normal.
She would wish him into normalcy, pray him into normalcy; their home would be a normal home. Surely
that was enough?

So Laura was right, of course. She had made an
icon of that word, "normal." It was a gift, and she had
tried to give that gift to Michael.

Tried and—well, it should have been obvious—failed.

She raised her head and regarded her sister. "You're saying I was the one who ran away . . . who hid."

"I believed that once. I don't think I can be so self-righteous now. I think we both ran away from it, each of us in our own way." She added, "Michael's different."

Fearfully: "What do you mean?"

"He never learned to be afraid of it. He's been asking questions you and I can't answer. Did we inherit this? Is it a miracle, or is it something we can understand?"

Karen shook her head. "There aren't any answers."

"We can't be sure of that. We never really tried to find them."

"How *would* we?"

"Karen, I don't know. But I think we would have to start at home, with Mama and Daddy. And we would probably have to talk to Tim."

"That's absurd."

"Is it?"

"We're safe here."

Laura said, "Are we?"

"What do you mean?"

She spoke in careful, somber tones. "The Gray Man. That's something else we never talked about. But he's the same man, isn't he? The same man we saw that night in the ravine, with Tim, all those years ago."

Karen was precipitated suddenly back into her dream, the dark streets of that other seaside town, cold cobbles against her bare feet, and the Gray Man (it *was* him), offering gifts from the cavernous hollow of his coat. And Laura remembered it, too; therefore it *wasn't* a dream, it was a memory; and only her desperate wanting had convinced her otherwise. She said, "He can't find us here."

"I would dearly love to believe that. Only I'm not sure it's true. We just don't *know*. And isn't that the point? We don't know enough to protect ourselves."

"You said we'd be safe here!"

"Safer than where you were. But I can't guarantee for how long."

Karen whispered, "I don't want to go back home . . . I don't want to dig up all that trouble."

Laura straightened the dish towel and hung it to dry. She walked to where Karen sat, put her hands on Karen's shoulders. The touch was cool, soothing. "Neither do I," she said. "You don't know how *much* I don't want to go home. I wouldn't do it for myself. You want the honest truth, I don't believe I would do it for you. But I think we should do it for Michael."

3

Laura slept downstairs that night, with Emmett.

The affair was on-again, off-again, usually at Laura's call. Emmett was almost pathologically easygoing about relationships. If Laura wanted to be his lover, fine. If she had something else to do or somebody else to see, well, he could live with that, too.

It was not an *unhealthy* attitude—it pretty much mirrored her own approach—but it lacked something in the way of passion.

But tonight she needed his warmth. She lay beside him in his bed, a beat-up four-poster he had acquired at a junk shop in Pueblo de Los Angeles, cradled in this outrageous down-filled mattress. They had made love and now the bedroom was dark and cool, a comforting place. Sometimes she liked to imagine Emmett's bed as a sailing ship drifting out to sea, timbers creaking. She thought that was a fine way to fall asleep.

Emmett sat up, lit a joint, offered it to her. She toked, but only lightly. She was afraid it might make her paranoid. It was good, though, to take the rough edges off things. Tonight she wanted gentility, calm, ease.

Outside the bamboo blinds there was darkness and the sound of the tide coming in. Emmett's big hand moved in time, stroking her shoulder. The sheet on Emmett's bed was light and cool as rain. Emmett toked deeply; she saw the tip of the joint flare in the darkness.

She said, not exactly meaning to, "What would you think if I went away?"

Emmett, whose reaction time was glacial even when he was not stoned, thought it over. Eventually he said, "Where are you going? How long?"

She moved her hand through the bristly hair on his chest. "Can't say where. Maybe for a while."

"Long time?"

"Could be long. What would you say?"

"I would ask," Emmett said thoughtfully, "whether you were coming back."

"Coming back probably for sure." She added, "You're dodging the question."

"You know the answer." He sat cross-legged, and she admired the way the trickle of moonlight played over the exposed ridge of his hips. Pale flesh like distant mountains. He said, "I'd miss you 'til you came back."

It should have pleased her. Oddly, it didn't.

She was annoyed both with Emmett and with

herself. What did she *want* him to say? "I can't live without you"? "Stay or I'll shoot myself"? She had cultivated a certain kind of relationship with him and she could hardly complain if he cooperated in it.

But (the irritation peaking now) it was not just Emmett, it was *everything*, Turquoise Beach, her life here. Karen's visit had jogged too many old memories. Laura had arrived here straight out of the heady psychedelic whirl of Berkeley at the end of the sixties, and Turquoise Beach had seemed like a distant colony, a gentler outpost of that same dizzying empire. And yet. And yet. In those days she had been full of energy, obsessed with the idea of going *beyond, further, deeper.* Since then, imperceptibly, by inches, her life had slowed. The final revelation, what they used to call the White Light in her sophomore LSD sessions, remained always out of grasp. And so the fervor cooled. Life became merely pleasant.

Her sometimes affair with Emmett was pleasant. It would always be pleasant. But Karen was—and this had taken Laura by surprise—a chastening example. Karen had showed up with her compulsive conformity, her exaggerated regard for the "normal," her fears all intact; but Laura saw the way she cared for her son—cared for him profoundly, wordlessly, wholeheartedly—and understood that her own passions were trivial by comparison; that her idea of love was something truncated and selfish. Karen loved Michael in a way that was genuinely *beyond, further, deeper.*

She felt a wave of vertigo from Emmett's highly potent grass. The bed seemed to rotate backward. The night had closed in, suddenly, like a wall.

Love, she thought, is a very dangerous thing.

Emmett stretched out, moving toward sleep. He turned his head against the pillow. "You know," he said distantly, "Mike was right . . . you are kinda spooky."

But time passed, a week, ten days, and she began to think she had been unnecessarily alarmed, unreasonably paranoid . . . until the evening Michael came home ashen-faced and said he had seen the Gray Man out along the beach.

Chapter Seven

....

"**W**ho is he?" Michael couldn't restrain the question any longer. "Where does he come from?"

But his mother and his aunt only exchanged furtive glances, as if to acknowledge some mutual guilt, a contract whose terms had come due at last.

He had climbed up the bluffs once again, the same place he'd talked to his aunt a couple of weeks back.

Michael understood why she liked this place. Turn one direction and you could see Turquoise Beach laid out between its hills in clean, logical blocks. Turn back and there was the ocean, sunlight glinting off the whitecaps. The height made everything seem far way and very still, very schematic.

Today even the air was calm. He stationed himself so that he could see the sandier part of the beach north of here, where a few people had laid out towels to catch this burst of late October sunlight. He watched the distant shapes of their sand-colored bodies and plucked out aimless tunes on the flat-top Gibson. He was a little more nimble-fingered now; he'd been practicing every day. He played Beatles tunes and thought with some amusement how impressed Emmett would be. Hey, he thought, if we stay here I'll be a songwriter; I'll call myself Lennon McCartney.

He had been exercising his other talent, too, these last few weeks.

Laura had taught him a lot. She had shown him the importance of discipline, control. "You have a great talent," she had said, "in the raw, but you have to learn to focus it—to *aim* it. It's the difference between going where you want to go and being tossed around in a storm. You have to know where you're going and you have to know how to get back."

She was with him the first time he made a door. In an angle of beach between two big stones Michael opened a passage and held it open while the two of them stepped through. Stepped from Turquoise Beach into the deserted shore he had glimpsed through the window of his fingers, seal herds moving in dark masses along the sand. He came into the sunshine with Laura behind him, and the seals looked up all at once, bobbing their heads with a distant, oblique curiosity. Michael understood that no one had ever hunted these animals . . . knew without thinking about it that this was a planet empty of man.

Laura guided him back, congratulated him, and told him not to do it again.

He was startled. "Why?"

"Because it's not a toy," she said. "Because it

might be dangerous. And there's another reason. I don't know for sure, but I think it might draw attention . . . I wonder if it isn't a kind of beacon light."

Because, Michael thought, unlike the seals, we *are* being hunted. She didn't say it but that was what she meant. Someone is hunting us.

Standing on the promontory, alone now, he made a tiny window between his fingers. Surely this would not attract attention?

And he looked between his fingers down at the distant beach and felt a first tentative rush of energy inside him . . . and then he hesitated.

Something familiar down there . . .

And in the circle of his fingers, Michael saw the Gray Man.

The shock was immense. He dropped his hands to his side, wiped them on his jeans as if he had touched something foul. He backed up slowly and then crouched down so the tall grass and the slope of the promontory would hide him.

He crept forward again, sweating.

The Gray Man, Walker, was still there, was down on the beach among the bathers in his gray overcoat and hat like a bad hallucination. Incredibly, no one paid him any attention. He was invisible, Michael guessed. It was magic. Walker could do that—make himself unnoticed in a crowd. None of this seemed unlikely anymore.

And now the Gray Man regarded him across that distance.

Michael felt exposed, naked. *He sees me.* He realized that Laura had been right, the Gray Man was drawn to his energy, maybe drawn whether he practiced it or not, drawn down through the hidden doors of the world; that he could be evaded but not ultimately escaped. He sees us, Michael thought.

He stood up. There was no longer any reason not to.

A communication had been established now, a contact. He peered down across the rocky beach at the Gray Man and the Gray Man seemed to swell and occupy the whole of his field of vision. Michael imagined he could hear the Gray Man's voice inside his head, softly insinuating.

You deserve an explanation, the Gray Man said. *I can give you that.*

No, Michael thought. No bargain. He was being hunted; he knew that now. He would be crazy to accept any kind of offer . . . he was crazy to be standing here like this, hypnotized.

But the voice was very compelling.

I know you, Michael.

He felt the truth in this.

I know you better than they do.

Walker moved toward the headland now. His motion was cautious, delicate; his eyes were on Michael's eyes. Even over that distance Michael felt the pressure.

The Gray Man said, *Come with me.*

Where? Michael wondered. Where does he want me to go?

The answer was immediate. He blinked and in the darkness behind his eyelids he saw an ancient industrial town, cobbled streets, tall black buildings, a stone gate engraved with the image of an eye and a pyramid. Well, hell, Michael thought, I could go there if I wanted. He was proud of his new abilities. I could find that place.

We can go there together.

It wasn't very far . . .

But he was distracted by a flicker of color on the beach. A little girl ran up from the shore, bright yellow one-piece bathing suit. She ran toward the Gray Man. She can see him, Michael realized. She was something his magic had neglected. She ran toward him and then hunkered down and stared at him, this mystery, the Invisible Man, or at least a man who wasn't dressed for the beach.

The spell broke as Michael's attention shifted. He gasped for air, realized that he had been on the verge of a terrible capitulation.

He felt the Gray Man's irritation radiate up from the shore like a brutal heat. In a gesture that was almost casual, Walker waved his hand at the little girl, and the little girl fell backward out of time: a motion Michael could only barely perceive, out and away into some chaos of possibility. The girl had vanished silently from the beach.

Michael hesitated a second, stunned by what he had seen. It was an act of murder as casual as the swatting of a fly.

He glanced back one more time at the Gray Man —at Walker—then turned to race down the grassy slope of the promontory, past these old whitewashed houses and their winter gardens, Emmett's guitar banging out crazy discords against his hip.

Far away, he heard a woman's voice calling a name.

His mother seemed paralyzed by the news. His aunt reacted more swiftly. She bolted the door and instructed Michael to pack his things. "I'll tell Emmett to lock up downstairs." And moved off toward the bedroom.

"Aunt Laura?"

She paused to look back.

Michael said, "Who is he?"

Her frown deepened. "We don't really know. I think . . . maybe we have to find out."

"We're leaving in the morning?"

"Yes."

"Where are we going?"

His mother broke the silence. Her eyes looked bruised; her voice was faint.

"A long way," she said. "Back home."

NOVUS ORDO

1

Cardinal Simon Palestrina—of the Vatican Congregation of Extraordinary Ecclesiastical Affairs, and now de facto a legate to the Court of the Novus Ordo—wrapped his cloak against the October wind and grimly regarded the approaching coast of the New World.

The bleakness of the coast was mirrored in the Cardinal's face. The severity of his expression, the pallor of his cheeks, had won him a reputation as a dour, almost Jesuitical scholar. In fact he was a Manichean Brother, and his countenance derived more from the periodic attacks of gastritis that had marked his entry into middle age than any surmised ecclesiastical purity. His friends were of course aware of it . . . but Cardinal Palestrina had very few friends. He suffers best, Palestrina often thought, who suffers alone.

For similar reasons, he had kept his own counsel through the course of this long transatlantic journey. In a sane world he would have made the trip by dirigible. The airships had been improved immensely since the days of the Teutonic tragedies. But the Curia was shamefully underbudgeted, even in light of events in the Mediterranean. Vatican conservatism, Palestrina thought dolefully; fear of potential allies . . . it could lose us this war.

Clutching the rail, he chastised himself with a vision of the Islamic hordes overrunning civilized Europe. A muezzin calling from the cathedral at Orvieto, ulemas hacking off the limbs of honest Christians. And here I stand, he thought, delayed a month on the tarry *Madonna of Avignon.*

It was not even a new ship. The rigging was ancient, the sails of much-mended hemp; the coal-oil engine belowdecks did more to pollute the immediate environment than to expedite the voyage. Cardinal Palestrina had spent his first week out from Genoa in a condition of relentless, rolling nausea. I will go home, he thought, and there will be wild Moslems in the basilica of St. Peter's, and I will seek out Fr. Oswaldo of the Funding Subcommittee in whatever dungeon they have clapped him in, and I will say, *I told you so.*

He relished this fantasy as the *Madonna of Avignon* entered the windy harbor of Philadelphia.

The city appeared to be everything Cardinal Palestrina had been led to expect of the Americans. The harbor stank. It smelled of dead fish and marshland. Every summer the yellow fever bred in this miasma and ravaged the city. The piers were old, the pilings layered with the dung of the harbor gulls. The distant towers of the city itself rose huge and black, sooty monuments to the industrial supremacy of the Novus Ordo, the New Order of the Americas. How desperately they had striven to emulate the festering valleys of the Rhine and the Rhone, how thoroughly they had succeeded.

Cardinal Palestrina, allowing the other passengers to crowd past him onto the dock, felt a pang of nostalgia for Rome. An old-fashioned city, obviously— it was older by several proud millennia than anything the Americans had built. He thought of the Vatican Garden, the Leonine Wall; he thought of the street sweepers crossing the Giardino della Pigna like an army, leaving the cobbles wet and gleaming in the morning sun . . .

A marvel. At least when the wind was not running from the Tiber.

But this was not an authentic nostalgia, he told himself, merely a reluctance. He did not relish his work here. He was a scholar, not an Inquisitor. He was only truly at home in the company of books. He had written a hagiography of St. Eustace that the Curia Romana declared "blemishless," and so he had been deemed trustworthy, bright but essentially incorruptible—or at least doctrinaire—and therefore suitable to carry out an act of ticklish ecclesiastical calculation. Perhaps more important, his English was very good. But the questions at hand were questions of means and ends, heresy and power, war and peace . . . above all, he thought, good and evil. And the dark powers were dauntingly active nowadays.

The thought was unwelcome. A spasm shot through his belly.

Sighing, Cardinal Palestrina clasped a handkerchief to his nose and descended into the New World.

* * *

He was met at the docks by a man named Carl Neumann, who drove an automobile.

The automobile was significant. The Jihadic Wars had interrupted oil traffic through the Persian Gulf; gasoline was prohibitively expensive. The Americans (Palestrina used the archaic term privately) possessed their own oilfields, of course. And their endless border crises with the Aztecs often involved mineral rights. Still, even here, an automobile was a rare indulgence.

Especially an automobile like this, large and low, immensely heavy—a kind of land boat. Palestrina, impressed in spite of himself, stowed his two small black bags in the auto's capacious trunk and climbed in beside Neumann. The smell of upholstery was sharp and oppressive.

Neumann said, "We're pleased you could make the trip, Your Eminence."

Palestrina understood instantly that Neumann was one of those government functionaries who would refer to himself constantly in the plural. Neumann wore a blue tailored suit, a narrow black tie, a fedora. They shook hands; Neumann engaged the engine. Periodically, as they worked their way south through a crush of horse-drawn trucks and cabriolets, Neumann glanced over at Cardinal Palestrina's black robes. Palestrina supposed this was the Waldensian legacy the Secretariat had warned him about: this mixture of curiosity and disdain. Annoying but, in its own way, useful. It would keep him on guard. It would remind him that he had entered a foreign country.

Not that he was likely to forget. Within the hour they had won through to a paved road leading south from the city; the forest closed around them. The Great Forest of the New World, Palestrina thought. It was legendary. Savages had lived here once. The auto-

mobile sped between endless aisles of trees. The
clouds opened to show a gaudy sunset; the night came
on quickly. The shadows behind the automobile
seemed suddenly very dense, and Palestrina thought
about wood sprites, elementals. But those were wholly
European terrors—he had read that somewhere. In
the New World the dangers were mainly secular.

Neumann spoke into the silence: "I'll be your liaison for the duration of your stay here, Your Eminence.
I'm afraid you'll have to get used to having me
around."

He smiled. Palestrina did not.

Neumann went on, "I can't help but wonder
about your name. Are you related to, uh, the famous
Palestrina?"

"You mean the Palestrina who wrote the
Marcellus Mass?"

"That's right."

"Are you a historian, Mr. Neumann?"

"Music lover," Neumann said modestly. "I collect
records. It was the *Missa Papae Marcelli* that settled
the issue of music in the liturgy, right?" Added, "A
terrific piece. Very moving."

Cardinal Palestrina disapproved of the secular recording of liturgical music. Though he himself did own
one recording, Giovanelli's *Jubilate Deo* on a Spanish
lacquer disk, a secret love: he played it on his tiny
electrical Victrola. "No," he said primly. "No rela-
tion."

Neumann seemed disappointed.

Palestrina said, "I'm really very tired. If you could
tell me where you're taking me—?"

"I'm sorry, Your Eminence. I assumed you'd been
briefed. We'll be in Washington by midnight. There's a
hotel room for you and I'll be your guide, your contact,
whatever. Then, of course, you're looking at a daily

commute to the Defense Research compound. There are people there you'll need to meet . . ."

"We'll be driving five more hours?"

"Afraid so, Your Eminence."

God help me. "And then, in Washington, I'll be allowed to see him?"

"See whom, Your Eminence?"

"This prodigy, of course. This monster you've created. The man who walks between worlds."

The silence in the automobile was brief but intense. The wheels ground against pavement. The headlamps played over deep grottoes of autumn woodland.

Neumann said, "Why, I assume so, Your Eminence."

2

Cardinal Palestrina's personal encounters with evil had been very limited.

Nevertheless he had a great respect for evil. Evil, this last century, had been what the Americans would call a growth stock. No one seemed exempt from it. Even the Church—he allowed himself a mildly blasphemous thought—even the Church had committed acts that might be called excessive. The Teutonic Inquisition, its oppression of the Jews and the Poles, doctrine wielded for political ends while Rome herself stood mute . . .

But that was history. History was replete with oppression. More important was that, lately, Christendom itself seemed threatened. Islam had swept like a brushfire through northern Africa, fomenting revolution against the Dutch, the French, the British; the

Russians were battling rebellious Moslems on their southern borders. The Oriental races had evicted the military forces of the Novus Ordo from their Pacific outposts and banned commerce with the West. There were small wars everywhere and larger ones seemed inevitable.

All the portents were ominous. On Palm Sunday in 1982 the image of the Prince of Darkness had appeared in a cloud of trichlorophenol above San Pietro in Vincoli—hundreds had been hospitalized. This last Christmas, a rain of doves had fallen on the Palazzo Venezia. Sicily had nearly succumbed to the Turkish fleet; the Mediterranean was endangered; troops had been mustered throughout Italy and Spain. The situation was desperate, or why would he have been sent here, eking out this dubious liaison with the Americans on the chance that they might in fact have produced a secret weapon?

Because, Palestrina thought, for all their naïve Protestantism and unrepentant superstition, they are more like us than the Arabs. *Salvandorum paucitas, damnandorum multitudo.* It went without saying. Also: politics makes strange bedfellows.

He slept a little in the automobile. When he stepped out into the fierce artificial light of the hotel vestibule he felt permanently bruised. His spine shrieked in pain. Neumann, perversely, was as fresh as ever. He smiled up at Palestrina through the window of the automobile like the framed painting of an especially insolent harlequin. "Can I see you to your room?"

"I'll find it myself."

"I'll be by tomorrow to pick you up. I imagine you can use the rest."

"Thank you," Cardinal Palestrina said dryly.

* * *

The hotel—it was called Waterwheel or Waterfall or some such fanciful name—overlooked the Potomac. It was in the Gothic style that had been so popular a half-century ago, a maze of courtyards and false spires. He checked in, rode the lurching elevator to the fifteenth floor, opened the door to a roomful of stale air, and collapsed into the bed. He slept without changing his clothes.

He woke in the dark hours before morning. He had slept deeply but briefly and he felt as exhausted as ever, dead in spirit. He offered a silent prayer and washed his face in the echoing tiled bathroom.

Feeling claustrophobic, he opened the curtains. Across the black gap of the Potomac he could see this American city breathing flame from its night foundries, sooty and dark. He pulled up a chair and sat drinking tap water from a hotel glass. The glass had been wrapped in paper: a novelty. So many new things. It occurred to him then that he was old . . . for the first time in his life, he *felt* old. As if to underscore the point, his belly clenched in a spasm.

He was old and he had never been so far from home.

So far from God.

Extra ecclesiam nulla salus.

But here, he thought unhappily, I *am* the Church.

He glanced at the phosphorescent hands of the bedside clock. It was 4:20 A.M. He felt bereft, spiritually empty. He put the glass on the windowsill; his head nodded forward.

He blinked, and suddenly it was dawn; the window was full of light and Carl Neumann was hammering at the door.

3

"It's an old project, really," Neumann said. "It began in the forties. A lot of research came together then. We had the talent—mainly refugees."

They drove through the city of Washington toward the Defense Research Institute. Traffic was light and mainly equine. The day had dawned cold and windy, and Cardinal Palestrina imagined he could smell snow in the air. Last winter a freak storm had struck Rome; ice had battered down the hydroelectric lines. The wet, pervasive chill had invaded his office in the Vatican and etched itself in his memory. Now the same unpleasant air poured in the automobile's ventilator grills and made Palestrina's knees ache hideously.

"Heretics," Palestrina said.

Neumann seemed puzzled. "What?"

"Heretics. Not refugees."

"Maybe both, Your Eminence. In any case, useful men. We had Einstein and Heisenberg on the run from the Inquisition, we had Russians like Lysenko. We had Dirac and Planck. And we supported their work. Some very unique ideas began emerging from that."

Palestrina had read profane philosophy; he was familiar with their ideas. "They were deemed heretics for a reason, Mr. Neumann."

"But surely the fundamental notions aren't terribly heretical? I know I'm treading on dangerous ground here"—his smile was fixed—"but the duality of nature, the light and dark creative forces, those are things your order recognizes, are they not?"

"Please don't lecture me on theology." To Neumann's chastened expression he added, more gently, "We also recognize a *moral* order."

"But it's not new—the idea of looking at nature objectively."

"Hardly. Descartes was hanged for it."

"But it's useful."

"Is that what matters?"

Neumann shrugged. "I'm not equipped to judge."

"God bids us all judge, Mr. Neumann."

"If you say so, Your Eminence."

The town was full of flags. The flag of the Novus Ordo was everywhere, the black pyramid with that single leering eye set in a field of red and white bars. Between the flags and Neumann's cheerful amorality, Cardinal Palestrina began to understand Europe's cherished horror of Americans: they feared nothing. Europe's bastard offspring, a nation of Waldensians and Calvinists and Freemasons and worse. A chaos of perverse beliefs, which they had the temerity to call freedom of religion. Maybe there *was* a secret weapon. Anything was possible in such a climate. Maybe the rumors were true.

"We gave these people a free hand," Neumann said. "We gave them the tools they wanted. There was criticism from certain sectors, of course. I mean, we're talking about kabalistic magic, trafficking with elementals, alchemy. And the secrecy was a strain; they fought among themselves. But they were brilliant men, and they shared this need to understand certain things—stars, atoms, the plenum itself."

"Theory," Palestrina said, wishing he could dismiss it as easily as that.

"They predicted," Neumann went on blithely, "that there was not a single plenum but many—worlds inside of worlds, if you can compass that, all divided by units of probability, which Planck called quanta. The theory predicted that it might be within the power of the human mind to penetrate those barriers."

Cardinal Palestrina wanted to say that this was nonsense, chimerical, a snare and a delusion. But of course it was *not* nonsense, or he wouldn't be here . . . Neumann wouldn't be telling him this. The Curia had some covert knowledge of the so-called Plenum Project; Palestrina understood that Neumann was being more or less open with him.

"I admired those men," Neumann said. "They were dedicated, they were serious. They were working at a very high level. Mind you, they didn't pay much attention to the practical applications. An army, say, or even one man, an assassin, who could pretty much move through walls, pass through any barrier . . . it took them by surprise that anybody might be interested in that. Some of them were appalled when we cast the finding spells, when we sequestered civilians who showed signs of latency. Well, there *is* a moral question, I'm the first to admit it. But rough measures for rough times. You can't make an omelet without breaking eggs, right, Your Eminence?"

Palestrina felt ill.

Neumann said, "The Institute's just around the corner."

They were deep in the government quarter now, vast stone structures crowding against the cobbled streets, a canyon of sooty architraves decorated with didactic friezes of the Virtues, of Capital and Labor striding hand in hand toward the ostensible future. The factories by the Potomac contributed a pall of oily coal smoke; on a bad day, Neumann had said, you couldn't tell noon from midnight.

But the Defense Research Institute was the most appalling of any of these structures. The sight of it made the day seem even colder. There was nothing here of the spirituality of the Vatican, an architecture striving toward God; nothing prayerlike in these black stone bastions, a fence of spikes rising automatonlike as the automobile approached. They drove beneath a pillared arch, the eye-and-pyramid motif engraved in the sooty keystone, and the temperature seemed to drop ten degrees.

The building was immense, prisonlike. It had its own powerhouse and commissary, Neumann said, its own shops and laundry. They passed through a second stone portcullis and Neumann identified himself to a guard. The guard presented a plastic tag for Palestrina to wear on his robe; his name was embossed on it. "We'll need a photograph of you," Neumann said, "but this will do for now."

Palestrina hated the tag, hated the association of himself with this place. The inner buildings loomed very large now and some of the windows were barred. He imagined he could hear the screams of the people the Institute had, in Neumann's ugly euphemism, "sequestered." But, he thought, surely all that is past?

"We had some trouble in the forties," Neumann admitted. "Congressional investigations, fanatics trying to close us down. It was a turbulent decade. That's over now, thank God. But it put our work back by at least a dozen years . . . and it allowed some of the lapses you may have heard about."

"The escape," Palestrina said. "The people who broke out."

"I don't like to use unnecessarily melodramatic language."

Neumann parked the car in a space marked PRIVATE—RESERVED. They climbed out, dashed through the cold to an immense iron door which Neumann opened with a key. The hallway inside was sterile with the light of aging fluorescent tubes; the doors were all painted salmon pink and numbered.

Neumann seemed amused by Palestrina's disorientation. "Follow me, Your Eminence."

"Where are we going?" Palestrina's reluctance was an imperative now, a physical resistance.

"My office," Neumann said. "Unless you want the grand tour right away?"

"I should speak to someone. Someone with rank . . . someone in charge."

That smile.

"You're looking at him," Neumann said.

Neumann said he'd been at the Institute for almost thirty years now, that his fortunes had fallen and risen with the Plenum Project, that he had been coordinating it independently for the last five years. "I'm not a scientist, mind you. But as far as operations are concerned, goal-setting, management, I have pretty much a free hand."

Neumann's office was sere, stony, and blank. Palestrina said, "I want to see this creature you've created."

"You make him sound like one of our homunculi."

"There are homunculi working as servants at the Vatican Library, Mr. Neumann. I assure you I wouldn't speak of them in the same tone."

At last—Cardinal Palestrina considered it a kind of personal triumph—Neumann's smile faded. "I hate to see you go into this with a negative attitude."

"I don't mean to insult your work—"

"Because, you know, the implications are tremendous. Even the Curia has acknowledged that. Frankly, it seemed like an extremely generous thing for the State Department to invite you here. We don't normally share this sort of material even with allies."

Palestrina bowed his head. "The stakes are considerable."

"The oil supply," Neumann said.

"I was thinking of the survival of Christendom."

Neumann's smile flickered faintly. "That, too."

"Show me the man," Palestrina said.

"Isn't that a little premature?"

"I know the history of this place. Do I really have to admire the architecture?" He leaned forward. "The Vatican acknowledges your nation's generosity. Nevertheless, a moral issue persists. That's why I'm here."

"A moral issue," Neumann said blankly.

"Means and ends."

"I don't understand."

Palestrina was not surprised. "Is he here?"

"Yes, he's in the building, but—"

"Then take me to him, please."

Neumann hesitated, annoyed, Palestrina thought, at being forced off his schedule. Finally he shrugged. "I guess there's nothing to lose."

4

The room was a gray stone chamber. Neumann agreed to wait outside.

Palestrina understood that, in a sense, he was at Neumann's mercy. He could not have found his own way here; he doubted he could find his way back out. The Defense Research Institute was literally a maze, corridors turning back on themselves or twining into blank stone walls. The building housed not only Neumann's Plenum Project but a dozen other deeply shrouded efforts: biochemical warfare, sorcels of invisibility, commerce with the dead. Every level in the bureaucratic hierarchy had its own fragmentary map of the building. The rumor, Neumann said, was that no single comprehensive map existed; no single architect had overseen the project and no living man understood the building as a whole. Neumann offered this as a legend, for its quaintness; Cardinal Palestrina found it only too easy to believe.

He entered the gray room from one of its two doors, sat down in one of its two chairs. Momentarily, the man he had come to speak to entered.

Only a man, Palestrina thought.

The man sat opposite him, silently, hands folded in his lap.

How ordinary he looked. A shabby old man in a shabby gray suit, a gray slouch hat on his head. In Rome, Palestrina thought, he would have attracted no attention. He would have been taken for one of the less successful bourgeoisie, an alcoholic shopkeeper or a retired subaltern from the cavernous bureaucracy of the Tribunals. Palestrina, scanning for omens of bad faith, found nothing more sinister here than a certain shiftiness about the man's eyes. But his own gaze was hardly fixed. The temptation to look away—somehow, to look away *from oneself*—was nearly overwhelming.

He said, "Do you have a name?"

"Walker," said the man in the gray suit.

The voice was odd: resonant but somehow toneless.

"Walker—?"

"Walker, stalker, hunter, finder." His grin was vulpine. "Walker is my family name."

Palestrina said, "Did you know your parents?"

"No, sir. I was crèched here."

Then it was true, Palestrina thought, what the Secretariat had told him before he left, what Neumann had implied. Men and women had been bred like cattle in this building. Surgical interventions: female ova plucked from living tissue and fertilized *in vitro.* Clonings practiced in sterile laboratories under fertility spells. The thought of it sickened him.

Walker added, "But I know who *you* are . . . you're the Papist."

"They call me that?"

"No one much talks to me. But I hear them say things."

"Then, do you understand why I'm here?"

"Something to do with war."

"Something to do, I profoundly hope, with peace."

Walker shrugged, as if to say, *It's all the same to me.* He said, "You're a judge."

"Yes, in a manner of speaking. Do you know what it is I have to judge?"

"Me," Walker said. The grin was persistent, child-like in a horrible way.

"Your usefulness," Palestrina said. "Whether you can help us, whether what you're doing can help us, in Europe."

"What I'm good for," Walker interpreted.

No, Palestrina thought. Not what you're good for, but whether you're good. Or worse: whether you are a purchase our moral budget can afford.

But he said, "In a way."

"Oh, I'm not good for much. They made me that way." He tapped his head. "But I can do a few tricks."

"Tell me about it."

"Spells. Binding and finding. It's slow work but I'm talented at it. And I can do the other thing, I guess you know about that."

"Traveling between worlds," Palestrina said. It still strained credulity. But here, in this room, this building . . .

"Across the plenum," Walker said, "yes."

"Could you do it now—if you wanted to?"

"Yes."

"You could go"—Palestrina held out his hands palms up—"anywhere?"

"Only certain places," Walker said.

"What places?"

"Where *they've* been."

The heart of the matter.

"My understanding," Cardinal Palestrina said, "is that you were a family."

"A long time ago," Walker said, and a shadow seemed to cross his face: not an emotion, Palestrina thought, so much as the shade of an emotion.

He said, "Would you like to talk about it?"

"They told me to answer your questions."

"Do you have to do what the people here tell you?"

"Yes."

"Tell me, then," Cardinal Palestrina said.

Walker closed his eyes and seemed to regard the memory directly.

"There were three of us," he said. "We were the best they could make. We had the talent. Very strongly. So they closed us in, of course . . . caged us with sorcels and spells. And it worked for a time."

He knitted his hands in his lap. Palestrina could not look away as the fingers laced and unlaced: old, bony fingers.

"They gave us one name apiece. Walker and Julia and William. We all had different parents, or no parents, but we used to think of ourselves as brothers and sister. William was the oldest. I admired him a lot. He was always surprising the doctors and nurses, doing things they didn't think he could do. I think William carried the whole plenum around inside him: he was that big, that powerful. He was like a god."

Walker's eyes shone with ancient feeling.

Cardinal Palestrina remained silent.

"Julia was very beautiful. Tell you the truth, Father, I felt kind of lost between them. William was big and powerful, Julia was beautiful and smart. Me, I was just Walker. Ordinary Walker. Oh, I could do the tricks, too. But not like *they* could. But that was all right . . . we had each other."

"Until they left," Palestrina said gently.

Walker's expression hardened. "They talked about it sometimes. I thought it was bad. A mistake. No good could come of it. But they included me. I appreciated that. 'They can't hold us,' William used to say. 'Not all their spells can keep us here.' And in the end, you know, he was right."

"But you stayed behind," Palestrina pressed.

"I couldn't go! Or I didn't want to go. Or I wasn't strong enough to go . . ."

"You don't remember?"

"I remember them begging me. We were all older then. By then I knew that Julia and William loved each other, that they loved me but in a different way. A *lesser* way. So we battered down the sorcels and we were going to go where no one could find us, worlds and worlds away from this place. But I couldn't or wouldn't and finally I told them to go while there was still time, just go and leave me . . . and they did . . ."

"They left you?"

"Yes."

"You resented that?"

"I don't remember."

"Why don't you remember?"

"Because the proctors took me. They took me to

the surgeons." He regarded Palestrina with his head cocked, an expression that was at once sly and pathetic. He said, "They operated on me."

Cardinal Palestrina experienced a twinge of abhorrence. "Operated—?"

Walker lifted his battered gray hat.

The scar was prominent, all these years later. It ran in a ragged circle from the tip of Walker's left ear past the orbit of his eye socket and up into the hairline. Walker traced it with his finger. "They opened up my skull," he said. "They took things out."

"Things," Palestrina whispered.

"Love and hate. Caring and not caring."

"And left—?"

"Obedience. Loyalty. They call it loyalty."

"My God . . . and you don't despise them for it?"

Shockingly, Walker smiled. "I don't think I can."

No, Cardinal Palestrina thought. No, this is too much: too much cruelty, too much obscenity. It recalled a kind of torture the Tribunals had not practiced for centuries.

They had cauterized a part of this man's soul, Palestrina thought . . . and how much could be murdered of conscience or outrage before a man was, essentially, dead?

So perhaps he was talking to a dead man.

The thought was chilling and unwelcome.

"You followed them," Palestrina said. "That's what you were trained for."

"Followed them for years." Again that distant look, Walker's old eyes gone diffuse. "It's hard work, you know. But I can smell them out. They leave trails."

"Julia and William? You found them?"

"Eventually."

"Brought them back?"

"Killed them."

Cardinal Palestrina blinked.

Walker said, "It was unavoidable."

His face was bland, affectless, smiling. Palestrina thought, He *is* dead. "But then it's over, surely? Your work is finished . . . the project is finished?"

"There were children," Walker said.

"I see . . . and they have the power?"

"They have it strongly. More strongly than they know."

"You've hunted them?"

"I've been close to them. Often! But it's not as easy as all that, bringing them back. These arms won't hold them. A cage won't hold them. That's the paradox! It's a lifework. Spells and geases are the only weapons we have. And they work less well far along across the worlds. But we're very close now." He bent toward Cardinal Palestrina; his breath was sour. "They've learned things in this building since I was young."

"I'm sure they have," Palestrina said faintly.

"And there's one other," Walker said. "Child of a child. Hybrid, but the genotype is true. He's what we worked for all these years. We'll bring him back. I'll bring him back. And he can do what you want, you know. He's powerful enough. A few adjustments—" Walker tapped the pale line of his scar. "He'll do what you tell him. Lead armies against the Holy Land if that's what you want. Call up forces across the plenum. Armies that would terrify a god, weapons that would devastate a city. It's all out there." Walker showed his teeth again. "Would that suit you? Is that what you're after?"

And Cardinal Palestrina thought, It might save us. Or damn us.

He moistened his lips. A cramp seized his belly; it was all he could do to keep from crying out. He drew a breath and said, "You can do that—you can bring him here?"

"Oh yes." Walker put his hands in his pockets, reclined happily against the chair back. "This time," he said, "we have help."

Part Two

....

HEARTLAND

Chapter Eight

· ·

They pulled in late Wednesday afternoon at a motel called the Stark Motor Inn somewhere west of Barstow.

Stark it was indeed, Karen thought. There was no shade but the meager shadow cast by a juniper rooted in the gravel courtyard; the tiny swimming pool out back stood pure and empty as a turquoise chip in the brown vastness of the desert. The room smelled of false lilac and air conditioning.

She reminded herself that they were back home now. Not home in the very specific sense—this desert was surely as exotic a place as she had ever been—but in a world where the verities were familiar: John F. Kennedy dead all those years ago, handguns for sale in the highway malls, no gentle bohemian ocean towns for people like her sister. The *real* world.

Home—the other kind of home—was still a long way off.

Michael unpacked his bathing suit and went out through the searing afternoon light to the pool. "Dibs on the shower," Laura said. Laura had driven all the way from L.A. and looked weary. From Los Angeles, Karen thought, and across a canyon of time. They had passed between worlds out on the empty highway, amid the scrub brush and the dust devils. Miracles and murders and hotels in the desert.

She read *Time* magazine while Laura showered. The news was as dour as it had ever been. AIDS was on the increase; there was trouble again in the Philippines. Laura emerged finally from the tiled cavern of the bathroom, toweling her hair. She had thrown on an old flower-print shift; the cloth adhered to the damp angles of her body and Karen was momentarily jealous of her sister's youth, preserved somehow while her own had slipped mysteriously away. Laura had never married. Laura was a single woman. While I, Karen thought, am that very different thing: a single mother.

Laura said, "They don't know we're coming."

Mama and Daddy, she meant. "No," Karen agreed.

"We should call them."

"We?"

Laura admitted, "I don't want to be the one."

"I guess you haven't talked to them all that much."

"I guess I haven't talked to them for years. I'm the wayward daughter, right? Bad seed. Anyway," she said, "they'll take it better from you."

* * *

But Karen had never liked telephones. She disliked the sounds they made, the click and hum of fragmentary dialogues, foreign voices holding foreign conversations. Long distance was the worst. There was something so lonely about a long-distance call: the extra numbers, like mileage, tokens of separation. She punched out the area code tentatively. Michael was still swimming, out there in the blistering light.

In truth, Karen had not been very good about phoning home either. She called every couple of months, sometimes less. And on holidays. But mostly she tried to call weekday afternoons, when the rates were higher but when Daddy was likely to be at work or out drinking. It was a long time since she'd spoken directly to her father. Years, she wondered, like Laura? Yes, maybe: maybe that long.

She imagined the phone ringing at the house in Polger Valley. The family had moved there the year after Karen went off to college, but she remembered it clearly. The phone was in the parlor. Fat textured yellow sofa, telephone on the walnut end table. Sunlight, maybe, sifting in through dust motes and the glacial ticking of clocks. Karen understood intuitively that none of this would have changed, that the Polger Valley house had become a kind of fortress for her parents, that they would live there until they died.

The buzz of the telephone ended abruptly and her mother's voice came crackling out: "Hello?"

"Mama?"

There was a brief, cautious silence down the long lines from Pennsylvania.

"Karen?" Mama said finally. "Is that you? Is everything all right?"

"I'm with Laura," Karen said.

It was bad, of course, blurting it out like that. Her mother could only repeat, "Laura?"

"Michael and I are with her. She's here, she's right here in the room with me."

The silence again. "I don't understand."

"Well, it's too much to explain. Mama, we're out here in California. In the desert. We're driving back East."

"Back here?"

"Yes, Mama."

The phone line stuttered.

Karen said, "Mama?"

"Yes . . ."

"Mama, is it all right?" Her own voice suddenly high and childish in her ears. "We'll be a few days, driving, you know . . . it takes time . . ."

"There's your father."

"I know. But it's all right, isn't it? You can talk to him?"

"Well—I will." Doubtfully. "I'll try." Then, "But if there's something wrong, baby, you know you should tell me."

"I can't do that now."

"Is it Gavin?"

"I'm not with Gavin."

"He phoned here, you know. He's looking for you."

That surprised her. "Gavin's not the problem."

"No," Mama said, "I didn't think so," and Karen wondered at the echo of old grief or fear there: had it been inevitable all along, this phone call, the journey back?

Karen said, "I love you."

The telephone crackled with static. "I know you do . . . I know it."

"Tell Daddy."

"I'll try."

"We'll see you soon, then."

"Yes."

The silence was sudden and vast.

Arizona, New Mexico, then the Rockies and an early threat of snow; the autumn plains. It was past the vacation season and so there was not much traffic on these big interstates, mainly diesel trucks. Nevertheless it was possible to think of this as a vacation. We're family, Karen thought, and we talk and we act like family now; we sing songs in the car and we eat at the Howard Johnson's. At times, suspended in the motion of the car, she would feel complete: memoryless and happy.

But it never lasted.

They stopped for dinner at a Trailways diner somewhere in Ohio. She was not sure where they were except that they had driven through barren wheat fields for the last hour and a half. Laura picked up a *USA Today* at the candy counter and carried it into the cafeteria with her. She folded it on the table so that Karen was able to see what she was reading. It was a page-two story on the Detroit murder stats for 1988 and Laura read it twice, frowning so intently that she seemed about to burst into tears. Then she looked up at Karen and said, "It's *not* normal!"—as if Karen had been arguing with her. "My Christ! It's ugly, and it's worse than that—it's so fucking *unnecessary!*"

The man at the next booth peered up from under his Cleveland Indians cap, blinking. The waitress, passing, neglected to refill their coffee cups.

Michael looked blankly at his aunt.

And Karen thought to herself, It's real, then. We are what we are and the Gray Man is real and he can kill people—children!—and my son, my only son, Michael, is in real danger, and we're going home, my God, after all these silent years, we really are going home.

Chapter Nine

....

They came over a long wooded ridge and Laura could see the town, then, shouldering up against the Monongahela River, one more fucked-up old mill town, the ancient coke ovens and rolling mills and blast furnaces fouling the air—but not the way they did when times were prosperous—and the slatboard houses and the row houses all built back in the twenties or earlier, when the railroads were making money and the demand was big for rolled steel and bituminous coal.

The sight of Polger Valley from this height invoked a rush of memory so intense that she pulled the car over to the gravel shoulder, her hands clenched on the wheel. She had never lived here—had left home a month before Mama and Daddy moved from Duquesne—but it was like every other place they had lived; it was like Duquesne and it was like Burleigh; it was like Pittsburgh with its hills and narrow streets. She looked at Karen beside her, Karen with her eyes fixed somewhere off beyond the river. "You drive," Laura said. "You know the way."

Her sister shrugged.

Laura walked around the car to the passenger side. Her legs felt hard and tense from driving. It was a cold, late, cloudy afternoon; the ragged hillside maples were spindly and bare. Streetlights blinked on in the distant, empty industrial alleys along the river.

Climbing back into the car, she glanced at Michael in the rear seat. He was gazing out blankly over the valley, lost in some thought. He had been like this —sullen like this—ever since California.

She rolled up her window. "Cold back there?"

He only shrugged.

Last week, in a hotel room outside Cleveland, Laura had asked him why he was so quiet these last few days. Karen had gone shopping for winter clothes; Michael was sitting on the bed, watching a football game with the sound turned down. He looked up at her briefly, unhappily. "Am I?"

"Yes. But not just quiet. *Pissed-off* quiet. So who are you mad at, Michael?"

He shrugged.

She said, "At me?"

"Do I have to talk about it?"

"No. Of course not. But we're living in each other's pockets and there's no way around that. It might make life easier if you did."

He shrugged again. "I just think it's stupid . . . all this should have happened before."

"All this?"

"What we're doing. Where we're going. What we're finding out." He straightened his shoulders. "I mean, you *knew* what you were. All your life. All three of you did. But nobody ever asked? Nobody said, Where did I come from, what am I? Not until *now?*"

He pressed his back against the wall of the hotel room, hugged his knees against himself. Laura said, "We were negligent and we screwed up your life—is that it?"

"Maybe. Maybe not just mine."

"So, Michael, who should we have asked?"

"Who are you planning to ask?"

Well, all right, she thought. He was bright and he had a point. But he didn't really understand. He was fifteen years old and everything seemed too obvious. "You don't know what it was like back home."

"I know, it was rough. But—"

"Michael, listen to me." She sat down next to him, and maybe he sensed the seriousness in her voice, because he was quiet again, not sullen now but attentive. She said, "I *did* ask once. I was maybe five, maybe six years old. I went to Daddy. I showed him what I could do. Made a little window for him. A window into some nice place, a child's idea of a nice place, a sunny day and, you know, flowers and meadows, and a deer standing there. I meant to find out whether he could do it. I think most of all I wanted to know what I was supposed to do *with* it, this strange little trick—what was it *for?*"

Michael said, "He wouldn't tell you?"

"I don't remember what he said. All I remember is showing him, wanting to ask him. And then I remember lying in bed. There were bruises on my face. Bruises on my arms. Five very clear bruises on my right arm above the elbow, and I knew he'd grabbed me there, that those bruises fit the shape and angle of his fingers."

"He beat you," Michael said.

"Yes. It sounds terrible, but . . . yes, that's the word for it."

"That's sick." Michael's outrage was obvious and heartfelt. "You must have hated him for it."

"No. I did not."

Michael frowned.

She said, "Do you hate your father? I mean, hey, he walked out on you. Walked out on you and your mom. That's a pretty big thing. You hate him for it?"

"No." Cautiously now. "But that's different."

"Is it? Maybe it's only a matter of degree."

"He never beat me."

"Should I have hated Daddy for that? Well, maybe you're right . . . maybe I should have. Tim did, at least eventually. But, Michael, I was too young. When you're five years old you don't have that kind of hate in you. You forgive. Not because you want to but because you don't have a choice. Can you understand that? Sometimes you forgive because there's nothing else you *can* do."

It was more than she had meant to say.

He looked at her steadily.

"But now," he said, "you *do* have a choice."

And there was nothing Laura could say to that— no answer she could think of.

They pulled up at the house just after dark.

It was an old row house on a hill that ran down toward the river, and behind it there was a steep wooded slope. The street was called Montpelier and it dead-ended against a chalky cliff.

This was not the greatest neighborhood. Some of these houses had been mended and repaired; many had not. Once upon a time, Laura thought, this would have been a street full of working people, Poles and Germans, but now, she guessed, most of these folks were laid off from the mills, and there were more than a few black faces peering out from shuttered windows as she parked beside the curb. Down where Montpelier met Riverside there was a big noisy bar; Riverside, a commercial street, was crowded with pawnshops, barred and locked at dusk.

Odd that her parents had stayed here so long. All my life, she thought, we moved every year, every two years. Sometimes because Daddy got laid off for drinking, sometimes for no discernible reason. Here, finally, they had settled. Maybe because they were alone together at last; maybe because Daddy had finally built up some seniority at the local mill.

Maybe because we left.

But now, she thought, we're home.

There was a yellow bulb burning over the porch. Karen parallel-parked and Laura unloaded luggage from the trunk. Michael hefted a suitcase in each hand. He regarded the house warily. "So," he said, "this is it?"

The screen door creaked open. Mama stepped out into the porch light. Laura's hands were shaking; she clasped them together in front of her.

"Yes," she told her nephew. "This is it."

Chapter Ten

. . . .

1

His mother and his aunt shared a second-floor bedroom, but Michael had the third floor of this old house all to himself.

He liked it up here. His grandparents were too old to climb the stairs, so everything was covered with a fine layer of undisturbed dust, and everything was antique: furniture, he guessed, they had been packing around all their lives. Michael was accustomed to the house in Toronto, a new house full of new things, as if nothing had existed before the year 1985; the Fauves' third floor was a shocking contrast.

His grandmother had come up once that first night, gasping on the stairs. She apologized for the clutter. "All this mess," she said sadly. "When Mama Lucille died we put all her stuff up here. So this is your family, Michael. See? This was your great-grandfather's rolltop desk. That big old bed belonged to my parents . . ."

The bed had sat for so long in this room, and was so massive, that the floorboards had curved around it. His mother aired the sheets and pillowcases for him, but the bed retained a characteristic odor, not unpleasant, of ancient down and ticking, of whole lives lived between its sheets. Sleeping there these last few nights Michael had wished he could make windows into past time as well as across worlds: that he could gaze back down the years and maybe discover the secret of his strangeness. Wished this old bed could talk.

He spent a lot of time up here. Considering the situation in the house, it was better to be alone. And, anyway, he liked to be by himself. Alone, he could let his thoughts roam freely. Nothing to fear up here, no Gray Man, only these old high corniced rooms with their ripply windowpanes and the winter sky showing through; only the trickle of the water in the radiator grills. Lying here, suspended in down and history, he could allow himself to feel (but faintly, carefully) the rush of secret power in himself, the wheels of possibility spinning in him; to contemplate a step sideways out of Polger Valley and time itself; to wonder whether Aunt Laura's instincts might not have been correct all those years ago, maybe there *was* a better world somewhere, a truly better world, and maybe he could reach it: maybe it was only a quarter step away down some hidden axis . . . maybe it was a door he could learn to open.

He thought about it often.

Downstairs, things were different. A week in this house had not inured Michael to all the silence and indignities.

His grandmother insisted on cooking. Every evening he helped her with the heavy china platters: chicken and gravy, roast beef and potatoes, meat loaf and boiled peas relayed steaming from the tiny kitchen to the dining room. Jeanne Fauve was overweight but not really fat; she was the kind of nervous woman whose metabolism runs fast. She was constantly in motion but the motion was inhibited, no large gestures but a lot of fluttering. Her hands moved like birds; her eyes darted like a bird's eyes. She wore her hair in white spring curls bound tightly to her head. Michael kind of liked her and he thought she might like him—she would stare thoughtfully at him when she thought he didn't notice. But if he looked directly at her, her eyes would dart away.

Tonight Michael helped her carry in a pot roast from the oven. Everything was in place: linen tablecloth, the china, the tarnished silverware. Everybody in their chair except Michael's grandfather. Michael sat down at the foot of the table. He was hungry and the roast smelled wonderful, but he had learned to be patient. He put his hands in his lap; the mantel clock ticked. His mother whispered something to Aunt Laura.

Then, finally, Willis Fauve came ambling in from the downstairs bathroom, where he had washed his hands. Willis was not really a large man, Michael thought, but he was a big presence in the room. His forearms were big and he wore polyester pants cinched over his expansive belly and a starched white shirt open at the collar. He had a small face set in a large head, blunt features concentrated around heavy bifocals. He wore his hair in a bristly Marine cut and his thick eyebrows made him seem to be always frowning. Most of the time he *was* frowning. Certainly he did not ever seem happy.

Sometimes he would come to the table drunk. Not loudly or conspicuously drunk, but his walk would be unsteady and he would talk more than he normally did: mainly complaints about the neighbors. He would sit opposite Michael, and his acrid breath would waft across the table. Willis Fauve was a beer drinker. Beer, he said, was a food. It had food value.

Tonight Willis was just detectably drunk. Michael thought of him as "Willis" because he could not imagine calling this man "Grandfather." Michael was acquainted with grandfathers mainly from TV: kindly, grizzled men in bib overalls. But Willis was not kindly; he was not even friendly. He had made it obvious that he regarded this visit as an intrusion and that he would not be happy until his privacy was restored. Sometimes—if he'd had enough to drink—he would come out and say so.

Willis sat down wheezing. Without looking at anyone he folded his hands in his lap and closed his eyes. Michael was supposed to do the same, but he kept his eyes open. "Thank you, Lord," Willis Fauve intoned, "for this food which you have seen fit to set before us. Amen."

Michael's grandmother echoed the "Amen." Willis began to circulate the pot roast. Michael took modest helpings.

He felt his grandfather's attention on him while he ate. He kept his eyes on his plate, worked his knife and fork mechanically. But he felt Willis watching him. His grandmother tried to make some conversation, the shopping she'd done, what the hairdresser had said, but nobody could think of anything to add and the talk ran out of gas. Michael had pretty much cleared his plate and was looking forward to the end of the meal when his grandfather said, too loudly, "You know what I call that shirt?"

Michael's shirt, he meant. Michael was wearing a Talking Heads T-shirt he'd carried with him from Toronto. Black T with a red-and-white graphic. Nothing spectacular, but he was moderately proud of the way he looked in it.

Nobody wanted to answer the question but Willis himself. Willis said brightly, "I call that a fuck shirt."

Michael regarded his grandfather with bewilderment.

"I see these kids," Willis said. "I drive by the high school every morning. I see the way they dress. You know why they dress like that? It's like sticking up their middle finger. It's an insult. It's 'fuck you.' They're saying that with their clothes."

Michael had observed that Willis, who complained about profane language on TV, loosened up in that regard when he was drinking.

Karen said, "Michael forgot to change before dinner."

Michael looked at his mother sharply. She returned the look, a warning: *Don't say anything . . . not now.*

"A fuck shirt," Willis repeated.

"Michael," Karen said, "go change." When he didn't move, she whispered, "Please!"

He stood up sullenly.

At the stairs Michael paused a second to look back at the dinner table, at the quiet tableau of the women with their heads contritely bowed, Willis Fauve still regarding him, frowning. They locked gazes briefly.

It was Willis who looked away. He said to Michael's mother, "You let him dress like that?"

Michael moved on up the stairs.

"A fuck shirt," Willis marveled, "at my dinner table."

But Michael understood the significance of Willis's complaint. It's not the shirt, he thought. You know it, I know it. It's not the shirt you're afraid of.

In his room Michael thought about Willis and about the silence at the dinner table.

This attic room looked out over the rooftops of Polger Valley toward the river and the mill. The mill dominated the valley like a black, crouched animal. The chimney flues were black and smokeless against a hard gray dusk. Michael put his hand to the window and the glass felt icy under his fingers. Snow soon, he thought.

He kept his T-shirt on.

It wasn't the shirt, of course; it was the power in him. Willis must have sensed that. Michael thought about what Laura had told him, some of the hints his mother had dropped. He understood that the T-shirt was itself irrelevant; that Willis might as easily have objected to his haircut, his shoes, the way he held his fork. What he really meant was: here is this new person under my roof and I don't control him and I don't like that.

Michael understood because the house in Toronto had operated the same way, though without the implied threat of violence. He recognized in Willis the shadow of his mother's cryptic silences. He had grown up in that silence. The vacancy of unpronounced words. This wasn't a new thing with Willis, only louder and more frightening.

He wondered whether that was the way it always worked in families, whether fears were passed on from generation to generation, like the color of a person's hair or eyes. Maybe it was like a curse, something you could never escape, something you carried with you whether you wanted to or not.

But, he thought, some things *do* change. Willis depended on his ability to scare people, and it worked: Michael's mother was frightened of him; even Laura was frightened of him . . .

But not me, Michael thought.

Not me.

He lay on his bed in the gathering dark and watched an early-winter snow begin to beat against the window. He felt the tremble of the power in himself and thought, Hell, I'm a long way beyond Willis Fauve. He doesn't scare me.

2

When Karen stopped in to say good night Michael was already dozing. Cradled in the old bed, he looked almost like a child again. Predictably, he still had the T-shirt on. Rather than wake him, she folded the comforter around him and tiptoed to the door.

He stirred long enough to raise one eyelid. And he said a strange thing, faintly, from the depths of his sleep.

He said, "Don't be afraid."

"I won't," Karen said. "Sleep now." She eased the door shut.

But she *was* afraid.

She was afraid of the Gray Man and she was afraid of her father.

It surprised her, the depth of her fear. Maybe it was predictable, maybe she should have expected it. After all, what had changed? Well, she was an adult now, she had been married, had lived on her own. Those things should make a difference. But they didn't, and maybe that wasn't unusual; maybe these angles of connection—parent to child, father to daughter—were permanent, timeless. Around Willis she was a child again, hapless and awed. It was not what he said but the force with which he said it . . . the absolute masculine certainty he projected. The words were like doors into a private blast furnace Willis Fauve kept stoked inside himself; through the words, she could feel the heat.

The next day, after Willis left for work, she helped her mother with the laundry; in the afternoon she carried the plastic laundry basket up to the second floor where Laura was waiting. Karen sat with her sister in the guest room folding sheets. The sheets were warm from the basement dryer; the fabric softener had imparted a faint, delicate scent of lavender.

Laura said, "We're not getting anywhere."

"I know," Karen said. This frightened her, too: this motionlessness. "It's harder than I thought it would be."

"It's hard because nothing's changed." Laura whirled a sheet out over the bed. "Everybody's older but nothing's different. They say you can't go home again, but the scary thing is that you can—it's too easy to step back into all the old mistakes."

Karen said, "Mistakes?"

"You know what I mean. He rules this house. You saw him at dinner, yelling at Michael. And we sat there. We took it. Nobody challenges Willis Fauve, no, sirree—not on *his* turf."

"Well, it is, isn't it? It is his turf."

"It was our home for twenty years, for God's sake! We lived under his roof like prisoners—it was only Tim who ever spoke up."

But, Karen thought, look what happened to Tim. Tim had disappeared out into the big world; for all anyone heard from him he might as well be dead. Maybe *was* dead. Maybe worse. Maybe the Gray Man had found him.

But she folded that traitorous thought into a dresser drawer along with the spare sheets. "Tim was braver than us."

"Brave or stupid. Or maybe he just liked getting bruised. But at least he fought back."

Karen thought privately that Tim was like a small frightened dog: the harder you kick him, the more he tries to bite . . . until he chews through the rope and runs away. Tim, after seventeen years of this life, had finally gnawed through his rope. She said, "We won't find out anything from Daddy."

"We haven't tried to find out anything from anybody." Laura smoothed the sheet over the mattress and slipped the two old pillows into their flowered cases. "It's Mama we should talk to."

"She won't like it."

"If we wait for her to like," Laura said, "we'll be here another twenty years."

It was undeniable.

"Now," Laura said. "We should talk to her now."

Karen hesitated and then wondered at her own reluctance. "Doesn't it scare you at all—what she might say? Don't you think about what it might mean —knowing?"

Laura walked with her to the stairs. They were

sisters now for certain. No time had passed; they were altogether children. Laura said, "I'm more scared of what might happen if we don't."

The house felt suddenly colder.

Mama was in the kitchen drying dishes.

How full of memories this house is, Karen thought. But it was not so much the house as the furnishing of it, the lay of things. The kitchen was like the kitchen in every other house they had lived in. The tile was peeling up, the cupboards were painted a dingy flat yellow color. Dish towels hung on a wooden rack; the dishes were stacked in a white Kresge's drainer. Cups on cup hooks, pot holders in the shape of roosters tucked behind the toaster, a hand-stitched sampler on the wall bearing a passage from Proverbs. It was late afternoon and the kitchen window showed a dismal backyard terrain of powder snow and hillside and empty sky. Daddy would be home in an hour or two . . . longer if he stopped to have a drink.

It was Laura who had the courage to say, "Mama, we need to talk."

Jeanne Fauve looked up briefly. "Talk about what?"

"Old times."

Mama stood still for a few moments, then set down the dish she'd been drying and turned to face Laura. Her expression was hooded, unreadable. "Wait here," she said finally, and bustled out of the room.

Karen sat with her sister at the kitchen table, tracing patterns with her finger in the chipped Formica. How old was this table? As old as herself? My God, she thought, we don't need to dig up the past: it's here, it's all around us.

Mama came back with a shoe box under her arm. She sat down at the table and pried up the lid.

Inside the box there were pictures.

Mama said, "These are the old days. All these photos." She emptied them onto the table.

Karen sifted through the pile. The photographs had aged badly. She remembered the various cameras Mama used to own: a Kodak Brownie, which had produced most of these mirror-finished black-and-white pictures; and later a big plastic Polaroid camera, the kind where the photograph rolled out by itself and then you had to wipe it down with some evil-smelling preservative.

"Here," Mama said. "The house on Constantinople . . . you remember?"

Karen inspected the picture. Daddy must have taken it: it showed Mama standing by their new car, a steely blue Rambler parked in front of the house. Karen and Laura and Tim stood listlessly in the background leaning against the porch railing. How bored we look, Karen thought. It must have been a church day: everyone was dressed up, Mama in her pillbox hat with the preposterous black mesh veil, Karen and Laura in white starched dresses. Tim wore a black suit and collar. How Tim had always hated those collars. It made his child face seem piggish, baby fat pushed up into his chin.

Briefly, dizzyingly, she remembered her dream, the ravine behind the house, the night they had passed into a grim world of Tim's devising. And not just a dream. It was a memory. It was as real as this photograph.

She thought, If we had taken Mama's Kodak Brownie through that Door we might have a picture now—a picture of that strange night city, a picture of the Gray Man.

In her mind the Gray Man said, *Your firstborn son.*

"Those were good days by and large," Mama was

saying. "Your father had steady work. And I think I loved that old house on Constantinople more than any place I've lived since. More even than this place."

Laura said, "Then why did you leave?"

Laura was focused, alert: Laura had not been seduced by the photographs.

Mama said, "Well, you know. You remember what I used to tell you kids? We're gypsies. We move around . . ."

Laura said, "That's not a reason."

Mama hesitated, then turned back resolutely to the photographs. "Here's the apartment in the West End. Karen, you were in fifth grade that year. That was your birthday party—you remember that? Here's where we moved in Bethel. That's Tim on the streetcar going downtown. Here we are with Mama Lucille taking the boat tour around the Point, I guess it was 1965 or '66, the summer we had so many fireflies. Oh, and here I am—I was skinny in those days—riding up the Incline with your father. Here—"

Laura said, "There aren't any baby pictures."

Mama remained silent, her eyes on the pile of photographs.

Laura went on, "It just seems strange. No baby pictures. And the way we moved. I mean, there was Constantinople Street, there was Bethel; there was the West End, there was Duquesne. And we could have stayed on. Daddy wasn't drinking so bad in those days. And I remember how we moved. Pack up and leave overnight. Like we were skipping out. But I remember how you always left the rent in a white envelope taped inside the door. So we were running, but not because of money."

Mama said sullenly, "Is that why you came back here—to stir up all that old trouble?"

"Is it so wrong to want to understand?"

"Maybe. Maybe there was a good reason we left those places."

"We're all grown up now," Laura said. "We have a right to know."

"If it would help you," Mama said vehemently, "you think I wouldn't have told you? It was only ever to protect you . . . it was only so you could lead normal lives."

Normal lives, Karen thought. She was passive now, a spectator in this exchange between her mother and her sister, thinking, A normal life is all I ever wanted. A normal life is what I wanted for Michael.

Laura said, "But we *don't* lead normal lives."

"But you could!"

"No. We can't. Maybe for the same reason you couldn't." Laura held up a handful of the flimsy old photos. They looked, Karen thought, like so many brittle leaves. "Is *he* in here?"

Mama looked fearful. "Who?"

"You know who. Is *he* in here? Is he looking over somebody's shoulder? Is he watching from the window across the street while Daddy waxes the Rambler? Is that why we moved all the time, because he found us on Constantinople Street and he found us in Bethel and he found us in Duquesne?"

Karen was holding her breath now. She thought of what Michael had said about the Gray Man on the beach, the way he had flicked that little girl out of the world with a gesture. With his eyes.

Mama said breathlessly, "You shouldn't even talk about him. It could bring him back. It's bad luck."

"It doesn't matter now," Laura said firmly. "He doesn't *need* luck."

"God help us," Mama said. The kitchen clock ticked; a wind rattled the windowpane. Mama added faintly, "He found you?"

"He found Michael in Toronto," Laura said. "He found all three of us in California. There's no reason to believe he can't find us here."

"So much time passed . . . we thought you were safe."

"Did you? What about Tim—is Tim safe?"

"I pray for Tim." Mama lowered her head. "I pray for him the way I prayed for you all these years."

Laura looked startled. She opened her mouth, closed it again.

Karen found herself speaking. "We need to know all there is to know." The words spilled out. "Not just for us. For Michael's sake."

"It almost wrecked us," Mama said quietly. "Do you understand? It could wreck us again . . . There's nothing I can say to help you."

"Please," Karen said.

Her mother looked infinitely pained and, in that protracted moment, impossibly old. Her cotton print housedress dangled limply from her shoulders. Outside, the wind raised up a whirl of snow.

"I can't," she said finally. "Try to understand. I never spoke to anybody about this. It's hard. Maybe later. I have to think . . ."

Then, at the front of the house, the door rattled and slammed. A draft of cold air swept in along the floor. Jeanne Fauve stood up, composing her face. "It's your father," she said, sweeping the photographs back into the shoe box. "I have to get dinner ready."

Chapter Eleven

....

1

The house was quiet that night, but Michael couldn't sleep.

The dark third-floor windows were shrouded with snow. The snow, he thought, should have melted; it was early for this kind of weather. But the temperature had dropped and the snow had deepened, cold air sweeping down the valley where the Polger met the Monongahela, whipping through these old blacktop streets.

Michael had spent the day exploring the town, walking from the north side to the south and back. He had bought a couple of paperbacks at a sad-looking Kresge's and stopped for warmth and a cup of coffee at the tiny McDonald's on Riverside, but mostly he just walked. One long depressing afternoon hike, one side of the valley to the other. The town, he had estimated, was about as big as Turquoise Beach, but older and dirtier and poor in a different way. Michael understood that many of the people in Turquoise Beach had volunteered for poverty, lived that way so they could paint or write or make music. But poverty in Polger Valley was an unforeseen accident, a disaster as tangible as a train derailment.

He had climbed a hillside until he could see all the sooty length of the town and the broad winding of the Mon, the steel mill and the gray highway, clouds rolling like winter itself from the northwestern sky. Standing there in his heavy coat, Michael felt the power in himself—stronger, it seemed, than ever before. It was like a current rising out of the depths of the earth, the old coal veins buried there, carboniferous ruins—it was a river running through him. He understood that it did not come *from* him but that he was a vehicle for it; the power was something old, eternal, fundamental. There was no end to it; by definition it was limitless. The limiting factor was Michael himself.

He thought, I can go anywhere I can imagine. The places he had seen were real places—as Turquoise Beach was a real place—but accessible only if you could dream yourself there.

He thought about this, walking home. He endured Willis's pointed stares that evening, thinking about it. He took his thoughts to bed with him.

He lay in the cloistered warmth of this ancient bed with the comforter pulled up to his chin and the wind sifting snow against the window.

He thought, *What we dream, we are.*

Some things would be closed to him forever. There were worlds he couldn't reach, worlds beyond his grasp. He felt them out there in the storm of possibility, tenuous doors he could not quite open. It made him think of what Laura had said about Turquoise Beach: *It's the best I could find.* She wanted paradise but couldn't truly dream it . . . maybe didn't really believe in it.

He figured Laura knew all this, understood that her ramshackle seaside bohemia was also a testament to her own limitations.

But at least she had tried. Michael thought about his mother, who hadn't, who pretended she didn't have the power at all—and maybe that was true now, maybe she *had* lost it. Maybe it atrophied, like a muscle. She had spent her life living up to the pinched expectations of Willis Fauve, trying to lead a "normal" life that was, when you came down to it, as ephemeral as Laura's paradise.

A better world, Michael thought.

Maybe there really was such a thing.

Maybe he could find it.

He felt sleep tugging at him. He felt, too, the maze of possibility, the twining corridors of time. He could walk that maze, he thought, pick a destination, feel for it, follow the tug of intuition . . . *here* and *here* and *here*.

He closed his eyes and dreamed a place he had never seen before.

He envisioned it from an immense height and all at once, a place where brightly colored cities stood amidst plains and wilderness, buffalo and redwood forests and busy towns where the rivers branched. He thought of names. They came into his mind unbidden, but with the feeling of real names, place names: Adirondack, Free New England, the Plains Nations.

He saw fragile aircraft swimming through a clean sky; the focus narrowed and he saw crowds thronging a city marketplace, caged birds chattering, acrobats in a public square, a man in feathers buying spices from a woman in Chinese robes.

And then he turned his head against the pillow, willed his eyes open, and saw only the dark outline of this attic room, the snow against the window.

The vision was gone.

Sleep, Michael thought longingly. Sleep now.

He lay in the dark and listened to Willis moving through the house, locking and checking the doors, maybe taking a last sedating drink before he climbed the stairs to his own long and dreamless sleep.

2

Laura shared the twin beds in the guest room with her sister, but tonight she couldn't sleep.

She sat up, glanced at the motionless form of Karen, then pulled a robe over her nightgown and went to the child-sized desk in the corner of the room.

It had been their study desk, hers and Karen's, years ago. How like Mama to keep it preserved up here. Laura switched on the lamp and blinked at the bright circle of light it made.

The desktop was bare.

She reached into the big bottom drawer and took out two bulky items. One was the shoe box containing her mother's photographs. The other was an immense, leather-bound family Bible.

Buried truths here, Laura thought sleepily.

She examined the photographs first. There were maybe thirty or forty altogether. She shuffled and fanned them like cards, painstakingly arranged them into a rough chronological order.

One of the pictures was very old, a ghostly image of Grandma Lucille with a tiny girl-child—who must have been Mama—and two older boys, Uncle Duke and Uncle Charlie. Charlie had died in Korea all those years ago; Uncle Duke had vanished out of a bad marriage. Laura could not deduce, from the photo, anything extraordinary about these people. Just Lucille Cousins and her three children by the railing at Niagara Falls—the date on the back was 1932. A sunny day but windy: everybody's hair was blowing around. Bland, sunny smiles. These people, Laura thought, were about as occult or supernatural as a shirt button. Maybe this was where Mama had derived her vision of perfect normalcy, from this smiling woman, her mother, the easy contentment in those eyes. Grandpa Cousins had died a handful of years after he took this photo; Grandma Lucille had gone on public relief. So here was this picture: the Eden from which Mama had been expelled.

The power, Laura thought, the specialness, must have come from somewhere else.

She had never met any of Daddy's family except Grandma Fauve, another widow. Laura remembered Grandma Fauve as a huge woman, obsessed with a mail-order fundamentalist cult she had discovered through radio broadcasts out of WWVA in Wheeling. She embroidered samplers with queer, threatening passages from the Book of Revelation; her bookcases spilled out pamphlets with titles like *Warning from the Sky* and *Living in the Last Days*. Laura, as a child, had looked very hard at her grandmother, peered deep into those dark unblinking eyes . . . scary eyes, in their own way; but she had never seen the power there, none of the recognition she had longed for.

Daddy didn't have it. Mama didn't have it.

She thought, Then we are flukes. Mutants. Monsters.

But the power was an *inherited* power . . . Michael had demonstrated that.

She leafed through the other photos quickly. The image of Tim caught her eye, Tim growing up in these old pictures like the frames of a silent movie. He looked less intimidating than she remembered. She remembered how Tim used to bully his sisters, even though he was the youngest—something in his voice, his bearing; or just his stubborn willingness to do what they wouldn't, to break not just one rule but every rule. But in the photographs he was just a child. His round face looked not threatening but threatened: a *frightened* child.

There were fewer pictures of Tim as a teenager, but in these she could detect at least something of his brooding sullenness. He wore a leather jacket that not even Willis's threats had been able to pry off him. Laura smiled and thought, A fuck jacket. He regarded the camera with his chin lifted and his lips set in a grim line. His eyes were narrow, fixed.

Laura looked at her lost brother and thought, How much do you know?

The power was immensely strong in him. He had gone on experimenting even after Willis began to beat him—but privately, warily. Laura remembered how Tim would go off back into the hills or down some lonely road somewhere. She suspected that he practiced his awesome talent there, but she never asked. She was not as prim as her older sister, but Laura had always been a little bit *afraid* of her power, of the things she might see or conjure. Karen believed what Willis told her; Laura did not, but was cautious; Tim—

Tim, she thought, hated all of us.

She closed away the photographs and hid the shoe box once more.

She opened the Bible. It was a very old family Bible with lined pages in the back marked BIRTHS and MARRIAGES and DEATHS. The Bible had belonged to Grandma Lucille and the pages were filled with her writing, looping fountain-pen letters, and then Mama's looser ballpoint script.

Laura bent over the brittle pages with their curious odor of dust and papyrus. Births from the turn of the century. She found Mama here next to Duke and Charlie. She found her cousin Mary Ellen, Duke's girl by a woman named Barbara before Duke ran off. There were mysterious branches of the family, people she had never met, names she couldn't recall.

She looked for her own name, for Karen's and Tim's.

But the names weren't there.

Karen's marriage was recorded—*To Gavin White, Toronto, Canada, 1970*—but not her birth. None of them appeared in the birth register.

Laura felt suddenly light-headed, breathless. Felt *fragile*—as if she might float out the window and into the sky. We were not born, she thought, so how can we exist? She thought of the fairy tales she used to read out of her big illustrated Golden Book. We are changelings, she thought. The goblins left us. She remembered those goblins from the pictures. Gnarled and huge-headed, with sharp noses and sinister bright eyes. The goblins left us, she thought, and now the goblins want us back.

She shuddered and pulled the robe tighter around herself. She closed the Bible and put it back in the bottom drawer with the shoe box of photographs on top. She was about to close the drawer when she spotted something at the back, a cluster of faintly familiar shapes, dust-shrouded and gray.

She pulled the drawer open as far as its runners would allow and reached inside.

Three things. She brought them up into the circle of the light.

A paperweight, clouded and opaque.

A tiny, pathetically simple baby doll.

And a cheap pink plastic hand mirror.

I remember, she thought excitedly. I *remember!*

She thumbed a layer of dust from the surface of the mirror and regarded herself. The old glass was bent and pitted. How she had loved this old thing. *The fairest in the land.* Who had said that? Another fairy-tale memory, she thought, a Golden Book memory. She repeated it to herself, aloud but faintly: the fairest in the land.

Ahh . . . but I'm not.

Her own eyes regarded her sadly from the shrouded depths of the mirror.

Truth was, she had grown old in that quiet California town. She had grown old almost without noticing: mysteriously, effortlessly. I was beautiful once, she thought. I was beautiful and I was young and damn if I wasn't going to change the world, or anyway find a better one. She had been caught up in that hot, brief burst of Berkeley idealism—all the things people meant when they talked longingly about the sixties. And it had burned like a fire in her and she would follow it out beyond the walls of the world and it would never, ever fail her.

But now I'm old, she thought, and I have spent twenty years watching the waves roll in and out. Twenty years of rose-hip tea and poetry and winter fog; twenty years of Emmett's facile, occasional love.

Twenty years of stoned equilibrium, she thought, and all this coming home won't make me young again.

The mirror made her feel very sad.

But these things, these toys, were meaningful. She could not quite recall their provenance, but they had the feel of magic about them. She would show them to Karen in the morning.

In the meantime she tucked them back out of sight in the drawer, switched off the light, and went to bed. In the darkness she could hear the snow beating against the window, a sifting sound like sand in an hourglass—twenty years, she thought, twenty *years*, my *God!*—and she watched the faint moonlight until it began to blur and she put her hand to her face and realized with some astonishment that she was crying.

That long night had not quite ended when Michael awoke, alone and desolate in the big upstairs bed.

He took his watch from the night table and held it up to the thin wash of streetlight that penetrated these old dusty windows.

Four A.M.—and he felt as wholly, mercilessly awake as if it were noon.

He sighed, stood up, pulled on his underwear and his Levi's. He stood a moment at the window.

No more snow tonight. Stars beyond the fading margins of cloud, old streetlights down the back alleys and shuttered windows of this barren coal town. His breath made steamy islands on the glass. His vision of a better world had evaporated entirely. He could not even remember how it had felt. No magic in this place, Michael thought, only these cold empty streets. He shivered.

He wanted to go home.

The trouble with coming awake at 4 A.M., he

thought, was that it left you feeling like a little kid. Vulnerable. Like you could cry at any minute.

These were things he had not allowed himself to think: that he was tired of being chased, tired of being afraid, tired of sleeping in strange beds in houses where he did not belong.

But these were thoughts a ten-year-old might have, and Michael reminded himself sternly that he was *not* ten years old . . . he only felt that way sometimes.

"Shit," he said out loud.

He padded barefoot down the stairs past the other bedrooms, down to the ground floor. He switched on the kitchen light and poured himself a glass of milk. The tile floor was cold.

Impulsively, he pulled his wallet out of the right-hand pocket of his jeans.

He opened the card case.

It was still there . . . the number he had pilfered from his mother's address book, his father's phone number in Toronto. Hasty blue pen scrawl on old green memo paper.

There was a telephone in the kitchen—an old black dial phone on the counter next to the cookbooks.

Michael looked at it and thought, But what's the point? Call long-distance, wake him up at 4 A.M.—or his girlfriend, for Christ's sake—and get him on the line and say what? Hi, Dad. I just spent a few weeks in California. Well, sort of California. Got to see Kennedy's funeral on TV. You should have been there.

Right.

But the ten-year-old inside him insisted, *Home.*

Bullshit. There was no home back there. Only an empty house, and his father living someplace Michael had never seen, with a woman Michael had never met.

That's not true, the ten-year-old said. *You could go back. You could make it be good again.*

Bullshit, Michael thought, bullshit, *bullshit.* How good had it ever really been?

Not that good.

But he was dialing in spite of himself. Standing half dressed in this cold kitchen listening to the hum and chatter of the long-distance lines . . . and then a muted, brittle ringing.

"Hello?"

His father's voice. Weary, irritated.

Michael opened his mouth but discovered that he was empty of words.

"Hello? What is this, a joke?"

He'll hang up, Michael thought. And maybe that would be best.

But he whispered, "Dad?"

Long beat of silence down the wires from Canada. Then, "Michael? Is that you?"

Michael felt a moment of sheer, bottomless panic: there was nothing to say, nothing he *could* say.

"Michael, hey, I'm glad you called. Listen to me. I've been frantic—we've been worried about you."

Michael registered the "we" as a very sour note.

"Michael, are you there?"

"Yes," he admitted.

"Tell me where you're calling from."

No, Michael thought . . . that would be a mistake.

"Well," his father said, "are you all right? Is your mother all right?"

"Yeah. We're okay, we're fine."

"Has she given you any reason for dragging you away like this? Because, you know, that's very strange behavior. That's how it looks to me."

Michael thought, You don't know the half of it. He said, "I just called to hear your voice."

I called because I want to go home. I want there to be a home.

"I appreciate that. Listen, I know this must all have been very hard for you to understand. Maybe we didn't talk about it enough, you and I. Maybe you blame me for it. The divorce and all. Well, fair enough. Maybe I deserve some of that blame. But you have to look at it from my point of view, too."

"Sure," Michael said. But this wasn't what he wanted to hear. He wanted to hear *You and your mother come home, everything's fixed, everything's back to normal*—some reassurance for the ten-year-old in him. But of course that was impossible. The divorce wouldn't go away. The Gray Man wouldn't go away.

"Tell me where you are," his father persisted. "Hell, I can come and get you."

And suddenly the ten-year-old was vividly alive. Yes! Come get me! Take me home! Make it be safe! He said, "Dad—"

But suddenly there was another, fainter voice, sleepy and feminine: "Gavin? Who *is* it?"

And Michael thought, No home to go back to.

The ten-year-old was shocked into silence.

His father said, "Michael? Are you still there?"

"It was nice talking," Michael said. "Listen, maybe I'll call again."

"Michael—"

He forced himself to hang up.

He looked at his watch.

4:15.

Chapter Twelve

....

1

Michael understood that it was his job to be the man of the family, which involved protection and standing guard.

The routine at the Fauves' house was that Willis would wake up early and Jeanne would fix him a big breakfast. Then Willis would head off for a day or a half day at the mill and Michael and his mother and aunt would venture downstairs. Nobody yelled "The coast is clear!" or anything, but that was how it felt—they would wait for the thud of the big front door, for the sound of Willis's feet on the porch. His old Ford

Fairlane would rattle out of the garage, and then the house was safe.

Grandma Jeanne insisted on cooking. Her breakfasts were heroic—cereal, toast, eggs, mounds of bacon—and Michael was always turning down second helpings. This morning she let him get away without protest, though, and he noticed the absentminded way she circled from the table to the counter, the odd looks Karen and Laura gave her: something was up.

He was only vaguely curious. He knew why Aunt Laura had brought them here and he was grateful that she was, maybe, beginning to get somewhere with it. He understood that this was necessary, sorting things out from the beginning, but he had already guessed it was not the whole job. Not by a long shot. Because there was still the problem of the Gray Man.

The Gray Man could find them anytime.

Michael bolted a big helping of scrambled eggs, considering this.

The kind of move they had made from Turquoise Beach would throw the Gray Man off their trail, but not indefinitely. He had followed them before and he would follow them here. It was only a question of time. And Michael's mother and his aunt were preoccupied, so it was up to Michael to stand guard.

Grandma Jeanne took his plate and rinsed it under the faucet. His mom put a hand on his shoulder. "Michael? We'd like to talk to Grandma Jeanne privately."

He nodded and stood. Grandma Jeanne would not face him; she stared into the foaming sink. Aunt Laura nodded once solemnly, telegraphing to him that this was important, he had better clear off.

"I'll be out," he said.

"Stay warm." His mother ruffled his hair absently. "Stick close to the house."

He was careful not to promise.

The temperature outside was still below freezing but the wind had let up. The sun was out, melting snow off the sidewalks; Michael's breath plumed away in the winter light.

He followed the same route he had followed the day before, along Riverside Avenue and out beyond the southern margin of the town, up the snowy hillside until he could see all of Polger Valley mapped out in front of him. He felt the power most clearly in high places like this.

In town, among people, it was blanked out by a dozen other feelings. Up here he could just listen to the singing of it, like some quiet but important song played on a radio far away. He felt it like an engine deep in the earth, humming.

It occurred to him how much all this had changed his life. Not too long ago his main worries had been his term exams and the logistics of enjoying Saturday night when you couldn't drive a car. All that was gone now—all washed away. But, Michael thought, it never really *was* like that, was it? He thought, *You knew.* You knew it before Emmett got you stoned that day in Turquoise Beach. You knew it before Dad left. Knew you were special, or anyway *different:* singled out in some way. Michael felt the power in him now and guessed he had always felt it, just never had a name for it. He had been timid of it, the sheer nameless immensity of it, the way you might be afraid of falling if you lived on the edge of some canyon . . . but he had loved it, too; secretly, wordlessly. He remembered nights coming home from some friend's house, winter nights many times colder than this, and he would be shivering in an overstuffed parka and the stars would be out and there would be an ice ring around the moon, and he would be all alone out on some empty suburban street; and he would feel the future opening up in front of him, his own life like a wide, clean highway of possibility. And there was no reason for it, no reason to believe he was anything unique or that his life would be special. Just this feeling. Time opening like a flower for him.

Still opening, he thought. He remembered his dream of the night before, the cities and prairies and forests he had seen. The vision had come across a great distance. He wondered whether he could reach it—whether he would ever be able to summon it back. Maybe it was *too* far; maybe it was out of his grasp, never more real than his dreams.

But he had seen it, and he felt intuitively that it *was* a real place. Maybe he could find his way there—somehow, someday. Maybe that was where his life was headed.

Maybe.

If they could deal with the Gray Man.

Walker, the Gray Man had said. Walker, stalker, hunter, finder . . .

Michael thought, He almost took me with him. That day before we left Toronto. Had me hypnotized or something, had me following him back down some ugly back door out of the world.

He remembered that place he had almost gone. He remembered the feel of it, the taste and the smell of it. And unlike the world he had dreamed last night, it was not very far away at all . . . Michael was certain he could find it again if he wanted to.

It might be necessary one day. It might tell them something.

Furtively now, he raised his hands in front of him.

This was probably not a good idea . . . he told himself so. But it was important, he thought. A piece of the puzzle. This was the step Laura or his mother would never take; this was Michael's responsibility.

He made a circle of his fingers.

He looked through that circle at the town of Polger Valley, calm under a quarter inch of snow.

Felt the power in him . . . looked again, looked harder.

The town changed . . .

It was recognizably the same town. An old steel-mill town on the Monongahela. Maybe even, in a way, better off. The mill was bigger, a huge compound of coal-black buildings strung out along the riverside. There were complex piers busy with odd wooden barges; the river was crowded with traffic. But the town was also dirtier, the sky was black; the houses hugging this hillside were tin-and-tar-paper shanties. There was snow on the ground but the snow was gray with ash; the trees were spindly and barren. The traffic down at the foot of this hill was mostly horses and carts; the one truck that ambled past was boxy and antiquated-looking. Michael caught a faint whiff of some sulfurous chemical odor.

He squinted across town to the police station and the courthouse, plain gray stone buildings a quarter mile away down Riverside. He saw the flag flying over the courthouse and recognized that it was not an American flag, not a familiar flag at all: something dark with a triangular symbol.

Bad place, Michael thought. You could feel it in the air. Poverty and bad magic.

This is *his* home, Michael thought: this is where Walker lives. Not this town, maybe, but this world.

He shivered and blinked away the vision. His hands dropped to his side.

Maybe they would have to follow Walker into that place. Maybe that was their only choice. It might come to that. But not yet, Michael thought. He felt soiled, dirty; even that brief contact had been chastening. He moved down the hillside toward Polger Valley—how clean it suddenly seemed—thinking, Not yet, we're not ready for that yet . . . we're not *strong enough* yet for that.

He was halfway home down Riverside, past the Kresge's and the Home Hardware, when Willis pulled up next to him.

"Hey," Willis said.

Michael stood still on the cracked sidewalk and regarded his grandfather warily through the rolled-down window of the Fairlane.

"Get in," Willis said.

Michael said, "I wanted to walk."

But Willis just reached over and jerked open the door on the passenger side. Michael shrugged and climbed in.

The car was dirty with fast-food wrappers and cigarette butts, but it smelled only faintly of liquor: Willis was sober today.

Willis drove slowly down Main. He looked at Michael periodically and made a couple of attempts at conversation. He asked how Michael did in school. Okay, Michael said. Was it messing him up to be out for so long? No, he figured he could make it up. (As if any of this mattered.) Willis said, "Your old man left?"

Michael hesitated, then nodded.

"Shitty thing to do," Willis said.

"I guess he had his reasons."

"Everybody has some goddamn reason."

Turning up Montpelier, Willis said, "Look, I know what it is you're running from."

Michael raised his head, startled.

"You can only make it worse," Willis went on, "doing what you're doing."

"I don't know what you mean."

"I think you do, though. I think you know exactly what I mean." Willis was talking now from way down in his chest, almost to himself. He downshifted the Fairlane and slowed, approaching the house.

Willis said, "Timmy used to go off like that. Off up into the hills or God knows where. And I knew what he was doing, just like I know what you're doing. I could smell it on him." Willis pulled into the driveway and on up into the tiny, dark garage. He pulled the hand brake and let the motor die. "I smell it on *you.*"

Michael reached for the door but Willis caught his wrist. Willis had a hard grip. He was old but he had hard, stringy muscles.

"This is for your own good," he said. "You listen to me. It *brings* him. You savvy? You go out there and make a little door into Hell and *he* climbs out."

Michael said, "What do you know about it?"

"More than you think. You don't give me much credit, do you?"

Michael felt Willis's huge anger rising up. He shifted toward the door, but Willis held tight to his wrist.

"My Christ," Willis went on, "didn't your mother teach you *anything?* Or maybe she did—maybe she taught you too fucking much."

Michael remembered what Laura had told him, how Willis used to beat them. He realized now that it was true, Willis could do that, he was capable of it. Willis radiated anger like a bright red light.

"Admit it," Willis said, "you were up in those hills opening doors."

Michael shook his head. The lie was automatic.

"Don't shit me," Willis stormed. "I'm a good Christian man. I can smell out the Devil in the dark."

It made Michael think of the sulfurous stink of Walker's world.

"I don't do that," he said.

Willis's grip tightened. "I won't have you drawing down that creature on us again. Too many years—I lived with that too goddamn long." He bent down so that his face was close to Michael's face. The dim winter light in the garage made him seem monstrous. "I want you to admit to me what you've been doing. And then I want you to promise you won't do it again."

"I didn't—"

"Crap," Willis said, and raised his right hand to strike.

It was the gesture that angered Michael. Made him mad, because he guessed his mother had seen that hand upraised, and Laura, and they had been children, too young to do or say anything back. "All right!" he said, and when Willis hesitated Michael went on: "I *can* do it! Does that make you happy? I could walk out of here sideways and you'd never see me go! Is that what you want?"

Willis pulled Michael close and with the other hand took hold of his hair. The grip was painful; Michael's eyes watered.

"Don't even think it," Willis said.

His voice was a rumble, gritty machinery in his chest.

"Promise me," Willis said. "Promise you won't do it again."

Silence.

Willis tugged back on Michael's hair. "Promise!"

Michael said, "Fuck you!"

And Willis was too shocked to react.

Michael said between his teeth, "I could do it

here! You ever think about that? I could do it *now.*"
And it was true. He felt the power in him still, high-
pitched and singing. He said without thinking about it,
"I could drop you down through the floor so fast you
wouldn't be able to blink—do you *want* that?"

Willis was speechless.

Michael said, *"Let go of me."*

Miraculously, he felt Willis's grip loosen.

He wrenched open the door before Willis could
reconsider. He stumbled down onto the oily concrete.

"You're lost," Willis said from the darkness inside
the car. "Oh boy . . . you are *damned.*" But there
was not much force left in it.

Michael hurried into the house.

2

"I don't like telling it," Mama said. "I can't tell it
all. I don't know it all. But I guess I can tell what I
know."

The kitchen clock ticked away. Karen and Laura
sat sipping coffee. Karen understood that silence was
best, that her mother was staring past these walls and
back into a buried history. Hard for all of us, she
thought.

Privately, Karen was frightened. The words pronounced in this room might change her life. Beginning now, she thought, the future is dark and strange.

Karen took another sip of coffee, waiting. Beyond
the steamy windows a still morning sunlight filled the
backyard.

"Well," Mama said. "I was a girl in Wheeling when
I met Willis. You know, this was all so long ago it seems
like a story. Your Grandma Lucille was working at the

Cut-&-Curl and that year I had a teller job at the bank."

She settled back and sighed.

"I met Willis through the church.

"It was a little Assembly of God church, what I guess nowadays they would call fundamentalist. To us it was just church. Willis was very serious about it. He went to all the functions. I was there every Sunday but I didn't do any work or go to the meetings much. There was a Youth Group that met in the basement and I went there sometimes. Willis was always there. He knew me from Group for most of a year before he worked up the nerve to ask me out. Maybe that seems strange, but it was different in those days. People didn't just, you know, jump into bed. There was a courtship, there was dating. But pretty soon we started going together. And I liked him well enough to eventually marry him.

"He was different when he was younger. I don't say that to excuse anything. But I want you to understand how it was. He was fun to be with. He told jokes. Can you imagine that? He liked to dance. After we got married a cousin of his got him a job at a mill up in Burleigh, and that was when we moved out of Wheeling.

"I guess it was hard for me being away from family and in a strange town and living with a man, all for the first time. Just being married, it was very different. Willis wasn't always as gentle or as interesting as he seemed when we were dating. But you kind of expect that. But he was doing a lot of overtime, too. There were days I hardly saw him. I will admit I was lonely sometimes. I made a few friends but it was never like Wheeling—it was always a strange place to me.

"We wanted children. Mostly I wanted them. I wanted them especially because the house we rented seemed so empty. It was not a big house; Willis was not making a great salary those early years. But it felt big when I was rattling around in it on my own. You clean up, you maybe listen to the radio a little bit, and the time slips by. So it was natural to think about children and how there would at least be company, even if it was only a little baby. The neighbors had kids and that woman, Ellen Conklin, she would come by in the afternoons and just drink one cup of coffee after another and complain about her life. Had a little brat named, I think, Emilia who never left her in peace. I mean a truly nasty child. But I envied her even that. A child— it would be *something*.

"But we didn't have any.

"We waited for five years.

"I didn't know to see a doctor or anything. I just thought you waited. And it would happen or it would not as God preferred. We went to an Assembly church there and one time I asked the pastor about it, privately. Well, he turned so red he could hardly talk. A young man. 'God willing,' he said—he used those words. 'Pray,' he told me.

"So I prayed. But nothing happened.

"I didn't know about fertility or about how it worked, except that the man and the woman were together in bed and that was how it happened. I wondered if we were doing something wrong. Because in those days nobody talked about it. Nobody I knew ever talked about it. I finally worked up the nerve to mention how we never had babies to Ellen Conklin and she said, 'Why, shoot, Jeanne, I thought you were doing it on *purpose.*' And it was news to me that there was a way to *not* have kids on purpose. It was confusing to me . . . why would anybody *not* want to? Which made Ellen Conklin laugh, of course.

"She said to see a doctor. It might be me, she said, or it could be Willis. And maybe it could be fixed.

"Well, I saw the doctor by myself. Willis wouldn't go. He just wouldn't hear of it. It wasn't the kind of thing Willis could talk about. So I went by myself, and in the end it didn't matter that Willis didn't go because as it turned out it *was* me—I was the one who couldn't bear children."

She looked at Karen and Laura, back and forth between them. "You know what I'm saying?"

Karen was trembling; she did not speak. Laura said coolly, "We were adopted?" Added, "I looked in the family Bible, Mama . . . I know we're not in there."

Karen felt suddenly adrift, a ship cast loose from its moorings.

Mama said, "Not adopted exactly. But I will tell you the story. What I know of it."

They were a strange couple (Mama said). They had been going to the Assembly church for almost two years, and they were immigrants.

DPs, most people thought, refugees from what was left of Europe after the war. No one could place exactly what country they might have fled. They spoke good English but in an odd way, as if a Dutch accent had mingled with a French. They looked alike. He was tall and she was short, but they had similar eyes.

They just moved into town one day and took up residence in a shack out on the access road. Obviously they'd been through hard times. They gave their name as Williams, so people were thinking, Well, here's somebody without papers, somebody maybe who came into the country through the back door—it was possible.

But they were not drifters. The man—he called himself Ben—had no skills but he was willing to work and he was a hard worker. You would see him sometimes at the back of the hardware store, pushing a broom or shelving stock. People said he never complained. And he had a family.

Three little babies.

The oldest was four. The youngest was a newborn.

I see you know what I mean. But wait—don't jump ahead.

People took pity on them because of this haggard look, a *hunted* look. In the Depression you might have mistaken them for criminals or hobos, but these were prosperous times and there was nothing criminal about them. And we were reading all the terrible stories then about the war—this was when the truth about the death camps came out. They weren't Jews but they might have been gypsies or Poles or who knows what. None of us really understood what had happened over there, only that a lot of innocent people had been hunted down and killed.

Ben seemed very serious about the church. I don't know if it was ever honest conviction, however, or just the urge to fit in. Sometimes at church I would see him a pew or three in front of me, standing there with the hymnal in his hand, not really singing but just mouthing the words. And he would have this utterly *lost* look, the way you or I might look if we'd stumbled into a synagogue or something by mistake and couldn't politely leave. I think he liked the processional best. He would always close his eyes and smile a little when the organ played. And he always put money in the plate—for a man in his circumstances he gave very generously.

I never thought he would abandon those children.

He seemed to like it well enough in Burleigh—and he loved those kids. You could just tell.

But this is the part I don't know much about. Willis never talked about it.

All I know is that there was trouble one night at the shack where they lived. Willis got a phone call and went out with some church people. He came back looking very pale and, you know, shaking. But he never talked about it. Couple of police cars were out there that night, people said, and some stories circulated but no two alike, so I don't know. Finally it was let out that Ben and his wife had left town, or maybe he had murdered his wife and run away—but I never believed that.

The pastor of our church took charge of the three children. There was a county orphanage two towns away but it had a very bad reputation—and these weren't registered children; they had no birth or baptismal certificates. In those days, in that place, people were more casual about such things. Well, the pastor thought of us.

He talked to Willis about it.

I don't know how much Willis liked the idea. But he knew I wanted kids and that I couldn't have any. Maybe the pastor or some of the deacons leaned on him. Anyway, he agreed. And I think that was a brave thing to do.

He brought you three home.

"I don't remember any of that," Karen said dazedly.

"Well," Mama said, "you were only just four years old—a young four at that. It's hardly surprising. And Laura was still in diapers and Timmy was just newborn."

"At least it makes sense," Laura said. "It puts some order into things."

"Does it?"

"There must be a reason we're the way we are."

Mama said, "You shouldn't even talk about that."

"But we are talking about it," Laura said. "Isn't that what we've been talking about all along? Mama, that's why we're *here.*"

Karen watched her mother stand up, pace nervously to the sink.

Mama said—faintly—"It frightened your father."

She turned to the window.

"I saw you do it once. I mean you, Karen. I remember that. It didn't seem like such a bad thing. You showed me. You were proud of it. You drew a circle in the air and there was a nice place in that circle—a lake, some trees, a flight of birds. Like a postcard picture. It was pretty and it was the sort of thing a child might try to draw with crayons. I wasn't frightened of it, not at that moment. Later I guess I was, because it was a miracle, you know, and frightening when you think about what it might mean. But you were so proud of it. Maybe somebody had showed you how, back before we got you. Or maybe you just knew. When I calmed down I said it was nice but don't do it again and *especially* don't show Daddy . . . I knew how he'd take it."

Karen thought, I remember that! So long ago, but the memory popped right back up. How it had felt, making that circle, feeling the power in her . . . she *had* been proud.

She thought, It's been so long! Once I was young and I could hear that song inside me, even when I didn't want to. Now I'm empty. Drained, she thought, like a bottle.

"It was always Daddy," Mama said, "who decided when we would move."

"The Gray Man," Laura said.

Mama nodded convulsively, her back turned. "You could call him that. I saw him once. One time only. Just before we left Pittsburgh. We were riding on the streetcar—I had some shopping to do. Karen, you were in school; but I had Laura and Timmy with me. And *he* got on the car.

"Timmy looked straight at him . . . both children seemed to recognize him. And I looked at him, too.

"I knew there was something wrong with him. He made me think of somebody who had been hurt somehow. When I was a girl we used to see veterans who had been gassed in France: he reminded me of that. He moved his head oddly; he had strange eyes under that old slouch hat. I thought he might be, you know, simpleminded.

"But then he sat down and looked straight at the kids and I saw them looking at him, and he smiled, and it was a horrible smile, and his eyes lit up in a terrible hungry way . . . and when I saw Tim smiling back at him I just felt faint, the way you would feel if you saw your child playing with a rattlesnake or something. I grabbed the kids and rang the bell and we got off at the next stop—*ran* off is more like it."

Laura said, "We moved after that?"

"I told Willis about it . . . and yes, we moved pretty much directly after that."

"Every time we moved, was it because of the Gray Man?"

"I think so. Mostly. Willis never talked about it."

"You never asked him?"

"Hardly ever. And he wouldn't answer."

We never talked, Karen thought. Nobody *ever* talked.

Laura said, "I wonder if this Ben Williams is still alive. Maybe there's somebody in Burleigh who would know . . . Mama, do you think so?"

Mama said, "You're determined to go stirring this up?"

"I don't think we have a choice."

"Well . . . I doubt that you'll be able to find anybody who can help. Most of that Assembly congregation must be scattered by now. The mill closed down years ago. A few of the men knew what happened that night when you three were taken from Ben and his wife. But they never seemed liable to talk about it. In a town of gossips, that is one thing people kept to themselves. And who else is there?"

Karen said, "There's Daddy."

Laura looked at her. Mama regarded her with obvious surprise.

"Your father," Mama began, "would never—"

But then there was the bang and rattle of the big front door, and Michael rushed into the house.

Chapter Thirteen

· ·

Karen found her son in his room, cross-legged on the bed and breathing hard. He looked up sharply when she came through the door.

"Michael?" She closed the door for privacy. "Michael, what is it?"

"Willis," he said.

Michael had been out in the hills south of town, he said, and Willis had picked him up and driven him back here. Willis wasn't drunk but he was angry. Willis had accused him of practicing witchcraft or raising demons or something . . . Willis had tried to hit him.

Karen felt a sudden chill. "How do you mean, tried?"

My son, she thought. *My father.*

Michael said, "I didn't let him."

"Michael, that's silly . . . if he wanted to hit you, he would have."

"I stopped him."

Willis might be older now but he was still strong and he was twice Michael's size. "How could you possibly stop Daddy?"

But Michael didn't answer, and Karen—thinking about Michael and Daddy alone in the car—guessed she already knew.

"You wait here," she said.

She asked downstairs, but Daddy hadn't come in yet. So she went out through the side door into the cold, hugging her sweater around herself and breathing icy plumes.

The garage door loomed open. It was not a garage so much as it was a shed, a barnboard box leaning cockeyed against the north wall of the house. The seasons had put big gaps and rents in it. The interior was dark in the wintry light.

She moved cautiously around the pitted chromed fenders of the Fairlane, along a wall lined with rust-flecked garden tools.

"Daddy?"

No answer. But there was a flicker of light in the car: Willis's cigarette as he turned toward her.

"Daddy," she said, "I'm cold."

He hooked open the right-hand car door with a weary gesture. "What do you want?"

"To talk," she said.

The door hung open.

Trembling a little, Karen slid inside.

Willis sat crammed against the driver's side, one arm up to cradle his head, the other resting on the wheel. The car was full of cigarette smoke. A crushed pack of Camels lay on the dash.

Karen looked at him, at his face. It took a certain amount of courage just to keep her eyes on him. She had seldom truly looked at her father; she had learned a long time ago that it was better not to. In her memory he was not a thing seen so much as a presence, a voice, a rumbling imperative. He was something fundamental, like lightning or thunder—and you can't stare down the weather.

But he was an old man in an old car—that, too.

She said, "You tried to hit Michael."

Willis exhaled and butted out the cigarette in the door tray. "He went running to Mommy—is that it?"

"I asked him about it."

"You ask him anything *else* about it?"

"No . . . should I?"

"Maybe. For instance maybe you ought to ask him what he was doing up in those hills this afternoon."

There was no way to avoid this anymore. She cleared her throat and said, "Daddy, I know what he was doing."

Willis looked at her once, startled . . . then turned away. His big hands gripped the steering wheel. He said after a time, "I used to think you were different. But you're not, are you? You're just like the other two."

It made her want to yell. I *am*, she wanted to say, I *am* different, you *made* me different! I'm what you wanted—Christ, *look* at me! But she forced away the thought and took a deep, deliberate breath. "I tried to bring Michael up to be normal. I really did. But he can't be forever what he's not."

"Well, what *is* he, then? Have you given any thought to that?"

No, she hadn't, but . . . "That's why we came here. To find out what Michael is. And what *we* are."

Willis just shook his head bitterly. "He threatened me. Did he tell you that? He threatened to drop me down a hole into Hell. And I . . ."

He seemed to stall in the recollection.

Karen said, "You believed him?"

"Wouldn't you?"

"Daddy, you scared him."

"He's like your brother. He's about as respectful. Less. Oh yeah . . . you did a great job on him, all right."

She said, "But I never hit him."

"Well, you should have."

No, Karen thought. I'm a grown-up woman now. I know better. "Maybe Tim was right," she said.

Willis regarded her angrily.

Karen said, "Maybe we *should* have hated you. Maybe the problem is we never did. You beat us and we loved you anyway. It was like loving a rock, but we did. Laura did, even though she won't admit it. Maybe even Tim did. At least when he was little. But you know what? If I had a neighbor who treated his kids the way you treated us, you know what I'd do? I'd call the police."

She was saying this and thinking it at the same time; it surprised her as much as it seemed to surprise Willis. He said, "You came here to tell me that?"

"I came here to save Michael's life!"

He frowned.

Karen said, "Daddy, the Gray Man almost took him. And there was a little girl killed."

Willis winced. "Christ Jesus." He shook his head. "You never told me . . ."

Karen said, "Who was Ben Williams? Who were our parents? Daddy, do you *know*?"

But he didn't speak. He stared at her and then he reached over and took a second pack of Camels from the glove compartment. He crumpled the cellophane and dropped it into the shadows at his feet, drew out a cigarette from the package, struck a match, and inhaled deeply. He held the smoke a moment and then said, with a meekness she did not recognize at all, "Your mother told you about this?"

Karen nodded.

"Well, shit," Willis said.

"But not the important parts. Daddy, we *need* to know."

He was silent for another long while. He smoked his cigarette down to the filter. Karen was about to give up and go back to the house when Willis suddenly opened his door. The overhead light flashed on in the car and the glare was sudden and harsh. He stepped out onto the concrete.

He stood hitching up his denims in the light of the garage. "You come with me," he said.

He took her up to the bedroom he shared with Mama.

It was a private place; Karen had not been in here even to help change the sheets. But she recognized the old oak dresser, the yellowing muslin curtains, the sailing-ship picture on the wall. They had owned these things forever. Daddy bent over the bottom drawer of the dresser, rummaged a moment, and then came up with a brown, ancient photograph, one that had not been included in Mama's shoe box.

Karen took it from him with a dawning sense of wonder. It was a church picnic photo. Men in shirt sleeves and hats, women in billowing sundresses, all lined up stiffly for the camera.

"That's him," Willis said. "Second man in the back row. That's Ben Williams."

Karen inspected this faint, small image of her natural father.

Ben Williams was a tall man with wide, bewildered eyes. His skin was pale and his hair was long and tousled. He held a leather Bible absently in one hand.

"The woman next to him," Willis said tonelessly, "is his wife. That blond one, there—you can't see her too well. The babies were off in the grass."

The babies, Karen thought. Me and Laura and Tim. We were there on this day—before everything changed.

Karen regarded the sad eyes of the man in the photograph. "Did he die?"

"Yes. He died."

She thought about it.

"Tell me," she said.

Willis said, "Are you certain you want that?"

She was not certain at all. But she nodded her head yes.

"All right, then," Willis said.

Well, Willis said, we always knew they were strange.

They had a look about them. We took them for DPs because of their accent and all. Reverend Dahlquist told them there was a Greek Orthodox church downtown in Burleigh—he thought that must be more along their line. But they said no, the Assembly was what they wanted. They were friendly and they joined the church and they tried to fit in, and after a while nobody thought much about it.

Not until that night.

(Karen, open the window. Your mother hates it when I smoke in here. But right now I need to.)

You understand, I wasn't there for the beginning of it. I heard some of this from Reverend Dahlquist. What happened is that Mrs. Williams came by the parsonage one night with her three children in tow—this was well after dark. She knocked for five minutes until the Reverend came down in his nightshirt and opened the door for her. Here, Reverend, she says, please keep these children safe, just for a little while, just for the night—please? Reverend Dahlquist said how come, but Mrs. Williams wouldn't say. Reverend Dahlquist wasn't pleased. But he told me later he took the children because he feared for them; Mrs. Williams was obviously scared half to death. He guessed Ben had maybe gone on some kind of rampage or was drunk or something. Not what you would have expected from Ben, but it was not too uncommon in that place. The Reverend fed the kids a late dinner and bedded them down. Might have gone to bed himself but he kept thinking of Mrs. Williams's face, how scared she had looked, and finally he started to worry that something might happen to her, maybe if Ben was that badly off he would hurt her in some way. So he telephoned a few of the church men and suggested we should drive out by the Williams place to have a look.

It was late to be driving but Charlie Dagostino and Curt Bloedell came by in Charlie's big Packard and picked me up. The three of us rode out there in the dark. Curt Bloedell had a little .22 caliber squirrel rifle with him, but I don't think he ever expected to use it. In fact, he didn't, not seriously—though maybe he should have.

We got to the Williams house at something past midnight. The house was dark.

Charlie argued that we should head back home.

Obviously nothing was wrong. I agreed with him, but Curt Bloedell wanted to knock and find out for certain —Curt always did love poking his nose in other people's business. We argued and finally Charlie said okay, we'll knock for Christ's sake, I want to go home and get in bed. And so we three went up the slatboard front walk together.

It was not a big house and in fact it was mostly a shack, one of those shanties you might see out along the county road. Tar-paper roof and it had a coal stove for heat in the winter. But Ben had fixed it up as nice as he could, and his wife had filled some old truck tires with creek dirt and planted them with morning glories and lily of the valley, which had bloomed. We weren't scared, except maybe of what Ben might say when we woke him up. None of us took this too seriously—Curt left his .22 lying in the car.

But before we could knock, the door opened.

A man stepped out.

He wore a gray trench coat and a gray hat. He looked foreign. He had a funny smile, standing in the doorway of that darkened house.

Maybe you know who I mean.

And I suppose then we ought to have been scared or at least suspected something had happened. But the strange thing is we did not. He looked at each of us in turn, at me and Curt Bloedell and Charlie Dagostino —in that order—and he just smiled and said "Good night!" in a childish kind of way, and then he walked down to the road and was gone in the shadows while we watched. We didn't ask who he was or what he was doing there. I swear I don't know why. My guess would be that he put some kind of spell on us. I could not say this to Curt or Charlie and they never hinted at any such thing to me. But as soon as this man was out of sight we all shook our heads and began to have the feeling that something was terribly wrong. And we were scared then for the first time. Curt Bloedell kept muttering "Jesus, oh, Jesus," and Charlie wanted to climb back in the Packard and run for home. But I said we had come to check on the Williamses and we should do that, and we were all thinking how strange it was that we could stand there talking out loud on the doorstep of the house and no one heard us, what was wrong? So I stepped inside and felt for a light switch because I knew the electric lines had been installed out here recently and so there would be light, at least. And I found the switch and I turned it on.

Well, they were dead.

They were worse than dead, really, because parts of them were scattered around the shack and parts of them were just missing. There was some cheap luggage on the floor and some clothes, as if they might have been packing to leave when all this happened. And some of the baby toys were lying around. And so much blood.

I can't describe it better than that. But it was terrible.

Remembering it is terrible.

I went outside and puked into one of the planters. Curt Bloedell ran to the Packard and got his .22 and started firing it into the air. I think he might have hurt himself if Charlie and I had not stopped him. He was sobbing like a child.

And I kept thinking, Those poor children!

We would have phoned for the police from that shack if there had been a phone, but Ben had never installed one. So we rode back to the parsonage (and it is a wonder no one was killed on that ride) and we told Reverend Dahlquist what had happened and he phoned the police for us.

We decided, in the time before the police came to talk to us, that we would not mention the children.

State custody would mean an orphanage or Christ knows what, and we thought it was better to deal with it inside the church—keep maybe a little closer eye on the kids that way. Plus Reverend Dahlquist and Charlie Dagostino's wife had heard about Jeanne's situation at home.

I suppose she told you about that, too?

I see.

The police talked to us and they were suspicious at first, but of course there was no way me and Curt and Charlie could have done anything like that even with the .22, and there was no blood on us or anything. We told them about the man we had seen and how the house had looked. Reverend Dahlquist told how he had sent us out there because he was worried about Ben getting drunk and beating his wife. And the police, I think because they couldn't figure out how or why any of this had happened, didn't seem to want to follow it up. As far as they were concerned it was two vagabonds that had died in suspicious circumstances— no more to be said. And none of the three of us talked about it after that.

But even now—even now I have dreams about it sometimes.

Karen didn't know what to say. It was too shocking, too horrible.

Willis said, "I don't understand it. I don't pretend to understand it. But I know what I felt the first time I saw Timmy doing that little trick of his. He was out in the backyard on Constantinople one summer night with fireflies all around him. You girls were inside and Jeanne was running a bath and I was out there watching the baby. He was chasing the fireflies. He would run across that lawn laughing and grabbing out. And then all of a sudden he reached out his little hand and drew a circle in the air. And the circle was full of that firefly light. And there were shapes in that light. Faces and bodies—things with wings. And it might have been anything but I thought—I was certain—it was Hell itself Timmy had opened up. And I could only think of that man in the gray hat and his eyes looking at me and Charlie and Curt Bloedell, and then of the blood and the parts of human beings in that shack.

"I took him—Timmy—and I beat him nearly senseless."

Karen said nothing.

"It gave me no pleasure," Willis said flatly. "I wanted him to be afraid of it. If that meant being afraid of me, then so be it. Whatever he had done, I knew where it led. It led back to that shack—those bodies."

"But it didn't work," Karen said softly.

"Tim always fought me." Willis rubbed his big callused hand across his face. "He hated me. You said as much."

"And when we moved," Karen said, "it was because of the Gray Man."

"I might see him in the street. Or one of you kids might mention him. Or Jeanne might see him. And so we would run."

"But he would always find us."

"Eventually."

Karen said, "You should have warned us before we left home."

"I always thought—it seemed like Timmy he was after. And I believed sometimes that it was Timmy who would bring him. Timmy was not afraid of that man. I don't know everything that went on . . . Timmy may have had some commerce with him." He ground the stub of his cigarette against the sole of his shoe. "For years I believed that man was the devil."

Karen understood that this was literally true, that her father had come out of an old tradition of hair-shirt fundamentalism, that he was quite capable of believing in a devil in an old gray hat. Considering what he had seen, maybe it wasn't so crazy.

She said, "Do you believe that now?"

"I don't know what to believe."

She watched her father staring morosely out the window. The afternoon light had faded. The air rushing over the sill was icy cold. She said, watching him stare into the gathering dark, "You *wanted* us to be afraid."

"Yes," Willis said tonelessly.

"Because *you* were afraid."

But he did not answer.

Chapter Fourteen

....

1

The day before they left, Jeanne Fauve took her daughter Laura aside and said in a whisper, "Where are you going from here?"

They stood in the parlor with the faded Persian rug and the relentless tick of the mantel clock. The air was still and dry; the furnace was humming. Upstairs, Michael and Karen were busy packing.

"I don't know," Laura said. "Up to Burleigh, maybe—see what we can find out."

"I think," her mother said, "if you're determined to do this, what you need is to talk to Tim."

Laura said, "You know where he is?"

"Not really. But we got this from him at Christmas . . . maybe it's useful to you?"

Jeanne took the card from the pocket of her quilted housecoat. It was not a Christmas card, just an ordinary postcard, a picture of the Golden Gate Bridge from the air, and the white buildings on the hills beyond it like some painter's dream of a city.

It was the only communication she had received from her son in the past ten years.

Laura accepted the card from her mother. She turned it over and read the message there. *Merry Christmas* was all it said, but she recognized the handwriting—after all these years—as Tim's. The message was mysterious; she could not discern either sincerity or irony in it.

But there was a return address there, too, crabbed and small at the top of the card. Someplace in San Francisco.

Laura looked up somberly.

"Thank you," she said.

"Be careful," her mother said.

2

That last night in the old house in Polger Valley, Karen stayed up and wrote in her journal.

Rustle of cold wind at the window, scratch of pen on paper.

I think about Daddy, she wrote.

The pen hesitated on the page.

She wrote, *I carry him inside me and I have carried him inside me longer than I knew.*

He means well, she wrote.

But then she scratched it out.

She wrote, *We think we live in a place or we know a person or we have a parent, but it isn't true. We are those things. They build us. They're what we're made of.*

I'm made out of Willis, Karen wrote. *I see him in the mirror more often than I like. I hear his voice in my voice.*

She discovered that her hand was shaking.

She wrote—bearing down hard with the point of the Bic—*I think about Michael, too.*

Michael is made out of me.

And in this dangerous thing we have begun— dear God, she wrote, *I wonder if that is enough.*

She closed the journal and was about to switch off the small desk light when Laura said, "Wait."

Karen turned abruptly. "You scared me . . . I didn't know you were awake."

"I didn't want to interrupt."

They were alone in the room with midnight snow heaped on the windowsill and the faint, far hum of the furnace. Karen wore a quilted robe over her nightgown; Laura was tucked up under a comforter.

"Been quite a visit," Laura said.

Karen smiled. "Hell of a visit."

"Foundlings," Laura said.

"Gypsies," Karen said.

"That's us." Laura sat up in bed hugging her knees. "Have you looked in the bottom drawer?"

Karen frowned. She had never been especially fond of surprises. And she was tired. But she opened the big drawer slowly.

"Oh," she said. "Oh, my God."

"You remember them, too?"

From among the toys Karen picked out the pink,

fleshy baby doll. It was tiny; it was naked; dust had infiltrated the pores of the plastic.

"Baby," she said. She looked at Laura wonderingly. "It *wasn't* a dream."

"None of it was ever a dream. That's the scary part, isn't it?"

Karen explained about the dream she had dreamt periodically almost all of her life, the house on Constantinople and Tim's doorway into that cold industrial city. Laura nodded and said, "That's more or less how I remember it. Tim was always the explorer. Still is, maybe."

She replaced the doll where she had found it. There was something unpleasant in the feel of the plastic. "You think we can find him?"

"I think we have to try."

"You think he still hates us?"

"You think he ever really did?"

"I don't know," Karen said. The question troubled her. "It's been so long . . ."

She yawned in spite of herself.

"Hey, me, too," Laura said. "Bedtime. Long drive in the morning."

But they left the light burning through the night.

3

Willis helped Karen carry the last bag out to the car.

Jeanne stood on the porch with a heavy cloth coat clutched around her. It was a cold day but clear; the sky was a deep winter blue. Everybody had said goodbye; everybody had waved. Michael and Laura were huddled in the car now; the engine was running impatiently.

Willis hesitated with his hand on the open lid of the trunk. His eyes were inscrutable behind his bifocals.

He put his hand on Karen's shoulder. He said, "You understand why I did it?"

She knew instantly what he meant by that. The fear, she thought, the not-talking . . . and the beatings.

She nodded once, uncomfortably.

Willis said, "But that's worth jack shit, right? Understanding doesn't make it better—right?"

She regarded him in his checkerboard winter jacket and his hunting cap, his gray Marine-cut sideburns and his stubbled cheeks.

"No," she said sadly. "It doesn't."

Willis said, "I wish you luck."

"Thank you," she said.

"If I could help—" But he wasn't moving. He was just standing there. His hands were limp and motionless.

Karen climbed in the car up front with Laura, and rolled up the window and did not look back. She did not want Daddy to see her, because she was crying, and how had *that* happened? What sense did *that* make?

4

Willis stood a long time watching the car disappear up the road.

There was a raw wind coming from the north down the valley of the Polger and his cheeks were red and burning, but Willis didn't care. He watched the car vanish around the corner from Montpelier onto Riverside, and stood a long time after that, hand up to shield his eyes against the sun, staring down these old row houses toward the far brown ribbon of the Mon.

He was surprised when he felt Jeanne's hands on his arms, his wife steering him gently up the porch.

"Come in and warm up," she said.

Her voice was kind. But the cold air lingered, the rooms were all too big, and the shadows were crowded with voices and time.

Interlude

....

NOVUS ORDO

1

Cardinal Palestrina was introduced to the upper echelons of the Washington diplomatic community, a few of whom were aware of his task here: the German envoy Max Vierheller and a man named Korchnoi from the Court of the Tsar.

Korchnoi drew him aside at a party at a Republican senator's Virginia estate: led him out to a glassed veranda and lectured him as snow fell beyond the perimeter of the hothouse plants.

"Of course you know," the Russian legate said in English, "it's not simply a matter of this weapon or that weapon." He gestured effusively with a goblet of

Aztec wine. "What the Americans are offering is their involvement in the war. Does it really matter what gift they choose to signify it? It's ceremony. Theater. The important thing is the prospect of an alliance between Rome and America. The infidels are terrified of it."

"Until recently," Cardinal Palestrina observed, "the Americans *were* the infidels."

"Hardly," Korchnoi said. "Heretics perhaps. A mongrel nation of Freemasons and Protestants—isn't that what the clerics say? But the industrial power, the wealth, the military strength . . . these are things you can see for yourself."

"Clearly," Palestrina admitted. "I have no objection to the alliance. Nor does Rome—the Vatican and the Senate are agreed on that. But there's more at stake than the fortunes of an alliance. You must have read *De Officiis Civitatum.* Adrian is a realistic pontiff but hardly a pragmatist. If we lend ecclesiastical approval to this project in particular—"

"Pardon me," Korchnoi said, "but you begin to sound like an ideologue . . . a Jesuit."

No, Cardinal Palestrina thought. The Jesuits had a rather more hard-nosed view of political reality. What I am, he thought, is a provincial bishop caught up in affairs beyond his station. *I should never have gone to Rome.* He might have been happy in some rural parish, vineyards and simple farmers and so on. He might have kept his scholarship down to a less conspicuous level. It was the unwise love of wisdom that had drawn him into ecclesiastical politics in the first place: a sin of pride or hubris.

Cardinal Palestrina was powerfully homesick.

"Rome and America," Korchnoi said, his eyes beginning to glaze. "America and Europe. Think of it . . . think of it."

* * *

In the morning Palestrina registered a Marconi message at the Vatican Consulate—essentially, that he had arrived and that the intelligence branch of the Congregation of Extraordinary Ecclesiastical Affairs had been largely correct in its surmises—and then hired a taxi to carry him to the DRI.

He despised this building. He had official identification now, a photocard clasped to his clothing. He walked from the front gate through the snow to the inner building, the tiny portion of it in which he had learned to navigate. He went directly to Carl Neumann's office.

"Is Walker still in the building?"

"For a time," Neumann said. "I thought you'd finished with him."

"A few more questions."

"Well, if it's necessary. We're happy to cooperate, Your Eminence, as long as circumstances allow. But do understand, we're approaching something of a cusp with this effort. Can you find the interrogation room by yourself?"

"No," Palestrina confessed. Humiliating but true.

"I'll take you there," Neumann said. "And I'll arrange for Walker to be waiting."

Once again, Cardinal Palestrina joined the Gray Man in this cold and windowless cubicle. Walker regarded him with blank expectation.

Palestrina extracted a notebook from his robes. He had jotted down some of the questions he meant to ask. Too, the notebook gave him something to do with his hands . . . an excuse for avoiding Walker's eyes.

He felt the hard contour of the chair beneath him. He felt an unpleasant churning in his stomach.

He began, "I want to make sure I have a fair and

accurate understanding of what you've told me. I apologize if I repeat myself. You were one of three original, ah, products of this research?"

"There were three of us," Walker agreed.

"And the other two escaped."

"Yes."

"They bore children."

"Yes."

"You killed those two, but the children survived."

The question seemed to trouble Walker. "The killing," he said, "was a mistake. I've admitted to that. I was punished for it. I had sorcels to bring back Julia and William, but it was the children we were most interested in. But the children weren't there! And William wouldn't say where they'd hidden them! So I reached out . . ."

The Gray Man faltered.

Cardinal Palestrina said, "You killed them both—with your own hands?"

"I sent them *home*," Walker said primly. "Certain *parts* of them. But of course you can't be in two places at once." He shook his head. "It was very bloody."

Cardinal Palestrina closed his eyes briefly.

He said, "You were instructed to do this?"

"No," Walker said. "I told you—I was punished for it."

"And you couldn't simply recover the children yourself?"

"They were too young to follow. They had no—" He seemed to search for a word. "No *song*. I couldn't *hear* them."

"But I assume you were able to trace them at a later date."

"When they began to exercise their talents."

"But you didn't bring them back."

"We wanted to make certain. No more mistakes.

We understood . . . Mr. Neumann explained . . . work like this takes time. There are spells that are best developed slowly. They come to maturity. But we planted the seed," Walker said, "when the children were very young."

"The seed?" Cardinal Palestrina asked.

"Bindings," Walker said.

"Bindings of what nature?"

"Vanity and anger and fear." The Gray Man smiled to himself. "A mirror, the kingdoms of the earth, her firstborn son . . ."

"Spells that would come to fruition in the future," Palestrina interpreted.

"Yes."

"Can you see the future?"

"No. But there are people here in the building who can. One of our other projects. 'As through a glass, darkly'—you know the expression? We rely on their advice. It isn't infallible but in this case it seems to be accurate."

"The sorcels are coming to fruition."

"Yes."

"Now?"

"Oh yes."

"And you're certain you can recover the third generation—the male child?"

"He's the one you want," Walker said. "I can bring him back."

Cardinal Palestrina looked up from his notes. "One other thing . . . something you said at our last session, something I didn't understand. You mentioned that you had help. What did you mean by that?"

Walker—his face old and lined but still disturbingly childlike—beamed at Cardinal Palestrina. "His name," the Gray Man said, "is Tim."

* * *

Cardinal Palestrina stood to leave the room, hesitated a moment, and finally turned back. An unscheduled question had occurred to him; he wasn't sure how to ask it.

Or whether he should. An Antiochene bishop from Malabar, visiting Rome for some ecumenical event, had once confided in Palestrina his belief that the profoundest of the venial sins was longing. As pride is the sin of the angels, longing is the sin of the clergy. Then, Cardinal Palestrina thought, I must be guilty.

He said, "What you call the plenum . . . is it infinite in extent?"

"There are worlds upon worlds," Walker said. "An infinity. That's what they tell me."

"But surely you can't see it, or feel it, or whatever you do—not *all* of it?"

"No. Not all of it. And I can only travel where *they* go. But sometimes I dream of other places."

Palestrina whispered, "Is *everything* out there—everything we could imagine?"

"Maybe," Walker said.

"Is—" But the Cardinal was embarrassed by his own question. "Is God out there?"

The Gray Man smiled faintly. "God is everywhere . . . isn't he?"

"And Paradise?" Palestrina said. "A world where mankind never fell from grace? The Garden, Mr. Walker? Is that out there too?"

Walker laughed.

"If it is," he said, "I've never found it."

Cardinal Palestrina turned away before Walker could see him blushing; the door clattered shut with a shocking finality.

2

Walker watched in bewilderment as the Papist emissary left the room.

He was inclined to like Cardinal Palestrina, who seemed like a well-meaning person. But he was disturbed by the Cardinal's nervous tics, his expression of barely restrained queasiness. And now this business about Paradise. It was not something Walker had encountered before, least of all in the corridors of the DRI.

Lacking other instruction, Walker returned to his own room deep in a subcellar of the Institute, down a corridor where sweating pipes ran overhead.

Walker's room contained a carpet and a framed photograph of the Rocky Mountains; a spring-mattress bed with a thin cotton blanket; and a television set with a round, bulky tube on a gooseneck swivel. He used the television sparingly. There was never anything to watch but the government channel, news and public affairs and a few shabby variety shows. Of these, Walker preferred the news. He liked the maps, the animated arrows darting across the Mediterranean toward Sicily. He liked the aerial photos of Turkish cities as European aircraft flew over them, props whirling, bombs tumbling like confetti.

He understood the political stakes that had brought Cardinal Palestrina across the Atlantic; he understood the war in the Middle East. Walker wasn't stupid. But—although he understood—Walker simply didn't care very much. There had always been wars and there would always be wars; there were wars everywhere. War had nothing to do with it. It was the search itself that obsessed him: the nagging sense of presence across those unfathomable distances. The complex, luminous web of magical obligation. A longing for the completion that this effort would bring him: a fulfillment.

Walker believed—although he seldom allowed the thought to become explicit—that he had lost something long ago, and that bringing Karen White's son Michael back to the DRI would return it to him. What was this lost thing? Well, he didn't know. Maybe something as ethereal as a scent, a memory, a feeling; or maybe something tangible, a reward. Something he had owned once; something which had slipped away. Walker often had dreams in which he lost his wallet or his hat, and he would wake up groping the bedsheets frantically—*it was here, I know it was here somewhere.*

But he never permitted himself to dwell on this. If he thought about it too much when he was alone—and he was almost always alone—his eyes would tear, his fists would clench. The DRI surgeons had cauterized most of his capacity for emotion, but the emotions he did feel were capricious and sometimes scalding. He tried diligently to suppress them.

But he wanted that lost thing back.

After dinner in the commissary Walker went to see Tim.

Neumann had given Tim a luxurious room on the third floor, high enough to afford him a view of the city, which was dark now, dark clouds rivering above it. Tim was at the window peering out. Walker, who was not stupid, and who understood the nature of the spells that had been cast over the years, was careful to stand erect, to fix a smile on his face, to assume an air of authority.

Doing so, he caught sight of his own reflection in

the window and thought, How old I seem! Of course, he *was* old. He had lost track of his precise age but he was certainly old enough to be Tim's father—that was in the nature of things. And Tim was a grown-up man. Not a middle-aged man but not a young man, either. Walker was vigorous but he knew that age and time were pressing him and he hoped he would not die before he recovered the precious thing he had lost.

He said, "You like the city?"

Tim turned to face him.

Timothy Fauve had changed a great deal over the last six months. Now his eyes were clear, his clothes and countenance were clean, he looked healthy. His dark hair was down to his shoulders but it was not matted. He had shaved. His hands were steady.

Tim said, "Hello, Walker." Added, "I don't think it's the kind of place you really like. Let's say I appreciate it."

Walker broadened his smile slightly. "You've come a long way."

"About as far as you can go. All kinds of ways."

"We won't be here much longer. Are you ready?"

"I think so."

This was more tentative than Walker liked. He frowned and saw Tim react with a wince. "You understand how hard we've worked to get to this stage."

Tim nodded vigorously.

"You know what we've done for you."

"Sure I do. Of course."

"And what's at stake."

"Yes."

"You're certain you're ready to finish it?"

"Absolutely," Tim said.

"Good." Walker relaxed. "How about a game of chess?"

He gave away odds of a vizier and a rook. Walker was a good chess player. Swift, methodical, and clean —he wielded the chess pieces like a surgeon wielding a knife.

Part Three

....

HOMELAND

Chapter Fifteen

·····························

1

They made it back to the California border three days out of Pennsylvania. Laura translated them in and out of a dry, hot world in which the roads were broad, traffic was light, and the horizon seemed always a little nearer. They stopped once at a roadside diner, but the menu posted over the counter was in a cursive script that looked more Persian than English—which implied, among other things, that their money wouldn't be any good. So Laura took them back onto an interstate and they pulled over at a Stuckey's outside Kingman, Arizona.

Karen said, "I didn't know you could do all this."

Her sister shrugged. "Neither did I."

"I was thinking," Karen said, "it might attract attention."

"I don't guess that matters now. There's attention on us already."

"It's a question of time," Karen said. "Do you get that feeling?"

"I think we should be in a hurry. Yes."

Karen ordered a club sandwich and a Coke. Michael asked for a hamburger and Laura ordered the salad. Waiting, Karen spread out her hands on the yellowed marble counter. "Things feel different now."

Laura said, "I know what you mean. I can do things I couldn't do before."

"Because it's more urgent. That's what I feel—the urgency."

The waitress brought lunch. Karen looked at Michael, who looked at his hamburger. Tides of sunlight bore down through the big green-tinted windows. Everything was still; the air-conditioned air was still. *Poised,* Karen thought.

"Eat up," Laura urged. "We ought to get moving."

It was Karen's first trip to San Francisco.

Gavin had been here a few times on business. He always said it was a beautiful city. And it was, Karen thought—from a distance. She liked the hills and the old white scalloped buildings; she liked the low clouds racing in from the ocean. But once you got into it, it was a city like any other city, same crowded sidewalks and diesel buses and neighborhoods you had to avoid.

They checked into a Ramada Inn on Market Street. The clerk accepted Karen's Visa card, but she wondered how much longer she could get away with that. It was an account she had shared with Gavin; now that she was gone, he would probably cut her off.

But there were more immediate things to worry about.

Each of them carried one of the three big suitcases up a carpeted flight of stairs to the second floor. The room was big and smelled faintly musty, but the sheets were crisp and the towels were clean. The bathroom was a temple walled with mirrors.

Laura unpacked the postcard Jeanne had given her. "We could go there tonight. It's not that far."

But Karen shook her head firmly. "It's late already. I'm tired."

"Well—food and a night's sleep sure wouldn't hurt. There's a coffee shop in the lobby—will that do?"

"I want to shower and turn in early," Karen said. "You two go, all right?"

Laura hesitated at the door. "Are you sure you're okay?"

"I'm fine. I just need some privacy."

Michael ordered yet another burger. Laura said, "You'll kill yourself with that stuff, you know. They shoot the cattle full of hormones. It's disgusting."

Michael smiled. "All of a sudden you're a vegetarian?"

"I just think, if you're going to eat meat, you should really do it. Big thick steaks from big fat cows. There used to be a restaurant not too far from here that would cook you a steak for a reasonable price. I mean real meat, not gristle and TVP."

"You used to live around here?"

"Berkeley. But that was a long time ago."

"The sixties," Michael said.

Laura smiled to herself. It always sounded odd when people said "the sixties" like that—like the name of a place, an address. "Yes," she said, "the sixties."

Michael took a big bite out of his burger. "You were a hippie?"

"That's really a dumb word, Michael. I always thought so. It's a *Time* magazine kind of word."

"Well," he said, "you know."

She nodded reluctantly. "I guess you could say that's what I was. A Berkeley hippie, anyhow. I came down to the Haight sometimes. I danced at the Fillmore—I guess that qualifies."

Michael said, "There was a thing about it on TV a couple of years ago. The Summer of Love."

Laura's smile receded. "The Summer of Love was nothing but hype. It was the end of everything. Ten thousand people trying to live in the Panhandle. You know what Haight Street was by the end of the so-called Summer of Love? It was where a lot of homeless teenagers went to get hepatitis. Or VD. Or raped, or pregnant. It was a disaster . . . everybody was talking about going away."

Michael said soberly, "Like you did."

"Yes."

"You went to Turquoise Beach."

"Well, that's where I ended up."

"Is that what it was like here—I mean when it was good? Was the Haight like Turquoise Beach?"

Laura shook her head emphatically. "The Haight was unique. It was full of all these crazy idealists, poets and saints—there's no way I can sit here and tell you what it was like. It was like holding the world in your hand. Turquoise Beach is good, you know; it's the best I could find. But it's slower there. There isn't the passion. There isn't—"

But she found herself faltering.

Michael said, "I didn't mean to get you upset."

He sat across the table from her, her sister's child, very eighties in a slash haircut and tight T-shirt. Strange to think that he had not existed in 1967. She thought suddenly, He could be mine, I could have had a child like this one, I could have raised him. Instead I moved away to Never-Never Land . . . where you can be young forever. Or almost forever. Or until you wake up one day, gray-haired and menopausal.

"I know what it's like," Michael said, and he was talking softly now, almost to himself. "Looking for a better world—I can understand that."

Laura put down her fork. "Do it," she said. Her appetite was gone. Her voice had hardened. "Do it, Michael. But look hard, all right? Don't give up too soon."

Karen showered and then stretched out on one of the big twin hotel beds. The mattress was hard—she had gotten used to the old plush beds back home— but that was all right. She had intended to order something up from room service, but she discovered she didn't feel like eating. She had opened the horizontal blinds, but there was only the blankness of the parking lot outside.

She looked at the telephone.

She picked up the receiver, thinking she might call room service after all. But when the hotel operator answered Karen found herself asking for a line out, and maybe this was what she had meant to do all along; maybe this was why she had sent Michael and Laura out on their own.

She called Toronto.

It was the number Gavin had left her all those months ago. She thought, If the woman answers I'll hang up. But maybe Gavin would be there. Three hours difference, she thought. Back home it was dinnertime. Maybe Gavin was having dinner in his girl-friend's apartment overlooking the lake. Maybe it was snowing. Maybe the drapes were open and they could see the snow coming down in the darkness over the lake.

She waited through the fourth ring and then the fifth and then her impulse was to put down the receiver, drop it *right now,* but there was a faraway click and then Gavin's voice saying, "Hello?"

"Hi," she said breathlessly. "It's me."

Gavin said, "Christ, Karen—where *are* you?"

"Pretty far away." But that sounded silly. "In the States," she added. She didn't want him to know exactly.

"What the hell are you doing down there?"

"We had to get away."

"Michael is with you?"

"Sure he's with me . . . of course he is."

"You know you left a righteous mess up here, don't you? I filed a report with the police. I had to let them into the house. It was strange. All those Mayflower boxes stacked up. It was like the *Mary Celeste.* And the school's been calling me about Michael. Have you got him in school, at least?"

"Michael's all right," she said defensively.

"Do you have a rational explanation for any of this?"

None that you would understand, Karen thought. "Not really."

"You had some kind of breakdown, is that it? You took Michael and you left town? Just like that?"

"Just like that," she said.

"You understand this looks very bad. This could weigh against you when it comes to custody."

She didn't understand at first. Custody of what? Then it dawned on her. "Gavin, that's crazy!"

"Obviously it's not something I anticipated. I mean, I was the one who left. I admit that. But I talked to Diane and it seems to us that Michael might need a more stable home environment."

"Stable?"

"Rather than being taken out of school and hauled all over the country." Petulantly: "I haven't seen him for months, you know. Maybe you think that's not important to me. But I'm his father, for God's sake."

Karen felt cold. She wondered why she had called at all. It had occurred to her that Gavin might be worried. She had wanted to reassure him.

He said, "Tell me where you are. Better yet, tell me when you're coming home."

"You can't just do that," Karen said. "You can't just give orders."

"That's not the issue, is it? Michael is the issue."

"You can't have him."

"I mean his welfare. His school. His health. I'll have to tell the police you called."

"Michael is fine!"

But it felt like a lie when she said it.

Gavin said, "It's not me you're letting down, you know. It's him."

"He's *fine.*"

"All I want is an address. Even a phone number. Is Michael there? Let me talk to him. I—"

But she slammed down the receiver in its cradle.

After dinner Laura and Michael walked a couple of blocks down Market Street. It was late and this was not the greatest neighborhood, but the street was busy with people. A middle-aged man with a Salvador Dali mustache panhandled them for change; Laura gave him a quarter. "God bless," he said happily. It made her think again of the Haight, of her Berkeley days. Of how much she had lost since then—slowly, without noticing.

Karen was asleep when they let themselves back into the hotel room. "You wash up," Laura told her nephew. "I'll take the last shift."

Ten minutes later the bathroom was hers. She took a long, deliberate shower, the water hot as she could stand it; she washed her hair and toweled herself dry as the steam faded from the mirrors.

The bathroom light was a merciless cool fluorescence and the mirrors were everywhere.

Old, Laura thought.

Look at that woman in the mirror, she thought. That woman thinks she's young. She moves the way she moved when she was twenty. She thinks she's young and she thinks she's pretty.

But she's kidding herself on both counts.

Shit, Laura thought. It's just depression and road-weariness and being scared. Hey, she thought, all you have to do is squint your eyes and blur away the wrinkles.

The wrinkles, the sags, the crow's-feet.

Too late, she thought. Too late, too late, too late . . . you're *old* now.

The fairest in the land.

Hardly.

Too late for love and too late for children. She had played too long before bedtime and now all the good TV shows were over and the lights were about to go off.

Maudlin, she thought. *You should be ashamed of yourself.*

Well, she was.

Bed, she told herself. Sleep. A person needs her beauty sleep.

She moved across the faded plush hotel carpet slowly, hearing the creak of her own frail bones in the silent darkness.

2

In the morning they checked the phone book, but there was no Timothy Fauve listed anywhere in the Bay Area.

"Means nothing," Laura said. "He could be using another name. Anything."

But, Karen thought, it wasn't a good omen.

After breakfast they drove to the address on the postcard Tim had mailed home.

It was a hotel in the Mission District. It was a boarding hotel, not the kind of hotel Karen was accustomed to; a derelict hotel, and there were homeless men squatting on the pavement outside. It was called the Gravenhurst, the name printed on an ancient rust-flecked sign. Karen gazed up at it with dismay. It was not the kind of place she could imagine going into.

But she followed Laura up the three chipped concrete steps to the door, Michael close behind her.

The lobby was dark and smelled faintly of mildew and sour hops. There was a barroom off to the right, a desk to the left. Laura stood at the desk and asked about Timothy Fauve. The man behind the desk was hugely overweight and seemed never to blink. He peered up at Laura and said he'd never heard the name. Laura said, "He was here at Christmas last year."

"People come through here a lot."

"Maybe you could look it up?"

The man just stared at her.

Laura opened her purse and took out a twenty-dollar bill. "Please," she said.

Karen was impressed. She couldn't have done anything like that. It just wouldn't have occurred to her.

The man sighed and paged back through a huge, old-fashioned ledger. Finally he said, "Fauve, Room 215. But he checked out months ago."

Laura said, "You remember him?"

"What's to remember? He was quiet. He came and went."

"Did you ever talk to him?"

"I don't talk."

Laura seemed to hesitate. "Is the room empty now?"

"Currently," the man said, "that room is not occupied."

"Can we look at it?"

"It looks like any other room. It's been empty since May. We had a water pipe break."

"Just for a few minutes?" She took another ten out of her purse.

The man put it in his breast pocket. "If you so desire," he said, and passed her the key.

But he was right, Karen thought. There was nothing to see. Just this long, dank stucco corridor; a wooden door with a lock and a handle; an empty room.

It was a cubicle. It was the size of a walk-in cupboard. There was a toilet stall behind a cracked door, a washstand but no shower. The walls were covered with gray plaster. The broken pipe had flooded the rug and mold was eating its way toward the door.

Michael said, "He lived here?"

"At least for a while," Laura said.

"He couldn't have been doing too well."

"We don't know why he was here," Laura said. "We don't know anything about him, really. We all lost track of him when he left home. But he was in this room—I can feel it."

Karen looked sharply at her sister.

"Things happened here," Laura said. "He traveled from here. It leaves traces."

"Traveled out of the world," Karen said.

"Yes."

She tried to feel it herself. It had been years since she had even allowed herself to believe such a thing was possible. But surely there was no point denying it now? She strained at the blank, empty volume of the room, trying to find a magic in it.

There was nothing.

If I could ever do that, she thought, I can't anymore.

She said, "Do you know where he went?"

Laura sighed.

"No," she said. "I don't."

Defeated, they moved silently through the lobby. Laura dropped the room key on the desk; the clerk didn't look up. Stepping outside, Karen shaded her eyes against the light, suddenly alarmed.

There was a man leaning up against the car.

He was only a little taller than Karen, and too thin, but he was reasonably well dressed. A starched white shirt and a pair of fresh Levi's. His eyes were narrow and his lips were set in a smile. Hands in his pockets. He looked up, and his face was pale in the sunlight.

For a moment she failed to recognize him. And

then the recognition, when it did come, made her dizzy.

Laura cried out, "Tim!"

The man's smile widened.

"Looking for me?" he said.

Chapter Sixteen

....

1

They drove to Fisherman's Wharf for lunch.

"You should let me show you around," Tim said. "Do the tourist thing."

Karen liked the restaurant. The waitress brought seafood in rich, buttery sauces; and out beyond the big windows she could see San Francisco Bay and the Golden Gate Bridge. The clouds lifted and a bright winter sun glanced from the tour boats lined up at the dock.

Laura said, "But we're not tourists. We don't have time."

"Well, maybe you do," Tim said. "Maybe things aren't as bad as you think."

"How did you find us?"

"I looked." Karen heard the subtle emphasis on "looked." He added, "And I knew you were looking."

"You can do that?"

He nodded.

But this wasn't the place to talk about it. Karen ate methodically, not much conscious of her food, stealing glances at her brother. His clothes looked good. He was healthy enough. But then why had he been living in a Skid Row hotel less than a year ago? Something was going right for him . . . but Karen noticed a faint, persistent tic tugging at the corner of his right eyelid and wondered whether something might also be going wrong.

Tim turned to Michael, who had ordered the Seafood Monterey when a thorough search of the menu failed to turn up any kind of burger. "Must be strange, discovering an uncle after all these years."

Michael shrugged. Michael had been quiet all morning. Quiet but attentive.

"A little," he said.

Tim said, "We should get together and have a talk sometime."

"Sure," Michael said.

And Karen felt a stab of uneasiness.

"Home," Tim said. "That's where I've been."

After lunch Laura drove to an extremity of parkland overlooking the bay. They sat in the car with the windows up and Karen watched a line of gulls wheeling down toward the water. It was quiet here and they were alone.

Laura said, "I take it you don't mean Polger Valley."

Tim laughed, and Karen was suddenly reminded of the old days: this derision. "Is that what you call home? Did it ever *feel like* home? Be honest."

"Mama and Daddy admitted a few things," Laura said.

Tim said, "Well, how about you tell me what you know."

So Laura told him what they had found out from Willis and Jeanne: about their natural parents, about the Gray Man. And Karen repeated the part Willis had told her—the shack on the country road outside Burleigh and the bodies he had discovered in it.

Tim listened intently; he was frowning when Karen finished. He shook his head. "I was aware of some of that from other sources. But it fills in some gaps."

Laura said, "You *knew?*"

"I was told."

"Since when?"

"Well, recently."

"Who told you—the Gray Man?"

The words seemed to hang in the cool air and for a moment Karen could hear the cry of the gulls.

Tim said, "Obviously I should start at the beginning. You want the long or the *Reader's Digest* version?"

Laura glanced back at Michael for a fraction of a second and said, "I think the short."

Tim was sitting up front with Laura, and Karen could only see the back of him, his profile when he turned, but she was watching him as closely as she could, relearning the look of him and trying to pinpoint what had changed. She remembered the sullen child in Mama's photographs. But he wasn't sullen now. He was, if anything, too effusive. Karen thought, Sometimes he talks like a salesman.

"I left home," he said. "I traveled a lot. I took a lot of jobs over those years. And I did some other kinds of traveling, too. But I always ended up back here . . . because I was familiar here; I know how to get along. Got along well enough—most of the time. But I had the same troubles you did. The Gray Man—I would see him sometimes. And more than that. Maybe you felt it, too . . . like being homesick for some place you've never seen. I swear I never did feel like I belonged here."

Karen saw Michael nodding fractionally.

"So," Tim said, "well, eventually I started drinking. And pretty soon that became a problem. I was in hospitals a couple of times. And then I figured out what you two seem to have figured out—that this is not something you can run away from." His lips compressed into a tight, grim smile. "We can run farther and faster than anyone, right? But not *away.*"

Laura said, "So what's the alternative?"

"To stop running *away,*" Tim said, "and start running *to.*"

"Meaning—?"

He said, "I found the Gray Man and I followed him."

There was another silence in the car.

"I'd done it before," Tim went on. "When we were kids. When I didn't know what he wanted. When I trusted him. You remember that night in the ravine —the old city on the coast?"

"Yes," Karen said, involuntarily.

Tim said, "Well, that's where he comes from."

But she had guessed as much.

He added, "That's where *we* come from."

She sat forward, wanting to deny it.

"It makes sense," Tim said. "Like it or not. Whatever we are, the Gray Man is one of us. You can't get away from that. There's this trick we can do, and no one else in the world can do it . . . except him. What does that suggest?"

Laura said, impatiently, "What did you find out?"

"We're related," Tim said. "We're family. The connections are kind of strange, but the closest you can get to it is—you might think of him as an uncle."

2

Michael listened to Tim's description of the Gray Man's world with increasing interest.

It was where they had come from (Tim said), and it was where they had been created. In an important sense, it was the only real home they had or would ever have.

It was not, he said, necessarily a *good* place. It was like this world: not distinctly good or bad but a little of both. It was not a utopia, but who believes in utopias? You had to take it on its own terms.

Things were different there.

History had happened a little differently. Rome and the Roman Church still dominated Europe; America had won its independence and had become a refuge for Europe's oppressed Protestants. It was not called the United States but the Novus Ordo, the New Order of the Americas, a major military and economic power. Rome had been jealous of the Novus Ordo for two centuries, but now there was a bigger threat: the militant Islamic nations of the Middle East and Africa.

The Novus Ordo, a heretical nation, was able to experiment with forces the Church wouldn't touch. Alchemy, kabalistic magic, astrology—it was all very different there, all very real. It was the Americans who first understood that the ability to walk between worlds might exist, that it might be a potent and accessible power. Maybe in the past it had occurred randomly, a wild talent in people who might never suspect they possessed it, who dreamed themselves haphazardly out of the world, or who used it to escape their families or their creditors. Now it was possible to identify those people, bring them together, take this thing to the limit.

Not necessarily as a weapon—though that implication was there, too—but as research. A learning tool.

That's where we came from, Tim said . . . or at least, that's where our parents came from.

Our *real* parents.

Michael said, "And the Gray Man."

"He's a failed experiment," Tim said. "He's insane."

Karen said, "He's hunting us. He's been hunting us all our lives. And he killed our parents."

They walked along the sea grass on this promontory, the three adults and Michael.

"Also the girl on the beach," Michael said. "I saw that. He just pushed her away—like killing a bug."

"It was never meant to happen that way," Tim said quietly.

"All these years," Karen said, "hunting us, finding us sometimes . . . you would think, if he meant to kill us, he would have."

Tim said, "I don't understand all his motives. But we're maybe not as easy to kill as those others. Our parents *trusted* him. He was a brother to them. So he could get close without suspicion. None of us ever felt that way."

Laura said, "Except you. You did."

Tim looked at her quizzically.

"That night in the ravine," she said, "in the alley. You talked to him like you knew him. If he had wanted to, Tim, he could have killed us all right then."

Tim said, "I think he wanted our trust."

"He seemed to have yours."

"I never spoke to him after that."

"And the things he gave us. Those toys. You know Mama and Daddy still have them stashed in a drawer? And the things he said. I always wondered about that. It was like a curse or an omen or something."

"Insanity," Tim said.

"You sound so sure of that."

"I talked to people," he said.

"People in that place—the Novus Ordo?"

"Important people."

"You just waltzed in and had a chat?"

"I established who I was."

"We're talking about what, a military project of some kind?"

"Research," Tim said.

"And they let you walk out again?"

"They understood," Tim said, "that they couldn't stop me."

"And you believed what they told you?"

"There's no reason not to."

Laura shook her head. "If this is true," she said, "then they want something. They must. Just like the Gray Man wants something."

"I talked to a man called Neumann," Tim said. "A real flesh-and-blood human being—not a monster. Nothing supernatural. He's operating what they call the Plenum Project. Sure, of course they want something from us. They need our help. So in a way I'm carrying that message. But, Christ, Laura, there's more to it than that. It's *home.* You understand? It's a place to belong." He looked at her intently. "Don't you miss that? Haven't you ever wanted that?"

"If it's home," Karen said—thinking now of what Willis had told her—"why did our parents leave?"

"They were running from Walker, not the Project."

"But you said they trusted him. That's how he killed them."

"They were *afraid* of him. But he was still family. They loved him." He scuffed a rock down this grassy incline toward the bay. "Hey, it happens, you know. People love people who want to hurt them. It's possible."

Chapter Seventeen

· ·

1

They dropped Tim off at a BART depot and drove back to the hotel. Time enough to talk again tomorrow. In the meantime there was plenty to think over.

Laura ordered up room service and Michael occupied the big chair by the window, ignoring a club sandwich, picking out barely audible chords on the Gibson guitar he'd carried across the country and farther. It was pretty obvious to Michael—listening to his aunt and his mother trying to sort all this out—that the appearance of Tim had thrown them for a loop. It wasn't what they'd expected.

Laura said, "He's not telling the truth. Or all of the truth."

"It's been a long time," Karen said. "It's hard to judge."

"Hard for you, maybe. I always could tell when Timmy was fibbing."

"He's not a child anymore."

"But he's still Tim."

The talk went on like this. Michael finished his sandwich and went down the hall for a Coke. When he came back his mom was saying, "It depends what he wants from us, doesn't it?"

"He wants us to go back there with him," Laura said, "to that place—the Novus Ordo."

"He hasn't said that."

"He will."

And Michael said, "Maybe we should listen to him."

The two women turned their heads as if they had forgotten he was here. Michael took another sip of the Coke and said, "The way you describe him, he sounds all right. I mean, he didn't get along at home—but under the circumstances who would? And he didn't give up. He had the talent and he followed it where it took him. I don't see what's wrong with that."

Laura shook her head. "You don't know him, Michael. You didn't live with him. He hated Daddy—and maybe even the rest of us—in a way that wasn't healthy. I don't think that kind of hate can just evaporate."

"At least he wasn't afraid."

"Not the way we were afraid," Laura said. "Not the *same* way."

He wasn't afraid of his talent, Michael thought privately, and he wasn't afraid to use it. He wasn't beaten into submission and he wasn't off living in some backwater beach town all these years. Surely that counted for something?

But he kept the thought to himself.

2

Timothy Fauve rode a bus back to his hotel, a good hotel close to the waterfront. He opened the room door with his key and Walker was inside, his big frame stretched out on one of the beds. One arm was crooked back of his head and the gray slouch hat was on his chest. He looked up at the sound of the door. "Hello, Tim," he said.

Tim eased the door shut behind him. "I didn't know you had a key."

"I don't need one."

Tim smiled shakily. "I guess not."

He switched on the lights and dropped into a chair. Walker wanted something. Or else Walker was checking up on him. He regarded Walker in the dimness of the room with a mixture of gratitude and uneasiness. He loved Walker, but Walker was very demanding.

The Gray Man said, "You talked to them."

"Yes."

"Did they listen?"

"I think so. I think they have some doubts. That was pretty obvious. But they'll come around."

"And Michael?"

"I think he's interested."

"That's what matters," Walker said.

"But it won't be easy," Tim ventured. "They're afraid of you. They know a few things."

Walker sat up. "What things?"

"How you killed Julia and William."

"We told you about that," Walker reminded him.

"Of course. But the way Karen described it . . . it seemed worse."

Walker was standing now. He was a big presence in the room. His back was to the window and he was a shadow, looming over Tim.

"You understand," Walker said, "it wasn't what I wanted to do. They had weapons . . . I reacted the only way I could."

"Karen didn't say anything about weapons."

"Karen wasn't there." Walker looked concerned. "We talked about this. I acknowledged that it was a mistake. If I could have avoided it, I would have. But we were less experienced then."

"There was something else," Tim said, wondering whether he was wise to carry on with this, but wanting an answer. "They mentioned a little girl—a beach in some California town—"

Walker's frown deepened. "What are you saying —that they have doubts, or that you do?"

"I'm just reporting. I thought you should know."

"But it troubles you?"

"Maybe a little. Say it raises a question."

"Were you on that beach?"

"No," Tim said hastily.

"I won't claim I've never done anything I regret. But it was a cusp, that moment on that beach. I was concentrating on Michael. And he was close . . . it might have been finished then, I might have brought him home. What I did was a reflex. It was instinctive."

"Still," Tim said. "A child . . ."

"I wonder what you would have done in the same situation."

Tim lowered his head.

"I know what I am," Walker said. "I acknowledge it. I live with it."

He put his big hand on Tim's shoulder.

"If I commit a sin," Walker said, "I atone for it. You remember how it was when I found you?"

But it was impossible to forget. He had been in a fleabag hotel in the Mission District—the same one his sisters had visited today—and he had weighed maybe a hundred and twenty pounds. He did day labor when he needed money and he drank Tokay and peach brandy and ate Kraft Dinners alone in his room, when he remembered to eat at all. Payday meant booze or cheap sex or maybe, very, very occasionally, a spoon of heavily cut heroin—Tim had been chipping on and off since '74, when an unemployed Detroit shift worker showed him how. Just recently, though, he had been doing up more often than he liked, the beginning of a habit he could not afford, and he was sick more often than not; he skimped on the Kraft Dinners. His weight was very bad for somebody his size. Soon it would interfere with the labor he was able to pick up, and without that trickle of money he would be in the street —he would be sleeping on the sidewalk. And that was bad, because Tim had learned that this was, ironically, the best of all possible worlds; he had opened many doors in his time but never to a place he wanted to live. Cold, cloistered, ugly worlds mainly. To fail here was therefore to fail utterly.

It was about this time Walker showed up.

Walker had appeared without warning, and it was like stepping into a dream, Tim thought, like something out of his childhood. Because he had known Walker once long ago. Walker had been his friend for a while. Walker had given him things and shown him things. But then Tim had grown wary of Walker and spent all these years on the road, avoiding him, because when you came right down to it he was frightened—scared of what Walker might want from him. And now here was Walker right in this shabby room with him, an old man but still a commanding presence, radiating calm and reassurance. Tim stared at him and Walker said—these precise words—"I never forgot you." And it was like being welcomed home.

"Everyone else forgot you," Walker said. "Except me."

Tim, who had gone three long days since spoon or food, began to weep.

Walker took him to the Novus Ordo and Walker got him dried out and straightened out and respectable. You don't need the bottle or the needle, Walker said, and through some magic Tim could not fathom it was suddenly so: that longing was taken away. Just utterly vanished. And he was grateful—filled with a wholehearted gratitude he had never experienced before. It was *better* than the spoon.

Walker showed him everything that could be his. His inheritance, Walker said. "It's what you were made for." Imagine a land, Walker said, a green land spreading out for miles, farms and cities and blue skies, and you stand on a hilltop, surveying it, and it's yours —it belongs to you.

An inheritance of lands and powers.

The kingdoms of the Earth.

"If you want it," Walker said. "If you do a little work for us."

Even now, in this hotel room in San Francisco, the memory was as bright and polished as a gemstone. My *place*, Tim thought, my *home*, that's what he promised me. And maybe, Tim thought, that was Walker's atonement for the accident on the beach. To find me and to make me well. It made sense. Anybody could have an accident.

But—

"Sometimes," Tim said, "I think we should just tell them the truth."

"I share that feeling," Walker said. "But you know they wouldn't understand."

"They don't trust you. Not . . . the way *I* trust you."

"Fortunately," Walker said, "it's not me they *have* to trust."

"All we want," Tim said, "is to take them home. Isn't that right? They would recognize it if they went there."

"I'm sure they would," Walker said—fading a little now, satisfied, turning down some hidden angle out of the world. "I'm sure they will."

"I'll talk to them tomorrow," Tim said. "I'll do a better job."

The Gray Man smiled and disappeared.

Tim—alone now—was reassured. He was doing the right thing. Or, if not the right thing, then the only thing. When you thought about it, he had very few options.

He feared Walker but he trusted him, too. And that was reasonable. It was that kind of relationship. A relationship of trust.

After all, Walker was the closest thing to a father Tim had ever possessed.

3

Michael lay awake for a long time in the leaden silence of the hotel room, no sound but the faint breathing of his mother and Laura in the darkness.

He liked the darkness and he liked being awake in it. In all these strange rooms—from Turquoise Beach to Polger Valley and all the way back to San Francisco—the one familiar thing had been the darkness. It was the next-best thing to home.

Home, he thought. A word Tim had used more than once.

Michael wasn't sure now what it meant.

Home was a dark hotel room out along some desert highway.

Or home was that distant world he sometimes envisioned—the "better world" he had talked to Aunt Laura about. He thought of it now, oceans and forests the way America must have been a hundred years ago; but vital, too, with crowded cities and markets. Roads and farms and big, delicate flying machines. He wondered if there was a city called San Francisco in that world, and, thinking of it, realized there was: but it was not as large as this one and the people in it spoke mostly Spanish and Nahuatl. Was that home?

Maybe.

What home was probably *not* was the suburban house in Toronto where he'd grown up. It was already a memory. A fading memory—it might have been a million miles away.

But Tim had talked about another home.

He called it the Novus Ordo. Michael said the words to himself, softly, in the darkness.

It's where we came from. It's where we were made.

Like Made in Japan, or Made in Hong Kong. Maybe, Michael thought—drifting now—maybe it's stamped on us somewhere. A birthmark or a tattoo. "Made in the Novus Ordo."

Maybe not such a bad place after all.

He felt it faintly down a distant corridor of possibilities—a door.

Doors and angles, Michael thought sleepily. It was only a sideways step from here. He could feel it and he could see it. It was cold, a cold place. He saw an old, dark industrial city—not San Francisco but someplace back East—tarry under a gray sky. He saw flames boiling out of factory towers; he saw a dark river winding away to the south.

It was not an appealing place. But Tim had said as much. It was not exclusively good or bad. It wasn't utopia.

But it was home.

The word echoed in his mind until it lost all meaning. Home, he thought, is where you belong. Where there's a place for you. Where you're understood. Where you can talk.

Home was no place he had ever been.

Unless Tim had found it for him.

Chapter Eighteen

....

In the morning, Karen rode down an elevator with Michael and Laura to the coffee shop, where Tim was waiting. A foggy morning. The fog pressed in at the plate-glass window and the far side of the street was lost in layers of cloud.

Tim said, "The question is, what do you really want? Why come looking for me in the first place?"

"To find out what we are," Laura said, "and to do something about the Gray Man."

It was past the breakfast rush and the room was nearly deserted. A man with a bucket and a mop did slow ballroom turns across the tiled floor. Karen sat with Michael in the central curve of a vinylette booth, content for now to let her sister do the talking.

Tim said, "Well, you have part of that. You know what you are and you know where you came from. As for the Gray Man—I guarantee you can't deal with him without help."

"Your help?"

"The help of the people who created him."

"The people you were talking about—the Novus Ordo."

"Exactly," Tim said.

"You want us to go there."

Laura shot a glance at Karen, who nodded to acknowledge it.

Tim said, "It would be the wise thing. Maybe the only thing. How many choices do you have?"

Laura said, "But we have to take your word on all this."

Tim drew back. His expression was cautious. "I'm not sure I like what you're implying."

"It's been a long time, that's all. Last time either of us saw you, you were Michael's age. You remember that? A bad-tempered teenager in a leather jacket. You had a tremendous chip on your shoulder."

He managed to look insulted. "You mean you don't trust me."

"I mean trust is a lot to expect. You're standing in the street one day and suddenly it's hi, sis, how are you? But it's been twenty years, Timmy. People change. Who *is* this guy, what does he want from us? I think it's a natural question."

Tim shook his head. He looked sad, Karen thought, but there was also a suggestion—very faint—of the contempt he used to express so freely.

He said, "This isn't new, is it? You come up to the edge and then you shy away. It's the way you've been living. Both of you. Well, it's easy to make excuses. But it won't solve your problems."

Laura blinked. "Why would you say that? You don't know anything about us."

"Maybe I was only fifteen, but hey, I had eyes. I have a memory."

"Just look at it from our point of view," Laura said. "Try to do that."

He seemed to bite back an answer. "I am trying. I'm just not sure what you want."

The waitress brought coffee in a steaming carafe. Karen watched Michael offer his cup and wondered when he had started drinking coffee. Maybe it began with puberty, like shaving.

She tried to focus her attention on the conversation but couldn't. What could be safer than a hotel coffee shop? But she felt uneasy here, exposed . . .

Laura said, "I would at least like to know what we're walking into."

"It's an old city," Tim said patiently. "It's called Washington and it's on the Potomac but it doesn't bear much resemblance to the city you know by that name. It's winter and the climate is colder than ours, so you can expect snow. There's a building called the Defense Research Institute. It's a government installation. There are people there who want to talk to you."

"They can help us?"

"I was given to understand that they can show us a way to travel without leaving traces—basically, a way to leave Walker behind."

"Have they done you this favor?"

"No. Not yet."

"So we're taking *their* word for it."

Tim assumed a long-suffering expression. "They can't hold us there. There's no punishment, there's only the reward. Obviously they don't want to give it away too soon."

"They want us that badly?"

"For their work. Nothing terrible. It's our *cooperation* they need."

A thought crossed Karen's mind. "How do we know *he's* not working for them?"

Laura and Tim turned to regard her. She reddened but pressed on: "I mean the Gray Man. He could be working for them. *He's* the punishment."

Laura considered this, nodded thoughtfully. "Maybe. How about it, Tim?"

"You're being paranoid," he said. "How often do I have to say this? These are reasonable people we're talking about. Not monsters."

Karen finished her coffee. Tim put down money for lunch and a huge, excessive tip. He said, "I've told you everything I know. What it comes down to is, I'm going back soon and I think you should go with me."

It was like an ultimatum. Karen heard it in his voice. It was a demand or a plea, or some bullying combination of the two. He had *not* changed.

There was a silence.

"I'll go," Laura said suddenly.

Karen gawked at her. Tim seemed equally taken aback.

"Tomorrow," she said.

More looks.

"Well," she demanded, "why not? The sooner, the better, right? But," she added, "only one of us. One of us will go. I'll go. And if everything looks all right I'll come back and bring the others." She looked intently at her brother. "Is that all right with you?"

There was an even lengthier silence. Tim looked at Laura, at Karen, finally at Michael. Inspecting us, Karen thought, for sincerity.

But why this distrust? What was *he* afraid of?

Tim said, "I think you're being unreasonably cautious. But all right—it's a beginning."

*   *   *

Karen said, "You don't have to."

Laura said, "I know."

They had gone back to the hotel room. Michael was in the shower; Karen was alone with her sister.

Karen said, "It's dangerous. I don't feel good about it."

"Well, Christ, I don't either. But I'm not a big enough prize to keep. I think Tim is duty-bound to bring me back. So I get a little tour, and maybe it's fraudulent, maybe it's designed to lure us there . . . but maybe I can learn something anyhow."

Karen said, "We're assuming he's a liar. That he might be working for the Gray Man."

"It's at least possible. There was that connection between them. I never understood it."

"But then it's too dangerous. You *can't* go."

Laura sighed and put her head back. "What choice do we have? Run and keep running? I don't want to do that. I'm finished with that. Anyway, it was never me he was after. Walker left me pretty much alone in Turquoise Beach. I'm not the prize."

That was true, Karen thought, but also frightening—the implications were frightening. "So who *is* the prize?"

"Not you or me," Laura said. "I think . . . ultimately, I think it's Michael they want."

Please, no, Karen thought.

But maybe Tim was *not* lying, maybe it was all the truth, maybe everything was okay.

Karen lay in bed and wanted to believe it.

Maybe it's true, she thought, maybe there really is a place we can call home. Not the kind of utopia Laura had set out to find in her town at the end of the continent, not Paradise, maybe not even an especially *good* place—but home, a real and true home where they belonged.

That would be good.

But she thought of her dream, which was not a dream, of the ravine behind the house on Constantinople and the darkness of a cobbled alley in an old smoky sea town. She thought of the lonely factories and warehouses and the black obsidian buildings. She thought of the snow that had begun to fall.

It was the kind of world Tim would have willed himself into. Karen had listened to her sister's speculations about this talent they shared. It was a talent as wide or as narrow as the imagination itself. Which is to say, the soul. She recalled Tim as a child and guessed that he had opened doors into a dozen or more of these sullen, haltered, chilly Earths. Maybe it was the only kind of door he *could* open . . . out of all the web of possibilities, nothing but these dark alleys and cold cities.

Drifting at last to sleep, she remembered what Laura had said: *It's Michael they want.* The words echoed in her head.

Not my son, she thought. Please not Michael.

And she thought of the Gray Man all those years ago, of the gifts he had given them, the gifts they had accepted, the gifts which had languished in a closed drawer for three decades.

The kingdoms of the Earth.

What did it mean?

The fairest in the land.

A riddle.

Your firstborn son.

She trembled, sleeping.

Laura, in the opposite bed, thought similar thoughts.

Walker's gift for her had been a mirror. The same mirror she had found in the desk back in Polger Valley . . . the mirror she could see clearly now in her mind's eye. It was a cheap pink plastic mirror and the chromed glass had corroded over the years. But it was obvious what Walker meant by it. It was his way of saying, You are vain. Your curse is vanity.

And it was true. She felt that now. It was what her life amounted to. Drugs were a mirror she had gazed into for a time. Turquoise Beach was a mirror, a magic mirror that cast up only pleasant reflections. Emmett was a mirror, and she had watched herself in his eyes.

And it all amounted to shit, Laura thought bitterly, and it had left her here, lonely and stranded on this shoal of time.

So, she thought, it *has* to be me. The logic was obvious. That was why she had offered to go with Tim. It was a good idea, but it was also a gesture: let me take this risk on behalf of someone else. For the first time, please, God, let me really care.

But she was frightened.

But that was all right. It was normal to be frightened. She was staring down the hard truths now, final confrontations, ultimate secrets.

She thought, I'll never sleep. I'm too wired to sleep.

But sleep crept up on her without warning.

She slept, and Karen slept, and the night rolled on, and when they woke the sun was shining and Michael's bed was empty.

Chapter Nineteen

· ·

The capital city of the Novus Ordo was dark and wintry and Michael wasn't dressed for it.

He had put on two shirts, heavy denim pants, and a Blue Jays baseball cap pulled down to cover the tips of his ears. But it wasn't enough. Wind came down these narrow streets like a knife and the snow infiltrated his sneakers.

The street was empty. He wondered whether there was a curfew in effect or it was just the weather. But it must be late here, too. These buildings were old and black and lit with sodium lamps at odd, uncertain intervals. Once in a while a bulky-looking automobile would chuff past, or a carriage behind a team of dray horses. The snow came down with a dry, sifting sound; Michael shivered.

But he was close. He could feel it. A few more of these long, narrow blocks and then right and then left again. He could not say where the knowledge came from, but it was immediate and sure; he had arrived here with it fixed in his mind.

But the weather was bad enough so that he would be in very rough shape if he tried to walk. So he stood in the meager shelter of a Gothic storefront—the sign said WATCHES, CLOCKWORKS, REPAIRS—and tried to flag down a ride.

Two cars passed by. The third stopped for him.

It was a huge gray vehicle with a black cylinder, a gas tank or maybe a steam chamber, projecting from under the hood. The right-hand door cracked open and Michael jumped inside.

The plush interior of the car was not much warmer than the street, but at least it was out of the wind. Michael looked gratefully at the driver. The driver was a middle-aged guy wearing Russian-looking furs and heavy gloves. They regarded each other a wary minute before the driver did something elaborate with the gearshift and the car rolled forward once more.

"Late to be out," the man said.

Michael nodded. "I didn't plan it this way."

"Caught in the storm?"

"Uh-huh."

"You could die walking around in those clothes."

The man's accent was odd, Michael thought, like a combination of Dutch and French. The tone was cautious and neutral. Michael said, "Well, you know how it is." There was no plausible excuse for his clothes.

"From out of town?" the man asked.

"Yes."

"Going far?"

"Not much farther."

"Give me an address. I can take you there."

But he didn't have an address. He hesitated. "I don't know the number," he said, "but I could give you directions."

"Good enough," the man said.

They drove in silence for a while. Michael watched as a huge, steaming snow plow passed them in an intersection, blue light whirling on its roof. Overhead wires hummed and clattered in the darkness. The buildings outside were odd, tall structures that looked like the pictures of Tudor houses he had seen in geography books; the ground-level windows were shop displays. This gave way to larger warehouse-style buildings and a few stone or concrete towers with false marble columns and gargoyles leering from the cornices.

Not a good place, Tim had said. But not necessarily a bad place, either.

Home, he had said.

But Michael shivered against the cold upholstery and withheld his judgment.

"Left," he said, following his instinct. "And right. Up here. Maybe a block or two . . ."

This new street was broader and hemmed in with tall obsidian buildings. Trolley wires were strung overhead. The rumble of the tires on the street suggested there might be cobbles beneath the snow. The growing sense of familiarity both excited and worried Michael. How could he have known which way to come? It was strange. But he *had* known. The instinct was strong, powerful . . .

"Here!" he said suddenly.

The car rolled to a stop.

There was a moment of silence, no sound but the snow hissing into the windshield.

The building was huge. There was a stone wall

that opened into a courtyard. Engraved above the
gate was the stark image of a pyramid and a single,
staring eye.

"Government building," the driver observed.

Finding his way here had been the easy part.

Michael had been awake long after his mother
and Laura fell asleep. He was so utterly awake in that
San Francisco hotel room that he thought he might
never sleep again. His thoughts ran like overheated
machinery. He was thinking about Tim.

Thinking about Aunt Laura following Tim back to
the Novus Ordo.

He understood what she meant to do. It made
sense. She distrusted Tim and she wanted to be sure
about what they were getting into. Michael knew she
was frightened and it was probably a brave gesture,
her offering to go.

But it didn't make sense. The more Michael
thought about it, the less sense it made. If a scouting
trip was necessary, why go with Tim—why trust him
even that far? He supposed Laura would not have
been able to find this place by herself . . . her talent
was not immensely strong and she had only been here
once, decades ago, as a child.

But, Michael thought, *I* can find it. He had felt it
already. In a curious way, he had been able to feel it
through Tim. Maybe this was how the Gray Man was
able to find them: this faint but discernible sense of a
road taken, a presence past. It wasn't something you
could put a word on. But he felt it in that hotel room in
San Francisco.

There was also the question of physical distance—
it was a city most of the way across the continent—but
Michael had come to understand that this was not a
substantial barrier either, that in the vortex of pos-

sibilities distance was as mutable as time. Washington or Tijuana, Paris or Peking: it didn't really matter.

He stood up in the darkness without waking his mother or Aunt Laura. He dressed in the heaviest clothes he could find. Now, he thought. There was no reason to wait. Laura was planning to leave tomorrow —so Michael would go first, would make her trip unnecessary. Just to have a look, he told himself, just to get a sense of the place. And then come back. Be back before morning. They wouldn't like it, of course. They wouldn't approve. But he was the man of the family. The responsibility fell to him.

Half a step sideways, a quarter turn in a direction he couldn't name. It was almost dismayingly easy. And then he was standing in a dark street up to his ankles in snow, flagging a ride to a building he had never seen, following an imperative so intense that he wondered whether he had ever really had any choice.

The odd thing was that the building was not better defended.

It looked like a fortress, iron gates and guard posts, but the big courtyard was open and deserted. Michael moved self-consciously through the drifting snow, his shadow multiplied by the harsh sodium-vapor lamps, shivering against the cold. He paused once and looked back through the open gateway. The car that had brought him here was still waiting, parked there, the motor cooling, and he thought that was strange. But it didn't matter. He pressed on toward the main building, a huge slab of stone and brick with random, cell-like windows. Sheets and veils of snow fell all around him. It was like being contained in snow, wrapped up in snow. The cold didn't feel so bad now.

The instinct or the compulsion he felt had grown

very strong. He followed it to the central slab-iron door of this building, which was slightly ajar. And that was odd, too. But Michael didn't think about it. A gust of wind carried snow down his collar, pushed him forward like a hand. *Inside*, it seemed to say. All right, Michael thought, that's where I'm going. That's where I want to go.

He entered the building.

The corridor was deserted. Half the overhead fluorescents were dark or flickering and a miniature snowdrift had accumulated inside the door. Michael pushed the door closed behind him; the clatter of it echoed down this tiled hallway like a handclap.

He thought, What *is* this place?

Home, he thought. The word was there in his mind. But not really his own thought: it was Tim's word. It sounded like Tim's voice. Or Walker's.

Michael shook his head and proceeded down the corridor.

The corridor smelled of Lysol and charred insulation. Some of these doors were open and some were not; the open ones revealed dark, windowless offices with gray metal desks. Periodically the corridor would turn left or right or fork in two or three different directions. There were no numbers and no helpful signs. Michael walked on regardless now, feeling the imperative inside him, following it, circling closer and closer to the heart of the building—as if it had an actual warm, beating heart—to whatever was waiting for him there.

It occurred to him that he ought to be scared.

Snow had melted into his clothes. His hair was cold and wet against his neck. His feet were numb. His sneakers made wet, rubbery sounds with every step. I should be scared, he thought, because none of it was the way it *should* be. Something was obviously wrong and he was the center of it; this empty building existed, in some sense, entirely for his benefit.

But there was no question of stopping or turning back. He could not even contain the thought; it didn't cross his mind. And that should have frightened him more than anything else—but in place of the fear there was only a faint disquiet. Just the outline of fear: as if the fear had been buried, as if the snow had covered it up.

He closed his eyes and walked with uttermost confidence. He came to a stairwell and followed it down, he could not say how far, but the air was warmer when he stopped. It was a hot, stale, enclosed air; it drew the moisture out of his clothes and it constricted his chest.

He arrived at a room. The room possessed a big steel door, but the door eased silently open at Michael's touch.

He stepped inside.

The room contained one wooden chair; otherwise it was empty. A bank of lights glared down from overhead. Michael was alone in the room. He had arrived, he thought happily, at the heart of the building.

But his sense of direction evaporated suddenly, and with it the inhibition that had locked in his fear. Suddenly he *was* scared, badly scared, profoundly scared. It was like waking up from a nightmare. He felt a panic boiling up in him. What was he doing here? What *was* this place?

He turned back toward the door but discovered with a dawning horror that he could not move in that direction. He tried but simply *could not;* his legs refused to function; he couldn't lift his feet. He could not even lean toward the door; could not make himself fall in that direction.

He felt the way a person trapped in a collapsed

building must feel: impotent and utterly enclosed. He wanted to scream for help but was afraid of the attention he might attract. But then, he must *already* have attracted attention. Why else was he here, unless somebody *wanted* him here?

There was a motion in the doorway and Michael shrank back into the wooden chair. He gripped the mitered edge of it and stared wild-eyed into the unattainable corridor.

A man stepped into the room with him.

It was the man from the car—the man who had driven him here.

The man stepped closer. He smiled. He seemed genuinely happy, and that was terrible in itself—he just radiated happiness.

"Hello, Michael," he said. "My name is Carl Neumann."

Chapter Twenty

·····················

"**M**aybe," Laura said, "he went out for a walk."

Which was at least plausible. It was obvious from the state of his open suitcase that Michael had dressed before he left. So, Karen thought, yes, that was a possibility. He could have slipped out sometime after dawn. Maybe he would be back.

It was a reassuring idea and at the end of a quarter hour she had almost convinced herself of it, at which point she became aware that the hotel room door was still locked and, worse, still chained—from the inside.

So he had not left the room after all. Not in *this* world.

Odd that it was possible to be calm at this revelation. She pointed out the chain lock to Laura, who said,

"God*damn,*" and punched out a flurry of numbers on the telephone. It was the number Tim had left. "Room 251," Laura said tightly, and then, after a long pause, "Fauve—Timothy Fauve. . . . He *what?* Oh, Christ . . . No. No, that's all right. Thank you."

The receiver rattled down.

"He's gone," Karen interpreted.

"Checked out this morning. Damn!"

So Michael was gone and Timmy was gone.

They have him now, she thought. He was the one they wanted and they have him now. That's what this means.

But Michael had only been gone a few hours at most. It was hardly any time. She wanted to reach back for him . . . unwind the clock until he was here in the room and she could grab him and hold him, hold him so hard that no one could take him away.

"One time," Karen said, "when Michael was just two years old—it was a couple of days after his birthday—I had him in a stroller and I was doing some shopping. We were downtown. It was almost Christmas; the stores were crowded. I was bending over a shelf and my back was to him. I was looking for that scented soap I used to send Mama every year—she loved that soap so much—but they didn't have it, so I was picking through the merchandise. It was like, well, there must be just one, it must be *behind* something. So I spent a lot of time rooting around, with these crowds just pushing past me. And they still didn't have what I wanted. So finally I stood up and I looked for the stroller. But it was gone. Gone with Michael in it. And I didn't panic. I just went cold. It was like the bottom had gone out of everything. I was dizzy but I was very systematic. I called out for him. I asked people, 'Did you see a stroller—a yellow flowered stroller?' And I worked my way down the aisle.

And then I saw it. It was like radar—I picked out that stroller in the crowd. It was way off down by the escalators. My heart started to beat hard. I ran over there. I pushed people out of the way—I didn't care. It was like the hundred-yard dash.

"And when I got there it was just this very confused old woman pushing Michael around. She had spotted the stroller and grabbed hold of it. She thought she was back in 1925 or something. I pried her hands off the push bar and she just looked at me, and there was such confusion and, I guess, grief in that look, I couldn't be angry. Five seconds earlier I was ready to tear her apart. But I just said, 'I'll take care of him now,' and she said, 'Oh. Well, all right. Thank you,' and went wandering down the escalator.

"But what I remember is that run. Spotting his stroller and just going full tilt after it. Nothing mattered but getting there. I'd never run like that before. Never in my life. But I wish—"

She faltered suddenly.

"I wish," she said, "I could run like that again."

Laura said gently, "Maybe you can. Maybe you have to."

Karen looked at her sister, trying to make sense of this.

"Maybe he left here on his own," Laura said, "or maybe he was taken. Either way . . . I don't think we have any choice but to follow him."

"Follow him *where?*"

"The most obvious place would be the world Tim was talking about. The Novus Ordo. But that's hardly specific. We have to *know* where he went—we have to feel it."

"Can you do that?"

"No. I want to! I've been trying. But it's like trying to follow smoke—I can feel him but it just goes away into the air." She focused on Karen. "Maybe you can do it."

But that was absurd, Karen thought. I don't have any talent at all. She told her sister so.

Laura said, "Karen, *I know better.* I know you've been trying to live a certain kind of life. And I know it's been a long time. But you were as strong as I ever was—all those years ago."

"We were kids!"

"It doesn't change."

"It *does* change!"

"You tell yourself that. But it was only ever a lie. Karen, do you understand what I'm saying? Because this is important. If you don't at least *try* to do this— well, maybe we've lost him. The Gray Man wins. Maybe we don't get him back ever."

And Karen thought, My firstborn son. Michael!

But I can't, she thought. Laura is mistaken. It's been too long.

But she sat in the silent hotel room with her sister's eyes on her, and all she could think about was that sprint, running after the stroller, Michael lost in the crowd. She had found him then. And how *good* it had felt—to run.

Michael? she thought. Was he out there now? Was it really possible to reach for him, to find him?

She felt a faint, sudden electricity . . . a kind of dizziness, as if the room had fallen away around her.

But that was bad. She knew that for a fact. It would be very bad to allow this back into her life, to give in to it now, to do the wrong thing. She thought of Willis Fauve. She saw his face in her mind, and it was the way he had looked twenty years ago, cropped hair still dark, his eyes like rain clouds under those huge brows. A bad and dangerous thing.

But Willis was just scared, Karen thought. Willis

was scared and in the end Willis had lost his children: they had run out of his life altogether. And now Karen was scared and Michael was gone. Maybe that was how it worked. Maybe it was inevitable, like a wheel turning.

All these thoughts flashed through her mind.

But he's out there, she thought.

That was the fact of it.

He's out there and maybe Laura's right: maybe I *can* find him.

So she closed her eyes and put away the thought of Willis once and for all and opened herself in a way she had almost forgotten. All you have to do is look, she thought. Worlds out there like petals on a flower. How long since she had done this last? A quarter of a century? But it was easy, and maybe that was the essential secret she had kept from herself all these years—the easiness of it.

And oh, Karen thought, how *much* she had forgotten.

Energy coursed through her body. Doors and windows, she thought, like a prism, like peering into a kaleidoscope and seeing it shift and change with every motion of your wrist. Every shard of colored glass a door, every door a world. And through one of them she would find Michael. She would spot him from a distance. She would run.

He had passed this way not long ago.

Her eyes were squeezed tight, but she saw a city, a dark complex of winding, snowbound streets, pale sunlight filtered through massed clouds, noisy automobiles and horses breathing steam.

She saw a dark building behind dark stone walls.

Instinctively, she reached out for Laura. "Take my hand," she whispered. "Now! I don't know how much longer I can do this!"

Felt Laura's fingers twine into hers.

It was as simple, she thought, as stepping over a threshold. You moved—but it was not quite a motion —in a certain direction—but it was not exactly a direction. Here and here and here. And then—

The cold air bit into her skin. She opened her eyes and saw the stone walls, prosaic and quite real, right in front of her. The walls were high and unassailable. But Michael was behind them. She could feel it. And she was lucky. The big iron gate was standing open.

Chapter Twenty-one

·····································

1

Cardinal Palestrina was awakened at dawn by the brash clattering of the telephone. Disoriented, he fumbled the receiver to his ear. The hotel switchboard announced Carl Neumann.

"Put him through," Palestrina said wearily.

Neumann's voice across the telephone exchange was shrill, piercing. "It's happening," he was saying. "You should be here as soon as you can."

Palestrina sat up. "So soon?"

"Right now, Your Eminence. As I speak."

"The boy?"

"The boy. And not only the boy."

Plucked out of thin air, Palestrina thought daz-edly. From a world beyond the world's edge. It was—in its own way—a sort of miracle. "All right," he said. "I'll be there."

"Excellent," Neumann said.

Cardinal Palestrina dressed hastily and drew a heavy fur coat around himself as he left the room. He stopped in the hotel lobby to buy a coffee in a waxed-cardboard cup—so hot it scalded his lips—and then hailed a taxi from the icy margin of the street.

2

Laura could not say just when or how she became separated from her sister.

It simply should not have been possible. The words repeated in her head like a cracked record: *not possible*. They had been together . . . she had been holding Karen's hand. It was like that time back in Pittsburgh when they followed Tim into what she guessed now was some distant corner of the Novus Ordo. They were like kids, clinging to each other.

After they arrived here they had moved through the snow to the black iron gates of this ugly building, through the long morning shadows across the court-yard. Michael was inside, Karen said. Laura couldn't feel it but she took her sister at her word. Find him and get out, she thought. Because we can do that: we can step sideways out of here anytime we feel like it.

It was a reassuring idea.

But then, if that was true, why hadn't Michael come home? How had they contrived to hold him?

But it was an unanswerable question. Just push on,

she thought. On down these twining corridors now, corridors like the roots of some immense old tree reaching deep into the earth. The air was stale and smelled like anesthetic, with some cloying scent laid over that, like cloves. Turn and turn and turn in the dim light. It became automatic.

And then she paused and looked for Karen and Karen wasn't with her.

The loss troubled her, but maybe not as much as it should have. She moved on in spite of it . . . not quite aimlessly, but without any goal she could name. It just happened. It was like sleepwalking. She *felt* asleep. She felt drugged.

That was it, Laura told herself: it was like being under the influence of some drug, not a mind drug or a stimulant but some sleepy narcotic, something syrupy and potent, the way she imagined opium must be. She moved down these antiseptic drab tiles thinking, This way to the Emerald City . . . through the poppy field . . .

The corridor narrowed until it was only a little wider than her body.

A bell was ringing somewhere. An alarm bell, Laura thought. Some sort of emergency in progress. But she ignored it, walking.

And then the corridor came to an end and there was only a room, a last windowless cul-de-sac revealed dimly through a final archway; and Laura thought, Why, *this* must be what I want, *this* is where I meant to go.

She stepped through the narrow doorway and saw a woman.

It took her by surprise. The woman looked so utterly ordinary. She was an ordinary middle-aged woman in familiar clothes, Levi's and a loose blouse, dressed maybe too young for her age. Her hair was graying faintly and the expression on her face was poignant, Laura thought, a mixture of bewilderment and longing. This woman, she thought, must have lost her way somehow.

But then Laura took a second step into the room —and so did the woman—and she realized that the far wall was in fact a mirror and that this sad middle-aged person was herself.

Her knees felt suddenly weak. Not me! she thought. That's not me, I'm not like that at all! I'm the *pretty* one, she thought—and, incidentally, what am I doing here, and where is everybody? Where was Karen, where was Michael?

She wanted to turn away but could not. Instead she took another step forward (and so did that sad, bewildered reflection) and she turned and saw—to her horror—that the side walls were mirrored, too, and facing each other at a canted angle, so that there were suddenly more images of herself than she could tolerate, an infinity of them, multiplied down dark mirrored aisles, all of them staring back at her with this same dumbfounded expression. Not me, she thought again, *none* of them are me, and she raised her hands as if to push them away, as if they were physical bodies crowding in around her. She wanted to leave . . . but she was, mysteriously, too weak to move; the door was too far away. *They can't keep us here,* she thought, and groped for a secret way out, a route back to San Francisco and the sunlight, a hidden door or private window.

But there were none. No doors or windows or angles here. Only the mirrors, like wells, drawing her down. She felt a surge of claustrophobic terror and saw the mirror-woman staring back at her wide-eyed, mouth opening in a scream; realizing all at once that she was trapped, that there was no way out and nobody here but herself.

3

Cardinal Palestrina joined Carl Neumann in his office in the Defense Research Institute.

The room was crowded. There was a man Cardinal Palestrina identified as a Pentagon bureaucrat—Neumann's superior. There were three of the Institute's seers, dwarfish creatures in cheap cotton smocks. There were two of the men Neumann called scientists, whom Palestrina preferred to think of as mages: the men who had cast the binding spells.

The sense of excitement in the room was palpable. It showed, especially, in Neumann. This was his triumph, the gratification he had deferred for too many decades. His face was flushed; his eyes darted around the room as if he were memorizing it, every detail of this day, the people present, their expressions. He looked at Palestrina and then approached him.

Palestrina said, "The boy is here already?"

"We've had him in containment for hours." Neumann grinned. "And the boy seems to have attracted the others. Bees to honey. It's all coming together."

"When can we see him?"

"Soon. We're waiting here until everything is in place. We have spells and geases twenty years in the making—and they're all coming to a peak, right here, right now. God, you can feel it in the air."

Cardinal Palestrina imagined he could. The air smelled odd, as if it had been singed in some vast, hot machine.

Neumann said, "We're just waiting for word from our seers."

The seers—the three dwarfish beings, who from the knotted closeness of their features must have been homunculi—sat staring into space. There was one for each of the three, Neumann said, Karen and Laura and Michael, each one linked in tandem to its subject. One of the creatures yawned and stretched as Cardinal Palestrina watched, and the gesture was so animalistic—so simian—that Palestrina suppressed a shudder.

The homunculus grinned at him from across the room, an animal grin.

Palestrina said to Neumann, "But can you hold them?"

"We're certain of it. This building is a cage—it's been designed that way. Since that original escape we've contemplated the problem and designed what we believe is an impenetrable barrier. You understand, not a physical barrier."

"Prison magic," Palestrina said.

"Exactly."

"Can you calculate that so precisely?"

"We believe so."

"It's been said—please don't take this the wrong way—the Americans have a genius for the profane sciences."

Neumann was in a generous mood. "But it's true," he said. "Look around."

Cardinal Palestrina drew a second cup of coffee from the urn in the corner. Too much would aggravate his stomach, but he felt he needed the alertness. So much was happening here.

Good things, presumably. After all, Palestrina thought, Neumann's arguments were hard to dismiss. His amorality was unmistakable, but the American un-

derstood the significance of events in the Middle East.
A weapon is a weapon, after all. Death, deceit, ravaged innocence: wasn't that what warfare *meant?* Cardinal Palestrina had been dispatched by the Vatican to
evaluate Neumann's secret weapon and its utility in
war. Also its position in the moral order . . . but
maybe that was finally irrelevant, a luxury the West
could ill afford. Is a sword more humane than a bullet,
a bullet more godly than a bomb? The news from
Sicily was very bad; bad enough, perhaps, to overrule a
delicacy concerning means.

But it was impossible to look at these grinning
homunculi and white-coated images without at least a
shiver of disquiet.

He found Neumann and said, "Assuming you
keep these people . . . can you guarantee their utility?"

Neumann seemed to resent the distraction.
"They can be revised into utility."

These words, Palestrina thought. These cool,
blank, terrifying words. Revised! "You mean surgery."

"It's delicate, obviously, but we're more sophisti-
cated than we were when we intervened with Walker.
This is a faculty of the imagination we're trying to
capture. It's like some fabulous rare butterfly. The
trick is to contain it without killing or crippling it.
Fortunately there are certain neural functions that
can be localized, at least generally. With the right
scalpel in the right place you can sever the will from
the imagination, cauterize the one without destroying
the other. We can make them work for us."

"But it's the boy you need . . . not the others."

Neumann looked at his watch. "What do you want
me to say?"

"Tell me the truth."

Palestrina was surprised by the tenor of authority in his own voice.

Neumann said, "This is not a confessional."

"You'll operate on them—you'll *fine-tune* your surgical procedures." (He thought, *I know these words, too.*) "You'll mutilate them and then use them or kill them, as it suits you."

Neumann said, "This *tone* of yours—look, I don't appreciate—" He stopped and recovered his composure. Cardinal Palestrina felt something of his own power here: legate from Rome, the ancient Imperium, Old Europe and all that implied. Neumann took a breath and began again: "These are moot questions, Your Eminence, or ought to be. In this kind of enterprise a certain amount of cruelty is built in. We all know that."

Cruelty and guilt, Palestrina thought. It amounted to Neumann saying, *Here is your share.*

The door opened then; Walker entered. Cardinal Palestrina flinched away from the man. Walker wore his customary gray clothing and gray slouch hat and was looking at Neumann now with a strange intensity of expectation, as if Neumann had promised him something, a gift, the answer to a question.

Neumann, consulting his seers, turned to the room and smiled. "It's almost done now . . . just a few more minutes."

The homunculi grinned among themselves.

4

Karen was not aware that she had lost her sister, or at least the awareness was not enough to make her hesitate. Her mind was fixed on Michael.

She had seen him.

It happened not very long after they entered this building. The silence of these long stony corridors had been oppressive and she was reluctant to break it; there was only the sound of her footsteps against the ugly green tile . . . and Laura's, until those faded. She moved steadily and purposefully, although she had never been here before, as if she possessed an instinct of direction, a cellular map. Michael was here somewhere. She knew it; his presence pervaded the building; the air was full of him. Somewhere very near now.

And then she saw him. She saw him at the end of this corridor, where it branched in an unequal Y to the right and to the left. Seeing him, she gasped and faltered. He looked oddly far away, an image through the wrong end of a telescope. But it was Michael. There was no mistaking his lanky figure, his untucked shirt and his baseball cap. He looked toward her but seemed not to recognize her; and then—agonizingly —he was gone again, retreating to the left.

Karen stumbled, then picked herself up and began to run.

She remembered the story she had told her sister, the old woman wheeling Michael away in his stroller and how she had chased after her. It should have been the same, she thought, this running now, but somehow it was not; there was no pleasure or relief in it; only a grim and breathless determination.

The corridor twisted again and she followed it in a long downward spiral. She could not estimate how far she had come or how far she might yet have to travel. There was only the image of Michael in her mind.

And then the corridor straightened and she saw him again—heartbreakingly, even farther away. "Michael!" She called out his name, and her own voice sounded strange to her, as shocking, in this dim doorless hallway, as a gunshot. "Michael—!"

But he was running . . . running *away from her.*

She gasped and began to sprint. She felt a kind of submerged panic, something that *would* be panic if only she could think more clearly. The important thing—the only thing that mattered now—was to keep him in sight.

She ran as long as she could run. Periodically Michael would stop, look back, and he was too far away for Karen to see the expression on his face, but she was afraid that it was a kind of taunting smile, a way of beckoning her on. It was cruel and she could not understand it. Why would he act like this? What was he thinking?

But there was nothing to do but follow.

When she could not run any longer she careened up against a stone wall. The wall was cold against her shoulder but she couldn't move, could only huddle against the pain of her struggling lungs. She looked up finally and saw Michael again, closer now, his face unreadable; she staggered forward and saw him sidestep through an archway. It was the only door Karen had seen in this labyrinth and she approached it warily. She understood now that something was wrong, things had gone wrong in a fundamental way, a way she had not foreseen. But here was Michael again —she saw him clearly through the empty doorway— alone in a small room watching her impassively, waiting for her. Karen made a small noise in her throat and stepped inside, reaching out for him.

But it wasn't Michael after all.

She blinked at the image, which would not focus. Suddenly this was not Michael but, horrifyingly, a thing the *size* of Michael, but smooth poreless plastic, and she recognized it: it was Baby, it was the doll the

Gray Man had given her all those years ago, grotesquely inflated and staring at her through painted china-blue eyes.

Karen bit the heel of her hand and took a step backward.

And then Baby was gone, too, and there was the final image—a fleeting impression—of some wrinkled, shrunken creature grinning madly at her . . . and then the space was simply empty, vision dispersed like smoke, and she was alone in the room.

She turned to leave. But she was tired. She was as tired as she had ever been in her life, and her feet wouldn't do what she meant them to do, and so she sat on the cold stone floor and folded her hands in her lap and closed her eyes—just for a minute.

5

"It's done," Neumann said.

Cardinal Palestrina listened to the cheering.

Chapter Twenty-two

....

1

Karen wasn't certain how much time passed.

She woke and slept and woke again, but the waking was partial and transitory. When she came fully to herself at last, she was in a room larger than the one she remembered; and there were old-fashioned-looking wooden chairs, and a single door—and she was not alone.

Laura was here, too, blinking at the light. And Michael. She felt a rush of gratitude. They were together. That, at least.

Tim was there, too.

She sat up—she had been lying on the cold floor—
and made her way to one of the chairs. Michael, doing
the same, gave her a look, a sort of "I'm all right," and
that was good. Laura struggled to her feet.

Tim, who was standing already, and whose expression was calm and endlessly patient, said, "You'll
feel better soon."

Karen could not at first understand what he
meant. It was like a message from another planet, a
foreign language. Feel better soon? Was he insane?

Laura said, "You *knew* . . . you were a part of
this."

Tim did not deny it. Karen looked at him with her
mouth open. Well, maybe he was capable of that. It
was possible.

He said, "Tell me if there's anything you need. If
you're hungry or you're thirsty. You don't have to suf-
fer here, you know."

Laura shot him an outraged look. Karen expected
some kind of outburst from her. But all she said was
"Go away," and her voice was flat and distant.

"I'll be back," Tim said, "later." He left through
the room's single door. And Karen understood, without having to think about it, that she would not be able
to follow, that the doorway was barred to her, that this
was a prison and that none of them would be allowed
to leave.

They had not been beaten or intimidated or tor-
tured; only confined. Karen tried to explain the trick
that had been played on her, the false image of Michael; but Michael began to look shamefaced and she
stopped, because he wasn't responsible and she didn't
want him to think he was. He was apologetic: "I only
meant to find out what we were getting into. I came
here because I wanted to save Laura the trouble."

Laura said, "If you hadn't gone they would have used me. A lure." She added, "Michael, I appreciate what you did. It took courage."

"It was stupid."

"Not in any way we could predict. Anyway, what we have to think about now is getting out of here."

Michael said, "We can't."

"You don't know that."

His eyes were empty, cynical. "You must be able to feel it. There are more than four walls in this room. I guess some sort of magic. We could walk out of any ordinary cage . . . so they had to build a special one."

Laura opened her mouth to answer, then closed it again. What he said was true and even Karen could feel it, a dulling, a suppression. Nowhere to look but up, down, left, right. It was ironic, in a way: all those years she had *wanted* to feel this, this utter ordinariness, to be anchored this firmly in one time and place. Well, here she was. But it was not an anchor; it was a leash; it was a chain.

She retreated to a corner and thought about Tim.

They had trusted him because he was family. But she guessed family had never meant that much to him. Maybe there was no reason it should. Family was Willis, with his flattop Marine haircut and his big fists. Family was Jeanne, taking him into her lap and laying an ice bag over his bruises. Those moments—Timmy bruised and curled in Mama's lap—were the only tender moments Karen could remember between Timmy and Mama, and she guessed there might be some connection there, a clue to Tim's willful meanness. I have been bad and beaten for it: now this is my reward.

So he doesn't care, she thought, that we hate him for it. He *wants* the hate. He would be rewarded for it: by the Gray Man, or the faceless magicians who had confined them here. She wondered what reward they'd promised him. But it hardly mattered. The kingdoms of the Earth. A paperweight.

She thought: Tim became the thing Willis always feared. So, ultimately, it was Willis's fault . . . this was the harvest of his frightened love.

But the question followed: Have I done any better?

All she had ever wanted was to protect Michael. And that was all Willis ever wanted, she thought, to protect *us*—he claimed so. But it wasn't enough. He had admitted that. *It's not worth jack shit.* He tried to protect us with fear, she thought, and I tried to protect Michael with ignorance. And here we are. It doesn't get worse than this. I wounded him, she thought bleakly, as badly as Willis wounded Tim. And here we are.

It goes on, she thought, the wheel turning, and it never gets better, and maybe that was the most frightening thing of all, that for all her wanting and all her trying she was not, in the end, any better than Willis Fauve.

2

Cardinal Palestrina moved quietly with Carl Neumann beside him to the open door of the cell.

"They'll hear us," he said.

"They can't," Neumann said, and his voice boomed down the corridor. "They can't hear or see us out here. It's part of the spell. Look: you can look at them. Go on, Your Eminence."

Cardinal Palestrina stepped reluctantly forward. He felt like a voyeur, a Peeping Tom. There was no visible barrier, no reassuring glass, only empty air between himself and these three people. And magic. But magic was so intangible.

They were asleep.

There were reed mats on the floor for them and blankets to help fend off the subterranean chill, for this was one of the Institute's lowest levels. The two middle-aged women and the teenaged boy slept with troubled expressions. Understandably, Cardinal Palestrina thought. They had been through so much. Kidnapped, held against their will . . .

He said, "Have you spoken with them?"

Neumann shook his head. "Only briefly to the boy, when he arrived. We're using the brother to break them in—get them accustomed to captivity."

"Ah, the brother. They talk to him?"

"Grudgingly. He's their only contact."

"The child," Cardinal Palestrina said.

"Yes. He's the important one."

"He doesn't look like much."

"It doesn't show," Neumann said.

An ordinary boy, oddly dressed. Hard to imagine him stepping across worlds. Cardinal Palestrina, who had considered himself credulous—and a model of faith—had discovered since his journey to America that his pedestrian mind balked at miracles.

Harder still to imagine this child as an effective weapon against the Islamic armies. He told Neumann so.

Neumann said, "But the potential is enormous. You have to understand—it's the *purity* of him. The others are all haltered in some way. Half-things. Compromised by their circumstances, or their genes, or their fear . . . or like Walker, hobbled by clumsy surgery. By comparison, the boy is a distilled essence.

Simple and potent. He can transport himself into the Arabic heartlands. Or carry our armies there."

"Surely not willingly?"

"When we're done with him," Neumann said.

The surgery. Cardinal Palestrina thought, *The cauterization of his soul*. The subtle cutting.

He said, "And the one who's collaborating—the brother—did you do that to him? Cut him in that way?"

"No," Neumann said calmly. "No, not Tim . . . we didn't have to."

3

"Soon," Tim said, "they'll be moving you out of here."

It should have been good news. Karen hated this room, its narrowness, the unsheltered corner toilet—and the pervasive numbness she felt here, the prison magic. But surely, she thought, they would not be moved to a *better* place. Not unless it was equally imprisoning, or they had been rendered somehow harmless. She did not relish the future. The magic worked on her like a sedative or a powerful tranquilizer; otherwise she might have been too frightened even to think.

Tim said, "It won't be so bad."

He was dressed in clean clothes, a little old-fashioned-looking, an odd cut, tweedy and Victorian. Probably that was what people here wore. There was something maddening about the way he looked—his cocked head and carefully inexpressive eyes, this attitude of *patience*. As if he were the one enduring some hardship.

Laura, across the room, stood up in the clothes she had been wearing for three days and said, "What did they offer you? That's what I keep asking myself. Why would you do a thing like this?"

Tim looked offended. Offended but patient. He said, "Why does anybody do anything? Maybe I didn't have a choice. Think about it. Maybe the reasons are obvious. I was serious, you know, what I said about this place. It *is* home. For me, anyway. And it could be home for you, if you would give it a chance. Home," he said earnestly, "is an important thing."

"The kingdoms of the Earth," Karen said, surprising herself.

He turned to face her, startled.

"A paperweight," she said. "I remember."

"I don't know what you're talking about."

"But you do. That's what they offered you." Sedated, distant even from herself, she was able to say this. It had been on her mind. "That's what they offered you. A place to rule. A kingdom. You relished that." She shook her head. "Bigger than Daddy. Oh, Timmy, you were always so literal-minded. You took everything so *seriously.*"

Incredibly, he was blushing. He drew himself up and said, "You make it sound like a fairy tale. But hey, it *is* a fairy tale. We're leading fairy tale lives. That should be obvious by now."

Laura said, "You *believed* them? These people—the people who put us here—you think they care about what happens to you?"

"They do. They have to." It was his vanity at stake now. "You'll see. You just don't know them. You—"

"I know they're capable of *this.*" This room, she meant; their imprisonment. "They don't care about you!" Scornful now. Chiding him. "It was only Michael they ever wanted."

"You pretend to know," Tim said. "You don't know a fucking thing."

He was not patient anymore.

"And now they have him," Laura pressed, "and what do you matter? You're nothing. Last year's model."

"All of us," Tim said hotly, "they want all of us. He's no different. Why is *he* special? He's just like the rest of us."

He waved dismissively at Michael, who was sitting in a chair, impassive, watching. Michael had been impassive for most of the last three days. The spell, Karen thought. It had this effect on all of them.

But now he stood up. He looked at Tim across the room and Karen noticed for the first time that they were approximately the same size: Michael was as tall as his uncle. For a moment he seemed somehow taller.

Tim—startled for the second time today—fixed his gaze on his nephew.

Michael glared back.

"You're wrong," he said. "I *am* different."

And what was that flashing on Tim's face now? Karen wondered. Was it fear? Was that possible?

The air filled with sudden electricity.

4

Cardinal Palestrina was with Neumann in his office when the homunculus burst through the door.

The creature leaped onto Neumann's desk and whispered something in his ear. With a mixture of fascination and loathing, Palestrina watched the creature's apelike features contort. But this was nothing like a smile.

Cardinal Palestrina had been finalizing the report he would present to the Congregation of Extraordinary Ecclesiastical Affairs. He had decided—reluctantly—that his finding would be positive; that he would suggest a joint European-American research effort involving the otherworldly child; that the strategic possibilities outweighed the ethical considerations. He would present his report to the consulate tomorrow and it would be forwarded by Marconi to the Vatican. Everything else would follow. Neumann would have his money, his prestige; in time, his ghostly armies.

But Carl Neumann stood up suddenly and his fists were clenched and his lips were taut; and Cardinal Palestrina thought, What is this? My God—what *now?*

"Something unforeseen," Neumann said tightly, "is happening at the cell."

Chapter Twenty-three

. . . .

1

Tim was wrong, Michael thought. It *is* me they want.

He had thought about this over the last few days—tentatively, ploddingly, under the blanketing influence of the prison magic. And he had come to some conclusions.

If they want me, he thought, it's because I'm different.

Laura had said as much, standing on the windy bluffs above Turquoise Beach. *It's more than I could ever do,* she had said.

And he remembered the way he used to feel, the

electricity raging up out of the earth, the vortex of time and place and possibility, and the way he had held it in his hands.

They want that, he thought.

But it was a new thing—this power. They had *anticipated* it, but maybe they didn't *understand* it.

And he let that idea lie fallow for a time.

Later he thought, How do you build a cage for an animal you've never seen?

It was an interesting question.

Well, you build according to what you know. Michael's grandparents—his natural grandparents—had once escaped a place like this. Tim had said so and there was no reason to disbelieve him, at least about this. So this room must be a bigger, stronger cage; they must have fortified their spells and their magic. But, still, wasn't that like building a wolf trap when you set out to trap a tiger? He thought, Hey, they don't know *me*.

But it begged the question:

How strong am I really?

He was new to his talent. It was not something he had much practiced. He felt the imprisoning magics around him like physical bonds, and he experimented, one night, fighting against them, exerting a counterforce.

But it was fruitless. Nothing yielded. He was alone and empty and all the countless doors of time and possibility had been brutally slammed shut.

So maybe he wasn't such a tiger after all.

He put all this out of his mind for a time. He slept, and when he woke he tried not to think about anything at all.

It was easy enough. The confining spells made it easy.

But then another thought drifted into his mind, not a thought so much as a daydream: it was the world he had envisioned at the Fauves' house in Polger Valley, and often since then.

Thinking about it made him feel better. It was a place, Michael felt certain, without prisons like this one.

He allowed himself to dream about it.

He drifted on the edge of sleep. It was a place and a daydream both. It was everything he felt when Laura talked longingly about "a better world." Maybe it was the kind of place she had been looking for when she found Turquoise Beach, a world she had reached for but could not grasp. And Michael discovered that he knew things about this world. He knew about the highways stretching from the watery French villes of the South up to the big northern cities of Tecumseh and New Amsterdam and Montreal. He knew about the rail lines running west across the prairies, the grain towns and Indian towns and cold switching-yard towns like Brebeuf and Riel. He knew about the Russian towns of the Northwest coast, where people still trapped for furs in winter. He knew about the Incan and Spanish cities of the Southwest, their freeways and temples and bright clothes and odd, raucous holidays. He knew that all this was called simply America and that it was not a country so much as a loose confederation, a kind of commonwealth. He knew that borders didn't matter much in this world. He knew that you could travel from Quebec to Coquitlam or Shelekhov to Cuernavaca without showing a passport. He knew that the market streets were rich with common goods, that any able-bodied individual could find a job in the cities, that the harvest had been bountiful this year.

But he knew this world best by its landscapes: geographies teased out of the air, as faint and unmistakable as the smell of rain. Salt marshes still in calm, empty southern noons; icy northern midnights bathed in radiant aurora glow. He had occupied these places in his dreams, walked these streets in his sleep. There was an affinity—an attraction. He thought, *A homing instinct.*

He knew all this as effortlessly as he knew his own name. He knew, moreover, that he could make himself a life in this place . . . that it was a place you could live without the quotidian threat of nuclear annihilation or imminent war, the daily roulette of robbery and violence.

A place where the Novus Ordo couldn't reach him.

A place where he would not be a freak.

And oddly it was this daydream—and not any struggling against his bonds—that made him feel suddenly freer, that opened his horizons for a tantalizing moment. He blinked and thought, *This* is what makes me different: *this* is what they didn't expect.

But then the walls and the ceilings closed around him and he was back in this room, which was only a room, and which contained him.

He stood up when he heard Tim talking about him. "You're wrong," he said. "I *am* different." And he understood by the expression on Tim's face that he had said something important.

Tim recovered fast. He drew back and stood up straight and made his face a bland mask of endurance. "I didn't mean to insult you, Michael. Sure, you're important. But so is Laura and so is your mother. And so am I."

Michael moved back toward Laura. Instinctively, he reached for her hand. She looked at him quizzically. But they touched and there was a flash—brief but significant—of real power.

Now, Michael thought. Now, while they're unprepared, or never.

"We're leaving," he said.

It was not an argument, just a flat declaration of fact, but he surprised himself by saying it. Laura's eyes widened and then she looked at him and made a tiny nod.

He reached for his mother's hand.

Tim said, "I don't think that's realistic. I don't think you've considered your position here."

Michael said, "But I have."

There was a kind of circuit going now, the three of them touching. He felt Laura's wounded vanity, his mother's passivity and resignation. And under that— buried but potent—these small, faint surges of power.

Gather that, he thought. Put it together.

A better world. Those forests and those cities. It was only a step away.

And Tim, sensing something now, said, "Hey—oh, Christ, *wait a minute*—"

No more waiting, Michael thought.

The room filled with a curious odor, hot motor oil and charred metal, like some huge machine gone into terminal overload. Far away, Michael thought he heard a savage and barely human howl of pain.

And the prison magic loosened a little around him.

Tim said, "God damn you, stop it!"

Karen reached out toward Tim with her free hand. She understood now what was happening; it was obvious. Tim backed off a step. Karen said, "Come with us." Adding, "It's going to be dangerous for you here."

But we don't have time for this, Michael thought.

He wasn't sure he could sustain the critical effort. An alarm bell was clattering in the corridor; he saw shadowy figures beyond the doorway.

Tim shook his head. "No!"

"They might kill you. They could do that."

Tim said defiantly, "Listen, they'll kill *you!* They won't let this happen! They'll send him after you and this time they'll let him fucking *have* you!"

The Gray Man, Michael thought.

"Timmy," Karen said, "it's not a game. You should have learned that a long time ago."

But Tim only shook his head, and Michael thought, *He looks like Willis . . .* it was odd, but you would swear they were blood relations. That anger. That *fear . . .*

Karen shook her head no.

"I'm sorry," she said.

And Michael thought, *Now!* But hesitated in spite of himself and felt the moment slipping away, a sudden recoiling.

I can't do this!

It was the voice of the frightened ten-year-old and Michael was paralyzed by it.

I can't do this! They're too strong for me! I want somebody to come get me—I want to go *home—*

But there was no home. He knew that now. Only his mother in this cell, his father living in bliss and ignorance by the side of a very distant lake. And Tim, of course, had lied; the Novus Ordo was nothing like a home.

The clangor of alarms. Feet in the hallway.

Laura's hand tensed against Michael's.

And he had then what he identified—a moment of lucidity among this shrilling noise—as a genuinely adult thought: that home is not a place after all but a thing you make, a territory you stake out. It was an act of will: a thing you *did*.

Karen sensed his hesitation, shot him a fearful look.

Laura whispered, "It's out there, Michael . . . please, I *know* it is."

Home.

He held the word inside him.

Those forests and those cities.

Home, he thought . . .

And then the walls gave way, and there was only time and possibility and a great and simultaneous motion; and Michael closed his eyes against the brightness and opened them on a high blue sky very far away.

Chapter Twenty-four

....

1

Cardinal Palestrina followed Carl Neumann into the empty cell.

Its emptiness was shocking and he could see that shock in Neumann's face, a numbed incomprehension. Neumann seemed to radiate loss, a grief as profound as if a child had died here. Timothy Fauve, the collaborator, stood motionless in a corner, stealing glances at Neumann the way an exposed field mouse might regard a passing hawk. For long moments no one spoke.

Finally it was Neumann who broke the silence,

with an action rather than a word. In a single motion he turned to the homunculus, which had followed him down these long corridors into the room, and kicked the unfortunate creature squarely in the ribs. It traveled some feet across the floor and came to rest limply against a wall. It looked dead.

Cardinal Palestrina turned away.

It's over now, he thought. There is no Plenum Project; there is no secret weapon. All this effort and constraint had come to nothing. There was the collaborator—Tim—the man cringing by the wall—but Neumann had explained that he was not, in himself, very powerful; that his talent was a crabbed, unsavory magic that opened narrow doors into ugly and marginal places; that his alcoholism and drug addiction had eroded even that.

And there was Walker . . . but Walker had been wounded with clumsy neurosurgery, gutted until he was nothing more than a passive psychic bloodhound, a hunting machine. So the Project had ended and probably Neumann's career with it; there would be censure, an enforced retirement.

And in the long run, Cardinal Palestrina thought, what else might this mean? A potential advantage in the war irrevocably lost; the alliance with the Americans weakened; years of entrenchment and bloodshed and compromise.

So this was a disaster. A terrible thing had happened today.

But Cardinal Palestrina felt the hammering of his own heart, and it was a kind of giddiness—a vicarious triumph: strangely, as if the Devil had taken a beating here today.

2

Walker learned from a distressed mage what had happened in the containment cell, and he hurried there looking for Neumann. Approaching down the hallway, he felt it himself—a rupture in the fundamental magics of the DRI, as obvious and as significant as a hole blown in a wall.

Neumann looked up as he entered. Just seeing Neumann's eyes, Walker registered the enormity of the escape.

But I brought them here, he thought. I did my part. It was a contract (though never written or spoken), and, Walker thought fervently, I fulfilled my part of it. Payment due, he thought.

But Neumann's expression swept away his certainties.

He thought for the first time, Maybe it's too late. Maybe they won't give it back—what they took from me. What I lost.

He touched his fingers to the scar running alongside his eye. He was not conscious of the gesture.

"It's *not* the end," Neumann was saying. He was addressing Palestrina, and there was a pleading note in his voice. "We can start again. Start from first principles."

Cardinal Palestrina shook his head. "You're talking about years. Generations."

"Not necessarily!"

"Our needs," Palestrina said, "are unfortunately more immediate."

"Needs!" Neumann was shouting now. "You never cared about that! Oh, you pretended. Strategic neces-

sity. The global view. You said all the words. But none of that ever mattered, did it? Just this priggish hand-wringing, this Jesuitical nonsense, the fucking *moral order*—"

But Palestrina merely turned and left the room.

Neumann's hands curled and flexed helplessly. He looked, Walker thought, like a wounded dog.

"Fucking Papist," Neumann whispered.

Walker stepped forward. His mind was whirling. So much had happened and he understood so little of it. Make me whole, he wanted to say; that was the bargain; you promised me that. But he knew from Neumann's face that it would do no good.

So he said, simply, "Do you want me to find them?"

Neumann focused on Walker—a blank, intent gaze.

"Yes," he said.

"And kill them?"

It was all Walker had to offer. It was everything. He understood how fragile the sorcels of entrapment had been, how long they had taken to devise—more than two decades since the day he had offered three gifts to three children: small potent binding magics. It was an edifice, moreover, which could not be rebuilt . . . certainly not within Neumann's lifetime.

"They're dangerous," Neumann said, performing (Walker guessed) this same calculation of loss and revenge . . . his anger and his hatred revving up like a machine, the machine that had operated this building for so many years. "They know about us here. That could be a problem." He sighed. "Yes, kill them."

Walker looked at Timothy Fauve, staring now openmouthed from his place against the wall.

"What about this one?"

"Begin with him."

3

Tim watched the Gray Man advancing.

His outrage was instantaneous. *Not for this,* he thought.

I didn't do any of it for this.

Christ, and how many miles had he traveled to come here since he left that house in Polger Valley two decades ago? How many fucked-up menial jobs and days without food and nights on some raw rained-out interstate hitching Detroit to Chicago to Des Moines to Points fucking West? How many empty bottles, how many insulted veins? How many lame dodges through crippled worlds like (admitting it now) this one? And for *what?*

So he could hand over his sisters to be killed? And be killed himself for his trouble?

No. Oh, no.

He looked into the eyes of the Gray Man, his fists bunched. He said, "I trusted you!"

Walker didn't laugh.

Home! Tim wanted to say. I came home! And you showed me! Kingdoms! Empires! You *owe* me that!

As Walker reached for him.

Tim stood up straight. He felt what Walker was about to do, some presentiment of it, the opening of the world's walls around him. He looked Walker in the eye, but there was no recognition there; only a shadow.

Walker touched him. All over now.

"Fuck you," Tim said. "You were never my father."

And tumbled away into chaos . . . only the echo of him left to bounce around these old stone walls.

Chapter Twenty-five

. . . .

1

"**W**e can't hide," Laura said. "I'm not even sure we can run."

But Michael was more optimistic. "Moving around helps. I think it'll gain us some time, at least."

So they thumbed a ride up the broad highway that ran between Ville Acadienne and the crossroads of the Urban North, startled into silence by the forests and the flights of birds, by the hugeness of this country they had come to. The driver said he was up from the Chickasaw towns, visiting his family there, and they were welcome to ride as far as he was going. So they traveled that night and a part of the next day north-ward, and when Laura admitted they didn't have any money—or none that was useful here—the driver bought them all breakfast at a roadside diner. He would have taken them farther but they demurred; he had done enough already.

They walked for an afternoon. At dusk, they knocked at the door of an old stone farmhouse and asked for shelter for the night. The woman who an-swered—a pretty woman in a peasant skirt and thick, rimless eyeglasses—said they could have the loft and leftovers, and it was a good thing the weather had warmed up.

Alone with a naked light bulb and what seemed like a feast of bread and cheese and faintly alcoholic cider, they talked about the future.

"We have to get back where we can operate," Laura said. "At least for a while."

Michael had thought this over. "Soon," he said. "But we're all right here for now."

"He'll come after us," Laura said.

"Probably."

She looked around. "Well. At least it's a friendly enough place." She regarded Michael curiously. "Have you been here before?"

So Michael told them about the Commonwealth, the way he had dreamed it, the cities and the wilder-ness, the flying machines and the highways and the railroads. The kind of place it was—how he had dreamed it, and then dreamed it real, and then dreamed his way out of prison with it. He wanted to tell them what it meant to him, but there were no words for it; he could only enumerate its features and hope they understood.

Maybe they did. He saw the way Laura looked at him, her intensity, and wondered if she hadn't dreamed of this place herself—faintly, distantly, a door she had never quite managed to open.

2

Karen sat back and listened to Michael talk, the roll of his voice now that the prison spells had been lifted. She wondered again whether he hadn't grown a couple of inches. A trick of the light or perspective, but she could swear he was taller, and there was something in his voice, a firmness, that was new to her.

The shadow, at least, of adulthood. And she realized suddenly that Michael must have passed his sixteenth birthday back in the prison of the Novus Ordo.

It was a disturbing realization.

After a time Michael went and sat in the broad loft window, surveying the tableland that stretched away into the darkness—standing watch—while Laura and Karen talked in small whispers amidst the hay. Because they had come so far, Karen thought, it was possible to think things that were unthinkable—even to say them. She found herself telling Laura what she had been thinking, about Michael, her failure. "What hurts is that I couldn't save him. All his life, I would look at him, I would think, I won't do to him what Daddy did to us . . . I won't let him lead that kind of life. But I was fooling myself." The wheel, she thought. Maybe she had never beaten him but she was as harmful an influence as Daddy had ever been. We bend our children, she thought bleakly; and our children, bent, bend *their* children; and the wheel turns, and it grinds out broken lives.

"But," Laura said, "you did save him."

Karen shook her head.

"I mean it," Laura said. "The only reason we got this far is because of Michael. His talent, the strength of it. But that's not a fluke or a mystery. Maybe any of us could have been like him. But we have chains on us . . . we have all the inhibitions Willis beat into us. I think the only reason Michael's different is that he isn't carrying around all that pain. No one ever made him afraid. Maybe you never prepared him for this—well, Christ, who could?—but you never made him afraid of himself. And that's why they couldn't cage him.

"So it comes to something," Laura persisted. "It *does* matter. You loved him, and that's not a bad thing. Maybe it's the only thing that matters. You loved him and you made him strong."

Maybe, Karen thought. But . . .

But she was drifting off to sleep now, leaving behind the loft and the cool air and the silhouette of the barn's old beam and pulley against a starry sky. She pulled this borrowed woolen blanket over her shoulders and let her thoughts meander.

I would like to believe that, she thought, what Laura said. It was a nice idea, the world as an upward-turning place, at least the possibility of improvement. But it was equally likely that there was some kind of natural law, a conservation of misery. Pain doesn't disappear, only gets changed into some other kind of pain.

If she had saved Michael from fear maybe it was only by taking that fear onto herself. Certainly she was frightened now. And it was not just the obvious fear, but a whole coterie of fears: mother fears, the fact that her son was in danger: and other fears beyond that, including the final and unavoidable one, that Michael had gone beyond her in some important way, that he was lost to her, a grown man, a separate creature, the last ties of blood and affection sundered by all this violence. That there was nothing more she could do to help him.

Not to matter anymore—surely that would be the worst thing?

But they had found a moment of peace in this curious place, the America Michael had found, and she allowed herself to sleep at last, lulled by the wind sounds and the rustle of an owl that had nested in the rafters.

3

Michael woke in the morning with his cheek pressed into the straw and a faint sunlight prying through the barnboards, and for a moment the only thought he had was that he was here, in the world he had begun to imagine in the old row house in Polger Valley. A *safe* place. And that feeling of security was so fine that he wrapped it around himself like a blanket and almost fell back asleep.

And then he remembered.

He remembered Walker; he remembered the hard stone prison of the Novus Ordo.

And sat up thinking, How do we run? Where do we run to?

—the only questions left.

He did not doubt that they would be pursued, were already being pursued, that their period of grace might amount to days at most. "They'll kill you," Tim had said, and Michael firmly believed it.

But he didn't want to leave any sooner than he had to. This was a tiny, rural segment of the world he had imagined back in Polger Valley, but it was real—

tangible, vast and complex and indefinably familiar. It felt like home.

"Home" had become a pretty ragged word and Michael was reluctant to use it even in his private thoughts, but it was the word he kept circling back on. Home, a place to live, a place to make a future.

Maybe.

Maybe.

Maybe sometime. Maybe even soon . . .

But he gathered up his Blue Jays cap and his spare shirt and hiked out to the highway with his mother and Laura behind him, a cool morning with frost coming off the casaba vines that lined this old stone wall, feeling nothing but the prospect of a warm day and a ride up to the market cities of the North—his mind empty but humming happily in the fresh sunlight— when suddenly a kind of sour electricity filled the air, and a man-sized space before him seemed to darken and then take shape, and it was the Gray Man, it was Walker, as inevitable as time and as real as the stones, standing there staring, his face looking somehow older and angrier now, his eyes wide and childlike as he reached out his big hands toward Michael.

Chapter Twenty-six

....

1

So he ran.

He took hold of his mother and his aunt and together they were gone, twisting down the secret corridors of the plenum as fast as he could take them.

2

White light and flickering darkness and this ceaseless motion . . . it was all Karen could do just to follow.

She felt Michael a step ahead of her and Laura a step behind, links in a chain, and the Gray Man in their wake, a dark presentiment, the shadow of a storm cloud.

She could not calculate the distance they traveled. There were no words for this kind of distance. The world—these worlds—had become a vapor, a mingled landscape too diffuse for the eye to comprehend. She felt disoriented, bodyless, lost in an indefinite betweenness, a fog of location. She felt stretched to the breaking point.

She closed her eyes and held on as hard as she could.

But it was exhausting. It was not only Michael's effort but her effort and Laura's. Exhausting, especially, because this was a talent she had not exercised since childhood; without Michael she would not have been able to do it at all. She felt a fatigue that was more than physical, an exhaustion of possibilities—it tugged at her like an anchor.

It was like that time in the department store, she thought, running after Michael. This same careless plunging into the unknown, down corridors and angles she had never dared imagine, a bursting through forbidden doors. But this time it was Michael who was doing the running, his skill or intuition. Periodically they lingered long enough to glimpse a landscape, some real and strange place, a grove of trees or a crowded lane; and she would think, *He'll find a place . . . somewhere the Gray Man can't follow . . .*

But the Gray Man was relentless behind them—she could *feel* him—and Karen was growing wearier by the minute. Worse, she began to suspect (and it was a grim, unwelcome intuition) that they were being somehow *herded;* that Michael's running had a desperation in it now; that these increasingly dark and half-glimpsed worlds where they paused were not entirely of his own choosing.

Too much for him, she thought.

Clinging to his hand as if it were the only real thing in this chaos, she thought, *Oh, Michael, I'm sorry—*

Because the fatigue was numbing, the distance was too great to bear.

She put her head up helplessly and saw a cold moon sailing through a black sky, worlds and worlds away from home.

And then she stumbled.

She fell. It was prosaic. She was, momentarily, as embarrassed as she was frightened. Her hand slipped away from Michael's; and she felt cut off, suddenly alone. But then Michael was with her, urging her up; Laura was lifting her.

Karen thought, *I know this place!*

She had slipped on the cobbled wetness of the alley. It was a dark night, wintry night, old gray moon in a black cheerless sky. Beyond the alley mouth she saw sooty Tudor-style houses with white ice bearding the eaves. A cruel wind came in from the sea.

It's always cold here, Tim had said.

It was one of his places, a cloistered industrial town by the sea, and she had been here before—once in her childhood and often in her dreams.

It might be some part of the Novus Ordo, a port town there, or it might be some analogous but unconnected world. But this was where she had met the Gray Man and this was a place, she felt, where his power must be considerable. It was here that Walker had begun to lay the complex spells that had almost—but for Michael—trapped them.

Therefore, a *dangerous* place.

Michael tugged at her hand. "Hurry," he said, but she could not; the fall had taken the last of her stamina. She looked at Michael helplessly and understood there was no need to explain; he had felt it in her touch. His eyes widened and then narrowed.

"Go without me," she managed.

Laura put an arm around her. "I'll stay. Michael, you go on. Maybe you can draw him away—"

"Just run," Karen said. "It doesn't matter, *run.*"

But then obviously it was too late, because the Gray Man was there with them, standing in silhouette at the mouth of the alley with the sea wind spitting at his back.

For a long moment no one moved.

"Go," Karen hissed. She felt dizzy with it, her own futility, Michael's silence: it was like watching him stand dazed between the rails with a train bearing down. And nothing she could do—nothing to save him. "Michael, *go,*" she said, but it was useless now, because here was the Gray Man reaching out, and she could see the stupid, implacable calculation in his eyes; and his hand, reaching, seemed to glow with dark electricity, strange ultraviolet lightnings.

3

Michael stood his ground.

He wanted to run. No, more than that. It was not just *wanting* to run. It was an urge so profound it went beyond fear, it was a screaming *need* to run . . . and yet he knew without thinking that, if he tried it, his legs would fail, the muscles would knot and bind.

He looked at the Gray Man and felt the keening of his own terror, a high note pitched beyond human hearing but which radiated through his body.

Nevertheless he stood his ground.

Because his mother was here, Laura was here . . . and because there was nowhere to run. He had exhausted the possibilities. Some final entanglement of binding magic had led him to this place and this was where the battle would be fought . . . if it amounted to a "battle" at all.

Michael, lucid in the maelstrom of his own fear, registered the absolute certainty in Walker's eyes.

He remembered the little girl on the beach, discarded into chaos like a rag.

Thinking, as Walker took another step closer, *But I'm not that little girl—I'm more powerful than that.*

Hadn't he proved it already? Hadn't he escaped the prison magics of the Novus Ordo?

But this was different.

The Gray Man was a killer, a destroyer: that was his nature. Michael didn't have those skills.

Now Walker took another step forward, fierce engine of death. Everything was in tableau: Karen struggling to stand up, Laura with her spine pressed up against the cold brick wall of the alley. The yellow streetlights flickered and hissed; the moon was bright and utterly still.

Michael remembered what he'd told Willis that time: *I could drop you down through the floor . . . I could do that.* But could he? Could he do that to the Gray Man, to Walker? No . . . not likely . . . but he squared himself and summoned a feeble trickle of the power, thinking, But I must.

It was a gesture. It amounted to nothing. The Gray Man smiled.

4

One more magic, Walker thought. One more trick.

There was a trick the mages had taught him, a trick he had never needed to use. Which, perhaps, he did not need even now; except that the boy was still in some ways an unknown quantity, a vehicle of unexpected strengths. So: magic.

Walker smiled and rearranged his own face.

It was less a physical change than a matter of suggestion, a spellbinding. The change was subtle but distinct, and he registered the effect in Michael's eyes, the shock and sudden terror.

Wearing his new face, the Gray Man moved closer. His smile was broad and authentic. He felt on the brink of completeness. Soon he would recover the lost thing. Soon he would be whole.

He regarded Michael with something like love.

"I came for you," he said.

5

Michael witnessed the transformation without understanding it. He was overloaded on all circuits and he could only register this figure, which had been the Gray Man . . . but which was now his father, was Gavin White, was Michael's own father holding out his arms and repeating those words—"I came for you"—

I came for you.

Yes. Please, God. Take me home.

Daddy, I'm *tired.*

But it wasn't Daddy.

It was a phantom, a monster. It was the Gray Man.

The Gray Man lunged out a hand and Michael felt the mask slipping, saw Walker like old paint through the chipped patina of this image. He raised his own hand to defend himself—or at least ward off this creature—but the shock of recognition had been profound; the power had drained out of him; he was empty as a cup.

Walker came to embrace him, and the cup filled up with fear.

6

Karen, watching, thought, You will not have him.

It was only that, a thought, barely articulate. But it rang in her mind. Everything was in slow motion now, a terrible ballet—Laura crouched to one side with an expression of helpless horror, Michael dazed and motionless, the Gray Man advancing by inches and millimeters, a slow trajectory, like some deadly thing falling out of the sky. And Karen, alone now in the sterile light of a streetlamp, thought to herself, You are the oldest. You have a *responsibility* here.

Daddy had been right about that. In that one thing, he was absolutely correct. It was her job; it was the job she had taken on herself. It was the job she had assumed in that crowded Christmastime department store a thousand years ago. And it was her weakness, too; it was the way they had seduced her. She thought about Baby, the doll this deadly man had given her. *Your firstborn son.* It was the weakness they had used to trap her, dangling images of Michael down the dim fortress corridors of the Novus Ordo. But maybe it was not only a weakness.

Maybe it was a kind of strength.

She looked at the Gray Man. He was moving toward Michael and Michael had raised a hand, but something passed between the two of them and Michael opened his eyes wide in shock. She could not see the mask Walker had adopted; it was a private and particular magic. But she sensed the change in Michael, his sudden weakness. She saw it in Walker's wide, eager smile.

She thought, You *will not* have him.

Maybe she said it out loud, because Walker did a curious half-turn; his trajectory slowed; he was still moving toward Michael but he was looking at Karen now.

And it was a strange look there in his eyes, she thought; not the dull-witted deadliness she had expected but something spontaneous; something older and deeper. A mingling of surprise and curiosity, an appraisal: *What do you have for me?*

As if she were bearing a gift.

Michael shook his head, as if some brief spell had been broken. Without thinking, Karen took two quick steps forward and reached to embrace Walker—to slow him down, at least.

You don't believe I can do this. Oh, but I can.

It was an instinct too sure and swift for words. She simply reached for Walker the way Walker had reached for Michael . . . reached out and *took hold* of him in a way she could not define.

But it was a real embrace, too. She could smell him. He smelled cold, like this alley. It was an alley smell, vacant and dark, like oil slicks and old masonry and abandoned buildings on deep winter nights. She had the sudden, curious sensation that he was entirely hollow—that if she squeezed hard enough he would crumble in her hands.

She saw Michael step away until his shirt collar brushed the wall. He shook his head, dazed.

And Karen felt the Gray Man tremble . . . summoning his energy now, redirecting it.

She closed her eyes.

She was aware at once of what Michael called the doors and angles of the world . . . an unfolding of possibility that was here and not-here, both, and how she might move in it. And she felt the chaotic places, too, the uncreated worlds and the dead, entropic ones.

Walker closed his own arms around her. It was a true embrace now, a mutual embrace.

She heard Michael's voice, faintly:

"Mom?" he said.

She understood what Walker meant to do . . . and what she must do to Walker.

She pulled back until only their hands were touching, a hot electricity running between them. Walker began a smile. She felt the withering force of his contempt.

And thought, *I know those places too.*

She said, "You will not have him."

His hesitation was momentary.

She looked deep into his empty gray eyes.

A gentle push, she thought, and this *opening* . . . a hole in the world directly behind him, and the rush and hiss of churning chaos.

She felt the coldness of it, colder even than this winter alley.

She thrust forward and into him with all her weight. He tumbled backward . . . and the vision of him was as sharply etched as a dream: of the Gray Man, of Walker—her broken uncle—falling away out of time altogether; and of the final expression on his face . . . not astonishment or fear but something Karen perceived, in this weightless moment, as *gratitude* . . . as if she had given him a gift, or returned to him some stolen and immensely valuable possession.

She blinked and gasped, falling after him.

Oh, the coldness! Chaos and wild entropy and a random dead nothingness: this was the hole she had opened for him, and she could not stop herself tumbling after—

But there were hands on her, warm hands suddenly pulling her back . . . and the door winked closed . . . and then there was merely this alley, this particular winter night, this ashen moon, and Michael and Laura weeping with her.

Chapter Twenty-seven

. . . .

1

Cardinal Palestrina boarded the Spanish diesel ship *Estrella Vespertina*, bound for Genoa with a cargo of jute and raw cotton and a handful of commercial passengers, on a fading late-winter day. The sky was cold and overcast, but he stood at the stern of the huge ironclad vessel and watched the harbor of Philadelphia draw away, wondering what consequences the events he had seen might imply.

For himself, nothing untoward. He had done his job as faithfully as it needed to be done, and in the end events had gone beyond him. Having proven his utility to the Curia, he might be allowed to carry on with his scholarly work. Assuming, Cardinal Palestrina thought, the war allows us such luxuries.

Ah, the war. But the news at the moment was not all bad. The Persian fleet had been turned back at the Balearics; the Turkish beachhead was isolated at Sardinia. European airpower would hold the day—for now.

So perhaps the loss of Neumann's secret weapon was not as tragic as it seemed. The shaky alliance between Rome and the Novus Ordo would hardly be strengthened by this miscarriage . . . but it was a temporary alliance in any case, doomed by its internal contradictions. Cardinal Palestrina doubted that the fate of Europe had been sealed.

As for what *truly* had been lost—

Well, that could only be speculation.

Night had fallen before they were out of sight of the New World. The purser approached Palestrina and instructed him, in mincing English, to go below—"It will only get colder, Your Eminence!" But Palestrina shook his head. "I'll be down shortly. Don't worry. I won't let myself die up here. I understand how awkward that would be."

And the purser smiled nervously and moved away.

There were the ship lights and the distant lights of land, the continent like some far-off world, the way Neumann's Other Worlds must have seemed, Palestrina thought, twinkling lights across an unimaginable gulf . . . and the thought made him sad, suffused him with an unwelcome melancholy. He allowed himself to wonder what might have been the outcome if this Plenum Project had not been solely aimed at creating a weapon; what wonders or terrors they might have found in that infinity, those Many Mansions. And he thought again of the land he had dreamed about, a world where Man had never fallen from grace, where it was warm, where the Garden grew, and there was innocence, and no one like Neumann, no serpent with his sweet poisonous fruit, and no death. We might have found it, Palestrina thought, touched it, walked in it— God help us, *if only for a moment—*

But the *Estrella Vespertina* sailed relentlessly eastward, and the distant lights sank below the horizon, and Cardinal Palestrina squeezed his eyes shut and went belowdecks, where the jute merchants sat drinking retsina and playing cards across a wooden table, and looked up at him unhappily, as if his sobriety would ruin their game, as if he reminded them of old sins.

2

Laura said, "What if I told you I was going away?"

Emmett, who had almost fallen asleep, turned up on his elbow and blinked. Behind him, moonlight streamed through a veil of bamboo blinds; the ocean rushed and sighed.

He tucked the sheet around her shoulders to protect her from the night. "I would remind you that you just got back."

Laura summoned her courage. "I meant going away permanently."

Emmett looked at her a long time and then shrugged.

It had been a good reunion and the lovemaking had been good, and she was reminded how much she had missed this man. But these were important questions, questions she had never allowed herself to ask:

as if they had signed a contract, *we will not mention these things.*

His eyes, in the darkness, were very large.

She said, "What if I asked you to go with me?"

"I would ask you where."

"Nowhere you know. Someplace strange. But not a bad place. You'd get along there, I think."

"This is mysterious," Emmett said.

"But I mean it," Laura said.

Emmett pondered this. "Sounds like you do."

"It's hard to explain."

"Witchcraft," Emmett said.

"Something like that."

"Really?"

"Really."

"I would have to trust you on this."

"Yes. It's too much to explain."

"I don't know," he said.

"Well, I understand," Laura said. "It's tough."

Emmett said, "I need time to think about it."

She closed her eyes and said, "I'm leaving tomorrow."

"Seriously?"

"Seriously."

"Hell of a thing to ask somebody."

"I know."

"What would you say if I asked you something like that?"

But she had thought about this a long time. "I would say yes."

He seemed surprised.

He said, "I have business here."

"I know."

"It's not the kind of thing a person can just do. Pick up and leave like that."

"I see," Laura said.

"Hey, you know how it is."

"Yeah. I guess."

She turned away.

And in the morning he helped her with her two big bags, all the things in the world she wanted to keep, and carried them downstairs for her, to the car, the little Durant parked in the gravel. It was a cool morning and the air was full of salt and iodine. Emmett didn't talk much and Laura didn't press it. She didn't know what to say either.

She opened the trunk and Emmett lifted her luggage inside. He slammed down the lid.

Laura opened the door and slid behind the wheel. Emmett closed the door for her. She rolled down the window and looked up at him.

"Lousy day for traveling," he said. "Looks like rain."

"Maybe not where I'm going."

"Somewhere sunny?"

"I think so," she said, sad but not wanting him to see it. "It's definitely possible."

"Well," Emmett said, "what the hell. I'm not especially fond of the rain myself."

She turned her face up. He was smiling. "Room for some guitars in there?"

3

Karen phoned Toronto from a hotel room in Santa Monica.

She was surprised at Gavin's voice. He sounded weary and uncertain. Older, maybe. Maybe things weren't going too well in the apartment by the lake.

He said, "I guess it's too much to hope you've come to your senses."

"Not the way you mean—no, I haven't."

"If you come home, you know, Karen, it'll look much better in any kind of custody argument. You're only hurting yourself by running away."

She said, "It won't be a problem for long."

"Jesus," Gavin said, "I wish I could figure you out."

"I don't think that's possible anymore."

"So why bother calling? To gloat?"

She was hurt. Brief but bitter—it was a taste of the way things had been. "Maybe just to hear your voice. Maybe to say goodbye."

"Don't be so damn sure you've heard the last of me. I'm quite capable of hiring detectives. Maybe I already have."

"I don't think it matters."

"Is Michael with you?"

"Yes."

"You're taking this risk—you're destroying his future."

But she didn't believe that anymore. He had lost the power to intimidate her. There was something familiar in the way he spoke, something in his voice she recognized; and she realized suddenly that it was Daddy, that it was Willis Fauve's voice echoing through Gavin. But it was vitiated, powerless . . . she had left all those voices behind.

She said, "Do you believe in the wheel?"

"Do I believe—what?"

"Things change," she said, "but do they get better? Is that a possibility? Can a wheel roll uphill?"

Gavin said, "You *are* crazy."

"Well, maybe."

"I can have you subpoenaed. You should be aware

of that. You're letting yourself in for a world of trouble.
You—"

But this was history.

She looked up and saw Michael watching her.

4

Michael knew it was his father on the phone.

Karen looked at him across the room, hesitated a
second, then offered the receiver to him. "You want to
talk?"

He thought about it.

Home, he thought.

The apartment by the lake.

Two different places.

Michael shook his head. "Tell him—"

"What?"

"Tell him thanks but I'm okay. Tell him I'm looking out for myself. Tell him . . ." Long beat, and then
Michael smiled a little. "Tell him maybe I'll come see
him someday."

Karen nodded solemnly. "Anything else?"

"Tell him goodbye."

Chapter Twenty-eight

· ·

The little Durant ran on gasoline, and that wasn't a common fuel here, but they drove as far as they could down a broad highway marked Camino del Mar, and when the tank ran dry they peddled the car to a scrap-metal dealer for a handful of Commonwealth money —enough to get by on for a while. The city down the road, the scrap dealer said, was Ciudad San Francisco, and there was work there . . . you could get by in English if you didn't know Nahuatl or Spanish. Michael said that sounded good but that ultimately they would probably be heading East.

"To each his own." The scrap dealer opened the hood of the Durant and gazed inside with patient puzzlement. "Personally, I *hate* snow."

*   *   *

Michael and Emmett played funny, clumsy guitar duets at the back of the northbound bus. Karen listened a while, to the music and then to the rumble of tires on pavement.

Almost dark now, the last daylight washing up this windy road, this folded coast. Tall pines and mountain shadows and a sky as broad and clean as the ringing of a bell. It was strange, she thought. Not just this place, but everything. You try to lead a decent life, maybe make the world a little better. And then you find out how powerful all the bad things are, how weak you are in the face of that. And so you think you're doomed to do it all over again, make the same mistakes everybody made for the last hundred thousand years . . . you live with that, admitting it or not, but with that defeat inside you, a black kernel of unhappiness.

But maybe—and here was this new thought again—maybe it wasn't true. Maybe if it was true she wouldn't be here. Maybe the wheel *does* roll uphill.

Cool air along this mountainous ocean road. She pulled her sweater close around her. Laura was sleeping now; the bus was quiet. Karen thought about her natural parents, who had died at Walker's hands. They had escaped the narrow cells of the Novus Ordo and found a town called Burleigh; Laura had discovered Turquoise Beach . . . and Michael had found this place, this quilted, radiant frontier world. A door, she thought, that hope had opened out of fear, imagination out of failure. And maybe that was the only door that really mattered.

The road veered to the right, a gentle rocking, and Karen looked out across the western ocean, which was still called the Pacific, and closed her eyes; and slept at last dreamlessly as the bus rolled down the angles of the night into the morning.

ABOUT THE AUTHOR

ROBERT CHARLES WILSON is a native of California who now resides on Vancouver Island with his wife and son. His short fiction has appeared in *The Magazine of Science Fiction & Fantasy* and *Isaac Asimov's Science Fiction Magazine.* His first novel, *A Hidden Place,* was published in 1986 and his second novel, *Memory Wire,* in 1987. He has recently completed his fourth novel, *The Divide,* to be published in hardcover by Doubleday Foundation.

A Special Preview of
THE DIVIDE
the new Science Fiction novel by
Robert Charles Wilson

Imagine losing your personality . . . feeling it slip
and alter, steadily changing, until the person living
in your body is no longer recognizable as *you*. Imagine being able to understand what is happening, but
powerless to stop it. Imagine . . . and you will understand the feelings of John Shaw. **The Divide** is his
story.

Shaw was a "designed" child—the product of a clandestine research project meant to create a superior
human being. But when government funding ran
out, Shaw not only lost the only father he had ever
known—researcher Max Kyriakides—but was left without the monitoring his altered body required. Now,
years later, he is a grown man . . . but a man whose
mind is not entirely his own. . . .

Such an ordinary house. Such an ordinary beginning.

But I *want* it to be an ordinary house, Susan Christopher thought. An ordinary house with an ordinary man in it. Not this monster—to whom I must deliver a message.

It was a yellow brick boarding house in the St. Jamestown area of Toronto, a neighborhood of low-rent high-rises and immigrant housing. Susan was from suburban Los Angeles—lately from the University of Chicago—and she felt misplaced here. She stood a moment in the chill, sunny silence of the afternoon, double-checking the address Dr. Kyriakides had written on a slip of pink memo paper. This number, yes, this street.

She fought a momentary urge to run away.

Then up the walk through a scatter of October leaves, pause a moment in the cold foyer . . . the inner door stood open . . . finally down a corridor to the door marked with a chipped gilt number 2.

She knocked twice, aware of her small knuckles against the ancient veneer of the door. Across the hall, a wizened East Indian man peered out from behind his chain lock. Susan looked up at the ceiling, where a swastika had been spray-painted onto the cloudy stucco. She was about to knock again when the door opened under her hand.

But it was a woman who answered . . . a young woman in a white blouse, denim skirt, torn khaki jacket. Her feet were bare on the cracked linoleum. The woman's expression was sullen—her lips in a ready, belligerent pout—and Susan dropped her eyes from the narrow face to the jacket, where there was a small constellation of buttons and badges: BON JOVI, JIM MORRISON, LED ZEPPELIN. . . .

"You want something?"

Susan guessed this was a French Canadian accent, the nasality and the dropped "th" sound. She forced herself to meet the woman's eyes. Woman or girl? Maybe nineteen or twenty years old: a few years younger than I am, Susan thought, therefore "girl" —but it was hard to be sure, with the makeup and all.

She cleared her throat. "I'm looking for John Shaw."

"Oh . . . *him.*"

"Is he here?"

"No." The girl ran a hand through her hair. Long nails. Short hair.

"But he lives here?"

"Uh—sometimes. Are you a friend of his?"

Susan shook her head. "Not exactly . . . are you?"

Now there was the barest hint of a smile. "Not exactly." The girl extended her hand. "I'm Amelie."

The hand was small and cool. Susan introduced herself; Amelie said, "He's not here . . . but you can maybe find him at the 24-Hour on Wellesley. You know, the doughnut shop?"

Susan nodded. She would look for "Wellesley" on her map.

Amelie said, "Is it important? You look kind of, ah, worried."

"It's pretty important," Susan said, thinking: *Life or death*: Dr. Kyriakides had told her that.

Susan saw him for the first time, her first real look at him, through the plate-glass window of the doughnut shop.

She allowed herself this moment, seeing him without being seen. She recognized him from the pictures Dr. Kyriakides had shown her. But Susan imagined she might have guessed who he was, just from looking at him—that she would have known, at least, that he was not entirely normal.

To begin with, he was alone.

He sat at a small table in the long room, three steps down from the sidewalk. His face was angled up at the October sunlight, relishing it. There was a chessboard in front of him—the board built into the lacquered surface of the table and the pieces arranged in ready ranks.

She had dreamed about this, about meeting him, dreams that occasionally bordered on nightmares. In the dreams John Shaw was barely human, his head unnaturally enlarged, his eyes needle-sharp and unblinking. The real John Shaw was nothing like that, of course, in his photographs or here, in the flesh; his monstrosities, she thought, were buried—but she mustn't think of him that way. He was in trouble and he needed her help.

Hello, John Shaw, she thought.

His hair was cut close, a burr cut, but that was fashionable now; he was meticulously clean-shaven. Regular features, frown lines, maps of character emerging from the geography of his fairly young face. Here is a man, Susan thought, who worries a lot. A gust of wind lifted her hair; she reached up to smooth it back and he must have glimpsed the motion; his head turned—a swift owlish flick of the eyes, and for that moment he did *not* seem human; the swivel of his head was too calculated, the focus of his eyes too fine. His eyes, suddenly, were like the eyes in her dreams. John Shaw regarded her through the window and she felt spotlit, or, worse, *pinned*—a butterfly in a specimen case.

Both of them were motionless in this tableau until, finally, John Shaw raised a hand and beckoned her inside.

Well, Susan Christopher thought, there's no turning back now, is there?

Breathing hard, she moved down the three cracked steps and through the door of the shop. There was no one inside but John Shaw and the middle-aged woman refilling the coffee machine. Susan approached him and then stood mute beside the table: she couldn't find the words to begin.

He said, "You might as well sit down."

His voice was controlled, unafraid, neutral in accent. Susan took the chair opposite him. They were separated, now, by the ranks of the chessboard.

He said, "Do you play?"

"Oh . . . I didn't come here to play chess."

"No. Max sent you."

Her eyes widened at this Holmes-like deduction. John said, "Well, obviously you were looking for me. And I've taken some pains to be unlooked-for. I could imagine the American government wanting a word with me. But you don't look like you work for the government. It wasn't a long shot—I'm assuming I'm correct?"

"Yes," Susan stammered. "Dr. Kyriakides . . . yes."

"I thought he might do this. Sometime."

"It's more important than you think." But how to *say* this? "He wants you to know—"

John hushed her. "Humor me," he said. "Give me a game."

She looked at the board. In high school, she had belonged to the chess club. She had even played in a couple of local tournaments—not too badly. But—

"You'll win," she said.

"You know that about me?"

"Dr. Kyriakides said—"

"Your move," John said.

She advanced the white king's pawn two squares, reflexively.

"No talk," John instructed her. "As a favor." He responded with his own king's pawn. "I appreciate it."

She played out the opening—a Ruy Lopez—but was soon in a kind of free fall; he did something unexpected with his queen's knight and her pawn ranks began to unravel. His queen stood in place, a vast but nonspecific threat; he gave up a bishop to expose her king and the queen at last came swooping out to give checkmate. They had not even castled.

Of course, the winning was inevitable. She knew— Dr. Kyriakides had told her—that John Shaw had played tournament chess for a time; that he had never lost a game; that he had dropped out of competition before his record and rating began to attract attention. She wondered how the board must look to him. Simple, she imagined. A graph of possibilities; a kindergarten problem.

He thanked her and began to set up the pieces again, his large hands moving slowly, meticulously. She said, "You spend a lot of time here?"

"Yes."

"Playing chess?"

"Sometimes. Most of the regulars have given up on me."

"But you still do it."

"When I get the chance."

"But surely . . . I mean, don't you always win?"

He looked at her. He smiled, but the smile was cryptic . . . she couldn't tell whether he was amused or disappointed.

"One hopes," John Shaw said.

She walked back with him to the rooming house, attentive now, her fears beginning to abate, but still reluctant: how could she tell him? But she must.

She used this time to observe him. What Dr.

Kyriakides had told her was true: John wore his strangeness like a badge. There was no pinning down exactly what it was that made him different. His walk was a little ungainly; he was too tall; his eyes moved restlessly when he spoke. But none of that added up to anything significant. The real difference, she thought, was more subtle. Pheromones, or something on that level. She imagined that if he sat next to you on a bus you would notice him immediately— turn, look, maybe move to another seat. No reason, just this uneasiness. Something *odd* here.

It was almost dark, an early October dusk. The street lights blinked on, casting complex shadows through the brittle trees. Coming up the porch stairs to the boarding house Susan saw him hesitate, stiffen a moment, lock one hand in a fierce embrace of the banister. My God, she thought, it's some kind of seizure—he's sick—but it abated as quickly as it had come. He straightened and put his key in the door.

Susan said, "Will Amelie be here?"

"Amelie works a night shift at a restaurant on Yonge Street. She's out by six most evenings."

"You live with her?"

"No. I don't live with her."

The apartment seemed even more debased, in this light, than Susan had guessed from her earlier glimpse of it. It was one room abutting a closet-sized bedroom— she could make out the jumbled bedclothes through the door—and an even tinier kitchen. The room smelled greasy: Amelie's dinner, Susan guessed, leftovers still congealing in the pan. Salvation Army furniture and a sad, dim floral wallpaper. Why would he live here? Why not a mansion—a palace? He could have had that. But he was sick, too . . . maybe that had something to do with it.

She said, "I know what you are."

He nodded mildly, as if to say, *Yes, all right*. He

shifted a stack of magazines to make room for himself on the sofa. "You're one of Max's students?"

"I was," she corrected. "Molecular biology. I took a sabbatical."

"Money?"

"Money mostly. My father died after a long illness. It was expensive. There was the possibility of loans and so forth, but I didn't feel—I just didn't enjoy the work anymore. Dr. Kyriakides offered me a job until I was ready to face my thesis again. At first I was just collating notes, you know, doing some library research for a book he's working on. Then—"

"Then he told you about me."

"Yes."

"He must trust you."

"I suppose so."

"I'm sure of it. And he sent you here?"

"Finally, yes. He wasn't sure you'd be willing to talk directly to him. But it's very important."

"Not just *auld lang syne*?"

"He wants to see you."

"For medical reasons?"

"Yes."

"Am I ill, then?"

"Yes."

He smiled again. The smile was devastating— superior, knowing, but at the same time obviously forced, an act of bravery. He said, "Well, I thought so."

They talked for a long time.

Dr. Kyriakides had already told her some of this. He had kept tabs on John, but surreptitiously, since it was a violation of his funding agreements to do so . . . and he had no illusions about the source of his grants. Susan was able to anticipate some of what John told her. But some of it was new.

He said, "It depends on what you call a symptom, doesn't it?"

The research project ended when John was five years old. He was adopted out to a childless couple, the Woodwards, a middle-income family living in a bleak Chicago suburb. The Woodwards renamed him Benjamin, though he continued to think of himself as John. From the beginning, his adoptive parents were disturbed by his uniqueness. He didn't always do especially well in school—he was contemptuous of his teachers and sometimes a discipline problem—but he read beyond his years and he made conversation like an adult . . . which, the Woodwards told him, was very disrespectful.

"Jim Woodward was a lathe operator at an aerospace plant and he resented my intelligence. Obviously, a child doesn't know this, or doesn't want to admit it. I labored for eight years under the impression that I was doing something terribly wrong—that he hated me for some fundamental, legitimate reason. And so I worked hard to please him. I tried to impress him. For example, I learned to play the flute in junior high. Borrowed a school instrument and some books. I taught myself. He loved Vivaldi: he had this old Heathkit stereo he had cobbled together out of a kit and he would play Vivaldi for hours—it was the only time I saw anything like rapture on his face. And so I taught myself the Concerto in G, the passages for flute. And when I had it down, I played it for him. Not just the notes. I went beyond that. I *interpreted* it. He sat there listening, and at first I thought he was in shock—he had that dumbfounded expression. I mistook it for pleasure. I played harder. And he just sat there until I was finished. I thought I'd done it, you see, that I'd communicated with him, that he would approve of me now. And then I put the flute back in the case and looked at him. And he blinked a couple of times, and then he said, 'I bet you think you're pretty fucking good, don't you?' "

"That's terrible," Susan said.

"But I wasn't convinced. It just wasn't good enough, that's all. So I thought, well, what else is there that matters to him?

"He had a woodworking shop in the basement. We were that kind of family, the Formica counters in the kitchen, Sunday at the Presbyterian church every once in a while, the neighbors coming over to play bridge and the woodwork shop downstairs. But he had quality tools, Dremel and Black & Decker and so on, and he took a tremendous amount of pride in the work he did. He built a guitar once, some cousin paid him a hundred dollars for it, and he must have put in three times that in raw materials, and when it was finished it was a work of art, bookmatched hardwood, polished and veneered—it took him months. When I saw it, I wanted it. But it had been bought and paid for, and he had to send it away. I wanted him to make another one, but he was already involved in some other project, and that was when I saw my opportunity—I said, '*I'll* build it.'

"I was twelve years old. I had never so much as touched his woodworking tools. 'Show me,' I said. He said, 'You'll never manage it. It's not a beginner's project.' I said, 'Let me try.' And I think now he saw it as *his* big opportunity . . . maybe this would teach me a lesson. So he agreed. He showed me how to work the tools and he gave me some books on luthiery. He even took me to lumberyards, helped me pick out decent woods."

John paused to sip his cappucino. "I worked on the guitar that summer whenever he was out of the house. Because it was an experiment—you understand? This would be the communication, he would see this and love me for doing it, and if he didn't—all bets were off. So I took it very seriously. I cut and sanded, I routed the neck, I installed the fretwire and the tuning machinery. I was possessed by that guitar. There was not a weekday afternoon through July or August I was out of the house. I was dizzy with lacquer fumes half the time. And when he came home I would hide the project . . . I didn't want him to see it until it was ready. I cleaned the tools and the workshop every day; I was meticulous. I think he forgot about it. Thought I'd given up. Until I showed it to him."

Susan said, "Oh, no."

"It was perfect, of course. Max probably told you what his research had suggested, long before it was fashionable science—that the neocortical functions aren't just 'intelligence.' It's also dexterity, timing, the attention span, the sense of pitch, eye-hand coordination—things as pertinent to music or luthiery as they are to, say, mathematics. Jim Woodward thought he'd found a task that was beyond me. In fact, he could hardly have picked one I was better suited to. Maybe that guitar wasn't flawless, but it was close. It was a work of art."

Susan said, "He hated it."

John smiled his humorless, raw smile. "He took it personally. I showed him the guitar. The last varnish was barely dry. I strummed a G chord. I handed it to him . . . the final evidence that I was worthy of him. To him it must have been, I don't know, a slap in the face, a gesture of contempt. He took the guitar, checked it out. He sighted down the neck. He inspected the frets. Then he broke it over his knee."

Susan looked at her hands.

John said, "I don't want sympathy. You asked about symptoms. This is relevant. For years I thought of myself as 'John' while the Woodwards were calling me 'Benjamin.' After that day . . . for them, I *was*

Benjamin. I became what they wanted. Normal, adequate, pliant, and wholly unimpressive. You understand, it was an act. They noticed it, this change, but they never questioned it. They didn't want to. They welcomed it. I worked my body the way a puppeteer works a marionette. I *made up* Benjamin. He was my invention. In a way, he was as meticulous a piece of work as that guitar. I made him out of people I knew, out of what the Woodwards seemed to want. He was their natural child—maybe the child they deserved. I played Benjamin for almost three years, one thousand and eighty-five days. And when I turned sixteen I took my birth certificate and a hundred-dollar bill James Woodward kept in his sock drawer, and I left. Didn't look back, didn't leave a forwarding address . . . and I dropped Benjamin like a stone." He took a sip of cappucino. "At least I thought I did."

"What are you saying—that *Benjamin* was a symptom?"

"He *is* a symptom. He came back."

The Divide is a poignant tale of love and loss, of real people caught in frightening circumstances. It is a prime example of the evocative writing we have come to expect from Robert Charles Wilson—and an experience of the heart. Find out for yourself, when *The Divide* goes on sale in December 1989 wherever Doubleday Foundation trade paperbacks and hardcovers are sold.